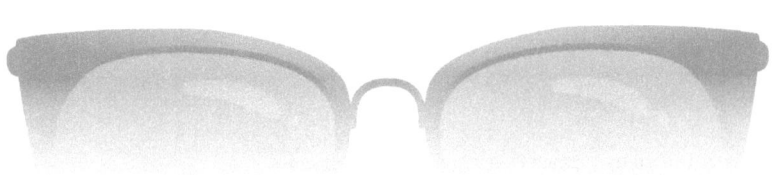

MEMPHIS GRACE

CATRIONA MCKEOWN

Memphis Grace

© Catriona McKeown, 2019

Published by Rhiza Edge, 2019
PO BOX 1519
Capalaba ,QLD 4157
Australia
www.rhizaedge.com.au
editor@rhizaedge.com.au

ISBN: 978-1925563719

Cover Design by Carmen Dougherty, Book Whispers

A catalogue record for this book is available from the National Library of Australia

For Emily,
who made my passion for inclusivity personal.

Chapter 1

People say I'm angry. And yeah, I *am* angry. I am angry at the world. Angry at Mikaela. Angry that something like *this* could even happen.

When we get the news about Mikaela it's a no-brainer—Nikki, Ellen and I skip school to wait at the hospital. I don't like hospitals. They bring back the worst memories; smells of sickness and fear, and yet with a hint of sweetness. The smell carries from the emergency department to the wards, from hospital to hospital. Whether you're there because you've cut your finger, or someone you love is dying, hospitals are the same.

And staff treat kids the same—no one's prepared to tell three teenage girls anything. While we wait for news of Mikaela, Nikki, Ellen and I flick through every possible social media site looking for clues of what happened; anything to distract us, to avoid seeing the man with a bloodied bandage to his head. The woman with the vomiting child. The old man with a weird rash on his face. But our feed continues on with life as usual, with no news of what we so desperately want to know.

Then Cooper arrives. He strides in, tall, determined, glancing at me with a look that lets me know that everything will be okay now. He's clearly distressed, and yet chats to the nurses and greets people as they walk around him like they're old business friends.

Despite his best efforts, no one tells him anything either; I can tell by the frustrated look on his face. Eventually he joins us, hugging us all in turn, but I'm last and he holds me especially tight, and for a little longer. My head rests perfectly on his chest, moving in and out in rhythm with his breathing. Cooper Dally—Mikaela's boyfriend—isn't the sort of guy you see in pain very often. But as he begins pacing back and forth with his hand to his chest, I wonder if I looked like that the last time I walked these floors. When Jesse died.

As Mikaela's best friend, I've hung out heaps with Cooper, but I avoid talking to him as much as I can. He's Mikaela's, and I knew from the moment I met him that being *just friends* with a guy like Cooper was never going to work for me. So, when Cooper comes over and sits beside me, his head in his hands, I fumble for something to say. His breath is heavy. He says nothing, which kinda says something. I tap my foot against his and give him a half-smile, and he smiles a little back.

He mumbles a few swear words under his breath. 'If something happens to her, Grace, I don't know how I'll go on without her.'

'Do you know what happened?' I whisper.

'No. Do you?' He's holding me captive, pleading to me with his eyes. Beautiful, big brown eyes.

'No idea.'

Cooper runs his fingers through his hair. 'Mikaela has been acting a bit weird lately.' He pauses. 'The last couple of times we've hung out, we've ended up fighting.'

'Really?' Mikaela hadn't said anything, but she doesn't talk about Cooper much. Cooper pulls his phone out of his back pocket; it's lit up with a message that's partially hiding a selfie of himself with his arm around Mikaela. They're both laughing; his eyes are mostly closed yet somehow they're still the highlight of the photo. He swipes away the message without reading it.

'Great photo,' I say.

He nods. 'Yeah.' He rolls the phone around in his hand. As he returns it to the upright position; it's gone black. 'We haven't had fun like that for a while.' Cooper unlocks the phone again and types a reply to the text.

'What do you mean that she's been acting weird lately?'

He keeps typing, but says, 'She's been picking fights about things that never bothered her before, not wanting to hang out with me, that sort of shit. Last time we hung out she even said she wasn't sure she still loved me.' He returns his phone to his pocket.

My jaw drops open. Mikaela and Cooper have been together for, like, two years. They're the ideal couple. Both of them perfect in every way. 'What—did she break up with you?'

'No.' Cooper shakes his head but it's not very convincing. He runs his hands through his hair again. 'I don't want to lose her, Grace.' Tears well in his eyes. He looks up to the ceiling.

'I'm sure she wasn't wanting that. You know what she's like. She gets all sullen but it only lasts a few weeks.'

'This was different, Grace. She's been different.'

His hands rest on his thighs and I consider putting my hand on his. They say physical contact helps when you're hurting, though I hadn't wanted it when I'd waited here for Jesse. Maybe hand-on-hand is too intimate. I decide I'd better not.

'I'm just scared ...' Cooper catches his breath. 'She's been more than just moody. She's been angry, kind of. Saying stuff about how she didn't want to be here anymore.'

'What?' I say, barely able to form the words I'm thinking. 'You don't think she's in hospital because ...'

A tear runs down Cooper's cheek as he pulls his shoulders up around his neck. I put my arm around him and feel him relax. I tilt my head so it rests on his shoulder and for the first time that day, allow myself to cry.

It's well into the afternoon when Mikaela's dad walks into the waiting room, dressed in a business suit, his loosened tie crooked against his white shirt. His tired eyes meet mine. I'm expecting him to welcome us, to be happy that we're all there to support Mikaela. Instead, he thanks us for coming and then tells us we should go home.

'Please, can't we see her?' I ask. I cast a sideways glance at

Cooper. Does boyfriend trump best friend in a hospital situation? 'Me, at least? We don't even know what happened to her.'

Mr Harper scratches the greying hair on his chin. 'All you need to know is that she'll be fine, she has people to take care of her now.' He lowers his voice. 'We caught her early, Grace. If we hadn't realised what she'd done ...' He shakes his head, as though clearing the thought from his mind.

'*Caught* her? What do you mean?'

Mr Harper's eyes confirm Cooper's suspicion.

My hand flies to cover my mouth. 'I can't believe it.'

Mikaela's dad goes to walk off.

'Wait,' I say. 'This doesn't make any sense. I need to talk to her. I need to know why.'

Mr Harper holds his hand out to stop me following him. 'We will get Mikaela through this on our own. Please, Grace. You and your friends should go home. It would be best for everyone, including Mikaela.'

Mr Harper turns and walks back through the closed doors, while my heavy jaw allows a deep, audible cry to leave my lungs. Cooper wraps me in his arms and leads me out of the hospital.

I don't fight to see Mikaela any more than that. Cooper calls a taxi and we leave the hospital not knowing if Mikaela knew we'd sat in the waiting room most of the day; not knowing if she knew that we cared. Not knowing what had made her do something like that.

We have big plans, Mikaela and I. We're going to university together, working at Mikaela's favourite cafe in Brisbane. Me, studying nursing; her, occupational therapy. We've even talked about getting jobs at the same hospital afterwards. Not necessarily in Brisbane; just somewhere in Australia. Anywhere.

Mikaela attempting to take her own life, and then disappearing out of mine, hadn't been part of the plan.

Chapter 2

The anger stays. What Mikaela did isn't supposed to happen. We're supposed to get up each morning and feel like crap and dress all the same and go to school and act as though we don't feel like crap, even though we all do. There is no opting out. We're supposed to go through it together and come out the other side. That's what is *supposed* to happen.

It's been five weeks and Mikaela hasn't returned to school. She's disappeared from Instagram, Snapchat, Facebook; she doesn't answer our text messages. She hasn't even looked at the messages we've left for her. And her parents are giving nothing away, they just keep saying she's going to be okay now. I haven't given up on trying to find out what happened to her, it's just that I keep hitting brick walls. It's like she really did die that day.

The latest rumour going round is that Mikaela has left town to go to boarding school. Miss Krensky basically confirmed it, though she says she's not supposed to talk about it. It's a knife to my heart, knowing my best friend tried to do that to herself and then ran away. From me. Cooper. Ellen and Nikki. Our future plans. With no contact. With no reasons why.

So, Mikaela is moving on from our life, from our dreams. But not me. I'm not giving up what I want most in life. I might have to do it alone, but I'm still going to graduate from teenage-world and go on to young-adult-world where I'll get a degree that will launch me into a new life. A better life. A life where friends aren't lying when they say they're okay, and I won't have to look through my sofa for spare change, and where someone walking out of my life won't make me feel like I'll never feel anything ever again.

Like they have. *Again.*

Five weeks can be a long time when you're walking around with a hole in your heart. I don't think I would have made it through without Cooper. Our midnight chats when neither of us can sleep; the knowing looks he glances at me in class if someone says her name; the way he randomly grabs my hand and squeezes it, reminding me we're going through this thing together.

I seem to be forever late for school now. My sister, Lisa Marie, has brought me to school again today, and even though it was just as much her fault as it was mine that we're late, she's stomped off to the office ahead of me.

The school ground is quiet and that after-rain smell fills the air as I make my way from the carpark to student reception. As I approach, a lone figure is sitting on a bench seat by the office door. Broad shoulders and surfer's leg muscles tell me it's Cooper, even though his head is down. He looks up, locking eyes with me. I take a step closer.

'Hey,' I say, with the plan to keep walking past, but he goes to say something.

'Hey, Grace. How you doin'?' His voice surges through me, the genuineness of the question, the knowing that he is the only one who really knows what my life has been like for the last five weeks. I smile. 'I dunno. Okay, I guess. You?'

'It was five weeks ago yesterday,' he says.

'Yeah, I know.'

'Do you think it's true that she's at boarding school now?'

'Yeah, I reckon there's a fair chance.' I massage the palm of my hand. 'I haven't heard from her. She's still not replying to my texts.'

'Yeah same. Five weeks and not a word. What's even with that, Grace?'

I shrug. 'I ask myself the same thing all the time.'

'Yeah, well, I've been thinking about this heaps, and I wanted to talk to you about it.' Cooper sits up straight, our eyes locking hard so I can't look away. My heart leaps to my throat like I'm thirteen again. But I'm good at playing cool; I've been doing it every day for three and a half years.

'You wanted to talk to me?'

'Yeah. Grace, you know her, maybe even better than I did.'

'Well, I thought so. Maybe neither of us really knew her.'

'Yeah, exactly. She's just dropped us, Grace. Moved on to a new life with no thought for those of us she left behind.'

It's like he's speaking my thoughts; thoughts I'd never dare say out loud.

'And I gotta say, Grace, I'm so sick of this bullshit. I'm sick of feeling crap and wondering what we could have done to make things different for her … so it never happened.'

'It would help if we knew what had happened to her; I mean, what got so bad in her life?'

'Maybe. Or maybe it would be better to just try to forget about the whole damn thing.'

'Some days I think that too.'

'You agree, Grace? Cause—' his voice is getting louder, stronger, '—I'm done. I've had enough of thinking about Mikaela and playing the "what-if" game. But I want to do this together; like we've done everything else together. I want to move on, really move on, together. What do you think?'

I frown. 'I don't know, Cooper. I still want to know why she did what she did.'

'We all do, Grace. But she's shut us out. It's time to do the same and get on with our lives.' He stands up and slaps his thigh with a flat hand. 'A fresh start, that's what I'm talking about.' He puts his hand out as though he wants me to shake it.

'Okay.' I take his hand. His handshake is firm, his grip, strong.

'Deal.' He smiles and holds my gaze for a moment longer than is comfortable. It makes my heart flip a bit and I force an awkward smile.

'Let's start with hanging out at lunch again, like we used to, yeah? I miss hanging out with you, Grace. With all of you. We'd been a good group of friends, hadn't we?'

I smile and nod. 'That would be great.'

I let go of his hand and start to walk away, but Cooper doesn't join me. I turn back. 'Are you coming to Form?'

Dimples appear on either side of his lips as he smiles. 'Soon. I'll see you up there.'

I get to my locker and have to force my frigid fingers to move as I put Jesse's birthdate into my combination lock. Although I don't think I'm ready to move on from Mikaela, or not consider her my best friend, I can't help but keep the smile plastered across my face. The lingering sweetness of Cooper's aftershave plays havoc with my senses as I try to stop the image of his smile from replaying over and over in my mind. As I throw my schoolbag into the locker, I hear a rustling behind me. Someone else is out of class. I glance around to see Jack Oskar.

My back muscles immediately tense. I don't like to be caught alone with that boy; he wants to talk to me about Jesse all the time. He says stuff like, *You know when Jesse died, there was nothing you could have done. You shouldn't feel bad about it; sometimes bad things just happen.* And then he raises his eyebrows and walks away again, as though Jesse dying hadn't been the most horrific thing that had ever happened in my life. As if my part in his death could be casually cast aside with a clinical cliché.

I lower my eyes and try to manoeuvre around him. His head is down as he scratches around in his bag. Then: 'Hi, Graceland,' as though he talks to me every day.

'Grace,' I say. 'It's just *Grace*.' I continue walking.

'But, your name *is* Graceland, Graceland.'

I wince each time he says my name.

Lisa Marie walks into her Form room just down the walkway. Three girls excitedly wrap their arms around her. I never understood how my sister came to be so popular at school, and why her popularity hasn't rubbed off on me. I turn to Jack. 'No one calls me Graceland.' His face is lit up with a stupid, goofy smile. 'Especially not you.'

His face falls and he tilts his head slightly to the side. 'Why especially me?'

I exhale heavily. 'You're late for Form, Jack.'

He pulls up his sleeve to reveal a large, chunky watch, as though this is a complete revelation to him. I walk away.

'Grace,' he calls, 'wait.' I climb the stairs.

Miss Krensky has marked me absent. 'You'll need to go to the office and sign in on the way to your first class, Grace, okay?'

I nod; no infringement for coming to Form late. Miss Krensky is generally pretty nice, but she's been especially cool the last five weeks.

Jack enters the classroom behind me. Miss Krensky calls him to the front.

I sit in the empty seat in front of Nikki. A new girl to our Form class is sitting next to her. I recognise her, though her hair is longer and she has heavy makeup on.

Nikki says, 'You remember Hayley Johnson, Grace?'

Sure, I remember her. 'Immanuel didn't work out?'

Hayley's eyes sparkle and she flicks her dark hair around like she's Barbie personified. 'Afraid not.'

'It's been eighteen months,' Nikki says.

'Impressive you lasted that long,' I say. 'Your decision or theirs?'

Hayley curves her lips slightly. 'A mutual feeling, I think.'

Miss Krensky is up the front talking about the upcoming cross-country race. I lower my voice. 'Why didn't they put you in your old Form class with Mel and Sissy?'

'I couldn't imagine.' Hayley laughs, drawing Miss Krensky's attention.

Ellen whispers to me, 'Hayley was suspended for bullying Mel, remember?' But I don't really. That had been when we were in Year 8—a lifetime ago.

'Perhaps they're hoping you girls will be a better influence on me.' Her eyes scan the classroom. 'I see things have improved during my absence.' She flashes a flirty smile as she catches Brad's eye.

'That's Brad,' Nikki says. 'He's only been here a few months. He's replaced Mark as Cooper's new lead guitar. But you'd remember Joe, sitting beside him? And Harry on the other side.'

'Hmmm, I've missed the Boy Band.' Hayley fiddles with a large hoop earring. 'I've especially missed seeing Cooper every day. There was no equal to him at Immanuel.' She pulls out a tube of lip gloss, applies it via the reflection in Ellen's glasses and smacks her lips. 'Mikaela's not his distraction anymore, I hear.'

'She left last term,' Ellen says.

Hayley chuckles. 'I heard.'

I go to ask her what exactly she'd heard when Miss Krensky interrupts. She's handing out forms and stops at Hayley. 'You were good at cross-country, Hayley, weren't you?'

Mirth simmers on Hayley's lips. 'I'm good at whatever I put my mind to, Miss K.'

Joe calls out across the room, 'That's the rumour, Hayley. But I'm available for practice any time you want.' He jabs Brad in the ribs and they chuckle.

Miss Krensky frowns a little. 'Well, here's hoping you put your mind to a variety of things now you're back. Especially English; you'll have quite a bit to catch up on.'

'I'm sure I will,' Hayley says, battering fake eyelashes. As Miss Krensky walks away, Hayley's lips purse together. 'So, both Cooper and Brad are single?'

The three of us nod.

'Hmmm, what a choice. Is Cooper still in this Form class?'

'Yes,' Ellen says. 'He must be away today. Or late, I guess.'

'Cooper's still pretty cut over Mikaela,' Nikki says. 'He's missed a fair bit of school.'

'Cooper's here. I was speaking to him before I came up for Form,' I say.

'What did you talk about?' Nikki asks.

I tense my lips to try to avoid the smile that's itching to return to my face. 'Just stuff. He's so sweet.'

'Sweet?' Hayley runs her tongue over her lips. 'I can think of plenty of words to describe Cooper Dally, and sweet is not one of them.'

I narrow my eyes. 'He's more than just a face, Hayley.'

Hayley laughs. 'True, that. He's a body as well. A damn fine body.'

I roll my eyes. 'You haven't changed much.'

'I'll take that as a compliment. And neither have you,' Hayley says, eyeing me up and down. 'You have so much potential hiding under your non-made-up face and hand-me-down wardrobe, Graceland. You and I could really shake things up in this school, if you were prepared to change a little.'

'It's just Grace, remember.'

Hayley raises her eyebrows. 'Oh, of course, Grace.' She throws her head back and laughs heartily.

'What's so funny?' I ask.

'Did Brad look over?'

'Yes,' I say.

'Good.' She smirks. 'It looks like I've come back at just the right time.'

Chapter 3

The following day I'm super late for school and don't arrive until recess. Distracted by trying to stuff the late-pass into my stupid uniform pocket, I almost run into Jack Oskar on my way to Science. I groan as I realise he's following me; twice in one week is more than enough interaction. 'Graceland,' he says.

'What do you want, Jack?'

He holds out something in his hand. 'You left your scientific calculator in Maths. They cost $28.50 at the newsagents. I couldn't find you after school, so I took it home.'

My eyes thin. 'Gee, thanks.'

Jack goes to speak, then pauses. 'You're being sarcastic, aren't you?'

'Yes, Jack.'

'You didn't want me to get your calculator for you?'

'You could have given it back to me in Maths.' I take it.

'I won't be there today. I knew you would need it for the quiz.'

'Right.' I'd forgotten about the quiz later today. Another fail coming my way. I try to walk off, but he's blocking me.

'Your friend Mikaela,' he says. I cringe. 'Is she alright? I heard she hurt herself.'

I bite my lip. 'I don't know, Jack. I haven't seen her.'

'What, not at all?'

I shake my head.

'You should try calling her,' he says. 'She could do with some friends. Friends can help when you're sad.'

12

I roll my eyes and try to prevent the stabbing in my chest slicing any deeper.

'You have pretty eyes,' Jack splutters. His feet are shuffling around like he's trying to remember the steps to a dance. He gives me a crooked smile but it's just creepy. 'Green eyes are not very common.'

I frown and step into his personal space. 'Yes, I know.' I'm almost touching him, but still he's not getting out of my way.

'Jesse didn't have green eyes,' Jack says. 'Of course, siblings often don't have the same eye colour, so that's not unusual.'

I stare at him. An image of a permanently eight-year-old Jesse sweeps across my mind. 'Jesse had blue eyes.'

'It's genetics, you know. You got green eyes. Jesse got Down syndrome.'

I shake the image from my mind. 'We've talked about this before, Jack. I don't want to talk about Jesse.'

Jack puts his head down. 'He was my friend. I miss him. That's why you should call Mikaela. I wish I could call Jesse, or him call me.'

'I need to get to Science.' I use the back of my hand to try and shove Jack out of my way. 'You need to get to class too.'

He allows me past.

'Next time,' I say, 'just give me the calculator in class.'

Jack is a few steps behind me, still mumbling about Jesse, as we round the corner to the Science room. Cooper and Joe come over to meet us. Mr Van Hayden is clearly late for class again.

Cooper smiles at me while Joe says, *Jaaaaaaack,* drawing out his name like he's happy to see him. Jack's whole body slumps in response to Joe's voice.

Cooper puts his hand around my shoulder. 'Is Jack annoying you?'

Heat rises to my cheeks and I say, 'No. Why would he be?' Even though he kind of was.

Joe's freckled face smirks from under his red, unruly hair. 'Jack can be pretty annoying, can't you, Jack?'

Jack's eyes remain fixed on his fidgeting hands. He's moving from one foot to the other, as though he's trying to find an escape route.

Joe moves closer into Jack and whispers, 'Aren't you going to look at us, *retard*?'

The word vibrates in my ear like a heavy gong. 'Hey, don't use that word, Joe, it's horrible. Jack was just giving me back my calculator.' I hold it up and flash it in front of the boys as Jack moves away. 'He hasn't done anything wrong.'

'Other than existing, you mean,' Joe says. I look at Cooper to back me up, but he's chuckling.

'Why are you being so mean?' I say. 'You know, not everyone can be perfect like you.' I don't mean to, but I look at Cooper as I say it.

Cooper raises his eyebrows. 'You think I'm perfect, Grace?' His mouth twitches at the sides, curving slightly.

I swallow hard, my chest tightening.

'I think she was meaning me, Coop,' Joe says, punching him in the arm. I catch Joe and Hayley exchanging a look, and he heads in her direction.

'Well, lesson learned,' Cooper says, looking at me. 'Be nice to Jack if you want Grace to like you.'

I open my mouth to say something, but nothing comes out. Mr Van Hayden arrives, arms full of paper and a laptop with a periodic table cover on it.

Cooper nods in Hayley's direction. 'Hayley Johnson's back and in full form.'

Hayley is laughing like Joe is funnier than Chris Hemsworth.
'Yep.'

Cooper's hand brushes my arm as we follow the last of the class into the science lab. 'Are you still up for some change for the better?'

'I'm doing my best to move on from what happened with Mikaela, if that's what you mean,' I say. 'And if you want change, you and your friends can start by being nicer to people.'

'Are you angry with me, Grace?' His face is soft, cleanly shaven, with just little tufts of hair creeping down past his ears.

I sigh. 'Maybe. A little.'

'Why?'

'Well, you just stood by and let Joe say all that stuff to Jack. You could have stopped him, he would have listened to you.'

Cooper shrugged. 'I don't think Jack would have even understood what Joe was saying.'

'You don't know that.' I put my hands on my hips. 'Being kind is always a choice, even if the person you're being kind to knows it or not.'

Cooper's eyes widen and a smile erupts on his face. 'Wow, you're so passionate, Grace.'

I can't help but smile. 'Yeah, well, I hope some of it rubs off on you.'

'I think I'll need help with that,' Cooper says.

I look over at Jack, who is sitting in a chair with his eyes fixed to the floor. 'What do you mean—moving on from Mikaela or being kind to Jack?'

'Both,' he says, a twinkle in his eye. 'Moving on to new goals, more kindness—that kind of shit.'

'Well, you can start by swearing less, too; Ellen doesn't like it. It makes you sound, I don't know, just like everyone else.'

'You don't ask for much.'

I shrug. 'The best way to change the world is to start with yourself.'

Cooper chuckles. 'I like that, Grace. Start with yourself. I can do that.' He tosses his hair a little as he wanders over to the back of the classroom to take a seat next to Brad.

I sit next to Ellen.

'You okay?' she asks.

I can feel the colour has drained from my face. I rub my cheeks to try to get the blood flowing. 'Cooper. Joe. Jack.'

'Ah,' says Ellen, giving me a knowing look.

Mr Van Hayden starts talking.

I lower my voice. 'Remind me that Cooper's not as good looking as my brain thinks he is?'

Ellen just chuckles. 'He seems a bit brighter today.'

I nod. 'He's starting to move on. He said he's keen for us to all hang out at lunch times again.'

'What do you think of that?'

'It's stupid that they stopped. I know Cooper was ridding himself of all things Mikaela, including us, but it would have been easier if we'd kept hanging out; it wouldn't have felt so much like she wasn't here anymore.'

Ellen indicates to Hayley up the back of the classroom. She's deliberately leaning over Joe to talk to Cooper. 'Do you think Hayley's arrival has anything to do with Cooper's improved disposition?'

'Maybe. More likely coincidence.'

'Well, she's not wasting any time with *her* goals. Do you think acting like that comes naturally to her?'

I shrug. Hayley is holding Joe's hand, a pen lid hanging from between her teeth, as she writes something on his arm.

'She seems pretty keen on Joe.'

'Then there's a fair chance she's not.'

Ellen raises her eyebrows. 'Who, then?'

'Cooper, most likely.' The words taste bitter. 'But it could be any of the others, I guess. Joe's the easy way into the group; he turns into a Labrador puppy as soon as a girl shows any interest in him.'

'She does keep looking at Brad,' Ellen says. 'Especially when she's laughing.'

I snatch a quick look at Brad in the back row. His high cheekbones and olive skin give him model looks, but it's his sweet nature that wins.

'Hmm, I don't know. I always imagined he was more your type.'

She smiles. 'Maybe. But no dating until I'm seventeen, remember.'

'Your parents are harsh,' I say. The boys seem to be scheming plans of their own at the back of the classroom. 'But it would be nice to be hanging out with them again.'

Mr Van Hayden's voice rings out, threatening to hand out infringements if people don't pay more attention. It's like he thinks school is all we've got going on in our lives.

Chapter 4

In English we're reading *Romeo and Juliet* aloud. I must have left my copy in my locker, so I share with Ellen. Five weeks ago, I would have shared with Mikaela.

Miss Krensky has her diffuser going in the corner, making the classroom smell like a regular lavender farm—she reckons the scent reduces stress. I rub my shoulders and the back of my neck to try to soften the muscles tugging at every movement—clearly the lavender isn't working for me today. I hate Shakespeare. But I need English to get into uni. For some reason, we need English to get into just about everything.

As we're given roles for the lesson's reading, the classroom phone rings. Miss Krensky talks for a moment then says loudly, 'Jack Oskar had some sort of accident during the break. Did anyone see what happened?'

The class is quiet. Joe puts his hand up. 'Yeah, miss,' he says. 'I saw Jack lying on the ground, but I figured he was making conversation with the ants, you know, as he does.' Joe high-fives the rest of the boy band, but Cooper catches my eye and leaves Joe hanging.

Miss Krensky places her hands on her desk and glares at Joe. 'I certainly hope, Mr Harding, that you and your band of merry men didn't have anything to do with Jack's injuries.'

Joe feigns innocence.

'He's so un-co,' Harry says. 'He probably fell over his untied laces. Everyone knows he can never get those things done up properly. Needs his mummy to do it for him.'

A series of sniggers move like Chinese whispers around the room. I glare at the boys.

'Hey, settle down, boys,' Cooper says. 'Jack must be properly hurt if he's in sick bay.'

The boys all stop and look weirdly at Cooper. I look back at Cooper, who smiles, raises his eyebrows and winks.

After English, I detour to the nurse, faking a headache to check on Jack. She lies me down and gives me the third degree about not drinking enough water. That, coupled with the hospital-grade smell in the room, just about brings on a real headache. The nurse gives me a tablet and as she leaves the room I glimpse Jack with bandages up his face and on his leg. He's talking to Vice Principal Reyl, who is taking notes on a clipboard.

When I join Ellen in Science after, she says, 'Mr Van's handing out a new assessment. You're just in time.'

I groan. 'Well that sucks.'

Ellen passes me a spiral booklet with a bright yellow pineapple on the front. 'There were some project books on the chuck-out table at Typo last week. I grabbed a pineapple one for you.'

I hold it to my chest and lean over to hug Ellen. 'You're the best, Ellen. Thank you.' I rummage around in my pencil case to see if I have a fineliner that still works.

Mr Van Hayden starts speaking. 'Okay, everyone, we're doing things a little differently with this assessment.' A general groan rolls around the classroom. 'Now, I hope you'll like the changes, actually. You'll have a lot more scope for presenting what you've learned, for a start. ' *Change?* I don't like *different*. There's a tightening in my chest that makes it difficult to breathe. 'The term's assessment will be a group project.' His words slap me into reality like a chemical-soaked lab coat.

Mr Van Hayden moves around the classroom in slow motion, his voice droning as he discusses all the different possibilities for the group project. I pick up the assessment sheet that's left for me and skim-read it. Sixty per cent of the assessment is group work. Forty per cent is evidence of learning. The swear word that comes to mind repeats itself over and over until it eventually bursts out.

'Grace, language,' Ellen whispers, a frown on her face.

'Sorry. But come on, a group project?'

Ellen gives my hand a reassuring squeeze. 'You'll be right, Grace. Mr Van has looked out for you from day one, ever since he realised Jesse was your brother. I'm sure after what happened with Mikaela, he'll be even more lenient. He knows you prefer to work on your own. He'll have put you in a good group.'

I shake my head. 'People always say teachers like me, or think they treat me different because of Jesse and stuff, but it's not true.' I run both hands through my hair. 'You know, I practically failed Science last term.'

Ellen laughs. 'Probably more like you *should* have failed Science last term. But somehow, you didn't.'

I wish I had the optimism Ellen has. Mr Van Hayden's busy at his laptop, mumbling under his breath, which makes the black slug-like hair over his top lip move like it's alive. How can anyone trust a man who has a *moustache?*

'What's he doing now?' I ask.

'Trying to find our groups. He lost the piece of paper on the way to class. How are you feeling?'

I raise my eyebrows.

'You went to sick bay with a headache, remember?'

'Oh, yeah,' I chuckle, playing with the tablet still in my pocket. 'A bit better.'

'And Jack?'

I narrow my eyes. 'How would I know?'

'Oh, well,' Ellen says, 'he hasn't come to class yet. And you were with the nurse.'

'He wasn't there.' I look at her out of the corner of my eye. 'But

I saw him bandaged up when I was leaving. He was in the office with Mr Reyl.'

'Oh?' Ellen says with raised eyebrows. 'You don't think the boy band would have done something to him, do you?'

Mr Van Hayden is clearing his throat at the front of the class. 'Right, quiet, everyone. I have found the list.'

I hope desperately Ellen will be in my group, but her name is one of the first to be called out. I wish Nikki was in the same Science class as us. She's really good at Science.

'Grace McKay,' Mr Van Hayden says, 'you're team leader in a group with Latisha, Seb and … Jack.'

His last word sticks. 'Jack?' I glare at Mr Van Hayden.

'Yes, Grace,' he says. 'Jack Oskar.'

He moves on, but time stands still for me. Latisha, the quiet girl who sits in the corner and never speaks to anyone. Seb, whose claim to fame is being able to drink Fanta and force it out his nose. And Jack Oskar, who can barely write his own name.

I collapse into my pencil case. Ellen's hand rests on my arm. She's speaking to me. The room is emptying. Noises. Voices. But Mr Van Hayden's words have caused a twisting in my heart. Definitely no favours from this teacher; he couldn't have put me in a worse group of useless, lazy, no-hopers.

'It'll be okay, Grace,' Ellen says.

'Who needs stupid Year 10 Science anyway?' I say into my pencil case. 'Who cares. I'll fail this year and make a fresh start next year, when those guys won't be in my class.'

'You may be overreacting a bit there, Grace.' She squeezes my hand, like a mother would do to calm a child.

I expel the air I've been holding onto. 'It's just … I'm not sure how much more stress my brain can take.'

We gather up our gear and head out of class. So much for moving on from the past five weeks. So much for a new start. I grab the headache tablet out of my pocket and swallow it.

Chapter 5

Hayley bounds up to us on Friday morning, holding her books like she's the bubbly blonde from an American sit-com. Except she's a brunette.

'Morning, girlfriends,' she says. Nikki kisses her cheek like she's from the same TV show. Then Hayley pulls me into an embrace. Her hair smells like apples.

'What's put you in such a good mood?' I ask.

She's smiling. 'What do you mean? I'm always like this.'

Perhaps she is. Perhaps the events of the past five weeks have left me unable to notice when people aren't under the same dark shadow I am.

Hayley is bouncing up and down on her toes. 'I hope none of you have plans for tomorrow,' she says.

'Nope,' I say. 'I was having lunch with Ed Sheeran, but he cancelled overnight.'

Hayley rolls her eyes. 'Is she always like this?'

Ellen shrugs. I fake a smile.

'Well,' Hayley says, 'I have something to put a real smile on your face.' She pulls her phone out. 'Have a look at this.'

Her iMessage is open. Nikki grabs the phone and scrolls through it as Ellen and I read from either side.

'The boys are inviting you to the beach with them tomorrow?' Nikki asks.

'Not just me, girls.' She tosses her hair about as she pulls it up into a messy bun. '*Us.*'

'All of us?' Ellen says.

'Yes, sweetness. All of us. Even you.'

I pull my phone out of my pocket and see there is a notification. I open it and find a few messages have just come through—and they're all from Cooper. Three of them were sent last night and another this morning.

I read them in sent order:

Hey, Grace. Hope you're okay after today? You looked pretty bummed by Mr Van's groups. Wish I'd been in your group ;)

Then, about 20 minutes later:

Hey, you don't need to reply. I'll catch you at school tomorrow. K?

And at 11pm:

Just letting you know I'm going to bed. So, if you reply to my message, I won't get it till the morning. Anyway, see you at school. Friday tomorrow! :)

And finally, one sent before I'd even gotten up this morning:

Hey, Grace. Can we chat today? I've got something I want to ask you.

As we start to head up for Form, I grab Nikki and hold her back. 'Hey,' I say, 'look at this.' I show her the messages from Cooper.

'Cooper sent you all this? Why didn't you reply?'

My cheeks warm. 'I've run out of data. Yesterday Brad showed me how to hack the school's wifi system, so the messages only came through when my phone connected just now.'

'Wow. Well, that's one way to look cool when a guy is messaging you.'

'Cooper messages me heaps at night, you know he does that. It's more, I don't know, like he's trying to get my attention or something?'

'You think?'

I catch the sarcasm, but ignore it. 'What do you think he wants to talk to me about?'

She shrugs. 'Your guess is as good as mine.' She raises her eyebrows. 'Perhaps you're Cooper's latest interest that everyone is talking about.'

Warmth floods up my body as Nikki walks up the stairs to Form. I grab her. 'Wait! What do you mean, Cooper's latest interest?'

'I overheard the boys talking. They seem to think Cooper has set his sights on someone new.'

'And you think it could be me?'

'Could be. Do you want it to be?'

My heart leaps in my chest, but I shrug like I'm indifferent to the idea. 'I don't know. I mean, he's cute and everything, but—' *He's Mikaela's.*

Mikaela's ex.

Nikki splutters. '—Cute? Grace, he's flipping gorgeous. And rich. It's a bit of a no-brainer, if you ask me.'

'Yeah, well, it's unlikely. Probably he wanted Hayley's number – and clearly he managed to contact her.'

'He treats you different to everyone else. You do know that, don't you?'

'No.' I bite my lip. 'What should I do?'

'Well, Grace McKay, talking to him might be a good place to start.' Nikki places her hand on my arm and squeezes it. 'I don't think he's at school yet, but you could always send a message.'

I roll my phone around in my hand. I'll have to hand my phone in once I get to Form. Nikki heads up the stairs, but I take a seat on the bottom step. I open iMessage and read Cooper's messages again. I'm starting to type a reply when a shadow falls over me.

'Hey, Grace.' Cooper peers over to look at my phone. 'So, you are talking to me then?' He sits down beside me.

I swallow and try to laugh. 'Yeah, sorry, I only just got your messages.'

'Should I have used Instagram?'

I shake my head. 'No. Well, yes, I use Instagram. And Snapchat. But I've run out of data. Your messages only came through when I got to school.'

'Oh.' Cooper chuckles. 'I didn't think anybody uses that pre-paid thing any more, except tourists perhaps.'

'Yeah, well, I do. And our router at home has died but Mum can't afford a new one just yet. I'm finding out that I go through data pretty quick.'

Cooper tilts his head to the side. 'What's your number? I'll top you up.' He's tapping things on his phone. 'Who are you with?'

'Aldi; but you can't do that.'

He stops. 'Why not?'

'Well, I don't know why you'd do that.'

He shrugs and taps his phone again. 'It's a kindness thing.' He looks at me, dimples wrapping around the curve of his lips. 'Don't you think?'

I give him my details, blood rushing to my heart. My phone pings to say the top up has gone through. 'Thank you,' I say.

'No probs. And hey, I didn't get to talk to you.' We're almost at the top of the stairs. 'Don't put your phone in the Form box today, yeah? Then I can message you in class and stuff.'

'Oh. Okay, sure.' I feel for the back of my phone in my uniform pocket and find the button to put it on silent.

Cooper's first text message arrives halfway through second period. It's a risky move, texting in Miss Krensky's English class; she can hear a phone vibrating from the next room.

I slide my phone out of my pocket and put it on my lap, hoping to look like I'm following along with the textbook. I take an extra big breath of Miss Krensky's lavender fragrance.

> You didn't ask why I was messaging you last
> night.

I look at him across the classroom and shrug. Another message almost immediately follows.

> I wanted to ask if you'd come to the beach
> with me tomorrow.

I text back.

> I know. Hayley told us.

> Yeah, but I wanted to see if you could come.

I run my thumb over the phone screen. There's nothing I would rather be doing.

> Sure, I can come.

Miss Krensky clears her throat excessively. 'That's your line, Grace,' she says.

I almost throw my phone into the air. My heart thumps in my chest. 'I thought I was Mercutio, and he's dead.'

'You are Benvolio, Grace,' she says. 'Who is pretty much the only young character who *doesn't* die in the play.'

'Oh,' I say.

'Naw, way to give away the ending, miss,' Cooper says.

Ellen shoves her book under my nose. It smells of years of student gloom and discontentment. I read the lines and scan ahead to make sure there are no more surprises for me. I relax a little. But then my phone vibrates again.

> Sweet cover up ;)

> It scared me to death. Can't we talk at
> recess?

Okay. But I wanted to check with you about tomorrow. You didn't answer my messages and so I asked Hayley to ask you all—but I wanted to ask you first. And I wanted you to know that.

I don't get what Cooper is up to. This makes no sense. Why would he want to make sure I could be there?

Sure, it will be nice to all hang out together again. Like old times.

No. It will be better.

For the rest of school, my thoughts are obsessed with what spending a day with the boy band will bring. In previous trips to the beach, back when Mikaela had been our glue, I'd been happy to hover on the outskirts. I'd watch as Mikaela moved confidently around the boys. It has been almost five months since we all hung out at the beach together—and now we have no Mikaela to be the centre of attention.

It's all the girls talk about at lunch. I toy with my Vegemite sandwich, avoiding saying much for fear of giving my feelings away.

'Does anyone need a lift?' Nikki asks.

'Yes, please,' I say. Who knows if I'll have a way to get there in the morning. 'So long as your mum won't mind coming over this side of town?'

'Nah. Mum's not working tomorrow, and I could do with a bit of a drive to get my hours up. I'm only on fifteen.'

'Right,' Hayley says. 'Let's talk clothes. What are we all wearing? I can't wait to show off this gorgeous red bikini I got on sale last summer. What is your swimsuit like, Grace?'

'Oh, I've got a blue one piece.' I force a laugh. 'I got it on sale a couple of years ago.'

Hayley's face drops. 'A one piece? Are you serious?'

I focus my eyes on the ground. 'I don't swim. I usually just watch from the dunes with Ellen.'

'The boys are surfing tomorrow, Grace. You can't sit on the beach and watch.'

'Why not?'

'Because, what if they offer us some lessons? It's a way in, Grace.'

I swallow hard.

'What's the weather supposed to be?' Ellen asks, diverting the conversation.

I open the app on my phone. 'Still a bit cool,' I say. 'Only twenty-five degrees.'

'Warm enough for summer dresses, though,' Hayley says. This starts a new round of conversation about jumpsuits and dresses and on what occasions it's okay to wear socks with slides. But it doesn't take anything away from the fact that I have no idea what I'm going to wear.

After school, I head straight for my favourite op shop. I try on three pairs of bikinis, two of which are too big and one that looks like it was owned by a five-year-old. I study myself in the changeroom mirror but can't help but see Hayley glaring disapprovingly at me. My stomach churns at the thought of being at the beach with Hayley and the boys. At least I won't have to worry about anyone noticing me. All eyes will be on Hayley and her red bikini. And any attention I've been getting from Cooper lately will soon be over. Tomorrow will end it.

I grab the few items I've tried on that are nearly acceptable and ask the lady at the counter if I can pay for them the next time I've got some money.

Chapter 6

The next morning, I stand in front of my wardrobe mirror and assess the damage Queensland's short winter has done to my body. Slightly bigger thighs. Hair that's more-sandy than blonde without the harsh sun around to bleach it. A fading tan that makes the freckles across my nose stand out more. At least my skin is now consistently white and not patchy brown. It's embarrassing to live in such a warm climate and not be able to gain that lovely, all-over tan most girls have here. Girls like Nikki and Hayley only have to walk out into the sun to get one; the sun loves girls like them. And most other girls can afford to fake tan.

I open my bedroom window. Outside the sun is kissing the ground and making it sparkle. There's a slight saltiness to the breeze that joins me in the room.

Lisa Marie opens my door without knocking and sticks her head in. 'Here's the Blu Tack you wanted.' She puts the sticky lump on my bedside shelf. 'Nice short shorts. A bit shorter than you usually wear. Where'd you get them?'

'Op shop.' I put my hand in the back pocket to show a hole.

'You wouldn't know, other than that. Are you going somewhere?'

'Beach.'

She raises her eyebrows. 'Boys?'

'Maybe.'

'It's been a while. Anyone I'd know?'

'Cooper and co.' I run my hands over my outfit.

'Again, with the boy band? Can't you girls find a new crowd to

29

hang with?'

I shrug. 'They're alright.'

'Brad's alright. Cooper's trouble.'

'And you know this because?'

'Haven't you heard? Once you get to Year 12 you know everything.'

I roll my eyes.

'Tom's picking me up in a minute. We could drop you off?'

'That's okay. Nikki's mum was happy to take me. Nikki's trying to get her hours up.'

'Do you want to get your learners?' Lisa Marie asks. 'Tom's offered to give you some lessons if you want to.'

'Tom?' I say. 'Since when would Tom offer to give me lessons?'

'He does like you, you know, Grace.'

'Then why does he always call me that stupid name?'

'Memphis Grace? It's his little joke. Remember the first time you met Tom and you told him off for calling you Graceland?'

'Only family members call me Graceland—and that's only because I can't stop you all.'

'Exactly. Since Elvis' mansion Graceland is in Memphis, it's his way of calling you Graceland without actually calling you Graceland. Like he's being part of the family, but not quite.'

I grunt.

Lisa Marie smiles. 'I think it's very clever of him.'

'Yeah, well, I think I'll leave getting my L-plates until Mum's a bit more up for teaching me.'

'Fair enough. Enjoy the beach.' Lisa Marie closes the door behind her.

I open Instagram and see Hayley has posted a picture of herself. She's wearing a sheer white dress. The red bikini glows beneath it.

My Target one-piece is peeking out from under my new shorts and crop top. They're the type of swimmers made for practicality, not fashion. Mum barely had the money when I found them on the throw-out rack two years earlier, but she relented. It helps that my boobs haven't grown since then, and I barely go to the beach.

'It's only one day,' I whisper to myself.

I pull off some of the Blu Tack and use it to put up an inspo quote I printed off Pinterest on my wall. It's about believing in yourself, and if you can't, then pretending you do, so that at some point, you will. There's a picture of a tennis player dressed in white in the background.

I whisper, 'I can believe in myself. I'm getting better at pretending. Eventually, I will.'

I throw a few things in a bag and head out to where I can hear Mum in the kitchen. I clear my throat as I walk into the room.

'Morning, Graceland,' she says, her head inside the fridge. Elvis is crooning from her phone, hidden amongst a week of unwashed dinner dishes. Mum's backside sways in time to the music. She pulls her head out and frowns. 'Togs, huh? After spending all that money on them, I'm glad to see them finally getting some wear.'

'They were, like, fifteen dollars, Mum.'

'And fifteen dollars is fifteen dollars that could have been spent elsewhere. Is it even warm enough for swimming at the beach yet?'

'Some of us are meeting there to hang out. I think the boys are surfing.'

'The boys?' Mum pulls herself completely out of the fridge. 'Who?'

'No one you'd know.'

She lets out a puff of frustration. 'When are you going? I thought we could watch a movie before I go to work. What's your favourite? *Love Me Tender*?'

'I don't have a favourite Elvis movie, Mum.'

'Sure you do. You know, you haven't watched *Follow That Dream* with me for a long time.'

'There's a reason for that.' I grab a banana. 'No one watches Elvis Presley movies anymore. No one listens to his music, either.' I pause. 'And no one, even when he was alive, named their child after his house. Everyone calls me Grace—can't you do that too?'

She moves her mouth to reply but I say, 'Nikki's picking me up. I'll go wait out the front.'

'Grace,' Mum says. Her blonde hair is pulled up into a high ponytail so her dark, doleful eyes are highlighted; an imitation-of-silk dressing gown flows down over her black bra and a pair of cotton short shorts. She could be pretty, if she wore a little makeup and stopped spending so much of her time living in the past. 'I want to spend more time with you. You and Lisa Marie. I hardly get to see you both now I'm working at Harry's. And, you know, after what happened with Mikaela and all ...'

'Sure, Mum.' I go over and plant a kiss on her cheek. 'How's next weekend? But not an Elvis movie. Maybe we could choose something from Lisa Marie's collection instead.'

'Sure, next weekend,' she says, but I hear the disappointment in her voice. 'I love you, Graceland, and I always will. You know that, don't you?'

I nod. 'Love you too, Mum.' And I head out the front door.

Chapter 7

Hayley comes up behind us as Nikki and I head towards the beach. Hayley's bubbling with excitement under her large sunglasses and floppy-brimmed white hat. The sun's glare on the sand hurts my eyes.

We round the corner of the headland; the breeze carries with it a hint of sunscreen and wet dog. In front of the surf club the boy band are talking to Ellen, surfboards in their hands. Most of them are in wetsuits with the top half pulled down over their butts, exposing bare chests. Cooper stands out amongst them, his olive skin extending down across his chest. His dark curls caress his brow as he talks animatedly.

'Who is that?' Hayley asks.

I follow her gaze. 'That's Justin—Brad's older brother.'

'Dang,' she says. 'Does he hang with the boys much?'

'Not usually. He's probably just their transport today.'

There are numerous remarks from the boys about Hayley as we approach. Cooper looks me up and down and I wait to see disapproval in his eyes, but his smile tells me something different.

'Hey, you came,' he says.

'I did.'

Hayley's introducing herself to Justin, who only seems mildly interested. The general discussion is about the disappointing waves.

'The wind hasn't picked up as much as we'd hoped,' Cooper says.

'Are you still going to surf?'

His eyes are narrow as they stare out over the water. 'Well, they're not real good surfing waves.' His lips are soft, his jawline firm. 'But they'd be great waves to learn on. Have you ever given surfing a go?'

I shake my head. For someone who lives on arguably one of the best stretches of coastline in Australia, I hardly spend any time on the beach. At least, not since Dad left.

'Want to?'

I pull my crop top down and wrap my arms around my stomach. 'You don't know me very well, Cooper. I'm not very good at that sort of thing.'

His lips curve. 'You don't know me very well, Grace. I'm a very good teacher.'

I give a little laugh. 'I don't doubt that for a second.'

'So, you will?' His smile widens to light up his eyes.

'Why not?' I say. *Other than it meaning I'll have to expose the entire beach to my ridiculous swimsuit.* 'A lesson sounds like fun.'

Hayley throws her arms around me from behind. 'Really? Lessons sound awesome.'

Hayley and Nikki are bouncing around in excitement, as though this was totally unexpected. Nikki doesn't even need lessons, since she can already surf, and I'm sure Hayley would have at least tried before. Ellen laughs, even though she'll have to sit out for it; she never seems disappointed at having to miss out on stuff because of her heart thingy.

Hayley throws herself at Justin, who puts his hands up, declaring he has stuff to do. She quickly turns her attention to Joe.

While Harry, Joe, Hayley and Nikki head straight out into the water, Cooper gives me the run-down on technique and balancing strategies, then points out the best waves. Brad spends the whole time talking to Ellen on the beach. She has on a large pastel-coloured hat that flops as she bobs her head around in response to Brad's questions. I see her smiling and laughing often. Cooper touches my arm and gains my full attention.

'Shall we give it a go?' Cooper asks.

I take off my shorts and t-shirt to pop in my bag.

'A one-piece, huh?' Cooper's mouth curves on one side. 'I didn't know anyone wore those anymore.'

I wince. 'Sure. Mostly little girls and their grandmothers.'

He laughs. 'Are you a swimmer? They look like the sort of togs you'd wear in squad.'

'No, they're budget friendly. You can't buy a decent pair of bikinis for under twenty bucks.'

'I guess not. Though, I can't say I've ever tried.'

'Shame. I'm sure you'd look great in one.' I smirk.

'Maybe. Not as good as you would, though.'

My eyes widen. I meet his gaze, expecting to see jest on his face, but he's deadly serious.

Cooper grabs the board, his biceps bulging as he lifts it effortlessly and tucks it under his arm. 'So, you think you'll remember what to do once we're in deeper water?'

I run through his basic instructions as we head out to join the others.

'You're a good listener. The perfect student.'

I laugh. 'I wish my teachers at school thought that.'

'School's highly overrated. There are plenty of other ways to make it in life, other than getting good grades and going to uni.'

'Really? You don't want to keep studying after school?'

Cooper shakes his head. 'Life is one gigantic lesson. Four years at uni is four years where I could be out making money in the real world.'

'What do you want to do after school then?'

'Start a business. That's where the real money is.' The waves ease a little. 'Come on,' he says. 'Now's our chance to get out beyond the breakers.'

Out in deep water, Cooper positions the board and wraps a strong arm around me to help me get up on it. His legs move rhythmically under the water, holding us in place as we wait for a wave. He talks me through standing up on the board once a wave rolls in. He pushes me off and I soar on top of the wave. I get to my knees, wobble, and make it to one leg up before I crash.

Cooper's right there beside me almost immediately. 'You okay?'

I take in a little water. 'I think so.'

He's grabbed the board and is holding onto it. 'That was awesome. Much better than most people do on their first go. Come on, let's try again.'

It turns out I'm not that bad at surfing. I even make it all the way to shore a few times.

We eventually head back to the surf club, where the boys place their boards onto the roof racks of Justin's car.

'Justin's still off somewhere,' Brad says. 'Want me to call him?'

'Nah, let's hang a bit longer,' Cooper says. 'Surf might pick up yet.'

'Well then, what about an early lunch?' Hayley asks.

'Great idea,' Cooper says, his eyes alight. 'I'm starving.'

Upstairs at the Maroochy Surf Club, the smell of baked bread mixes with freshly brewed coffee, making my stomach rumble. I hang back while everyone lines up to order. I have my wallet in my bag, but I know there are only a couple of dollars left in it. Awkwardness brews inside me as the line dwindles down to the last few people. The guy behind the counter asks what I want.

'Um,' I say. I'm scanning the menu desperately for something I might be able to afford. A stab of pain flicks through my chest; Mikaela usually shouted if we went out like this. Even a bowl of chips would do. I can't sit at the table and have nothing.

Cooper leans in from behind me. 'What are you thinking? Are you keen to eat?'

'Um,' I say again. The guy behind the cash register taps his fingers on the counter.

'There's no rush,' Cooper says. The guy stops tapping.

'I don't know.' I try to buy some time by rummaging through my bag to get my purse.

Cooper puts his hand on my arm. 'Hey, let me shout. You deserve it after that stunning performance on the board this morning. In fact, how about we share something? What's your opinion on pineapple on pizzas?'

I sense my face turning a darker shade of pink. I try to stop the relief from escaping out of my mouth. 'Um, okay, sharing would be great. But I have to warn you, I'm a with-extra-pineapple kind of girl.'

'A girl after my own heart,' he says.

He brings me back a drink from the bar as well—raspberry lemonade.

'How'd you know I love this drink?'

He leans in close and whispers, 'I have my sources.'

We sit around a table with a view over Maroochydore Beach, Cooper on one side of me, Ellen on the other. Each of the boys take turns telling their highlight of the morning's surfing lesson. As the only real novice in the group, Cooper sings my praises—how I triumphed over the waves in just a couple of hours.

'You want the last piece?' Cooper asks, pointing to the pizza.

I'd barely managed two pieces. 'It's all yours.'

He nearly swallows it whole.

Outside, the cloudless sky shows little sign of providing the boys with some wind for their waves. As the boy band mumble about trying a different beach for surfing, Hayley proposes we walk down toward the pier. The boys agree.

Hayley and Nikki run ahead to do handstands down by the water. Hayley is paying particular attention to Cooper, and the way he's responding suggests she's caught his attention. And it's no wonder; Hayley has the body of Khloe Kardashian and the wardrobe to go with it. I manoeuvre myself to fall in step with Ellen and Brad but they're deep in conversation. I fall back and walk alone.

The beach is filling with people. An older couple pass by us, matching in their blue shirts, sandals dangling carefree from their hands. An overwhelming sadness pours over me. With my one-piece swimsuit and hopeless excuse for a Queensland tan, there's little hope any boys will ever be interested in me—at least, not in the way they are interested in Hayley.

'You're being quiet this afternoon, Grace.' Cooper is suddenly walking next to me. 'Not feeling sad about our previous trips to the beach together, with Mikaela, I hope.'

'No.' My heart leaps into my mouth, making me stutter. 'I—I must just be tired after the surfing this morning.'

'Good.' He undoes the buttons on his shirt, exposing his chest to the sun. It's hard to look away. 'I mean, not good you're feeling tired, though. Surfing can be quite exhausting, especially since you are using muscles you wouldn't normally use in that way.'

'I'm sure I'll be sore tomorrow.' I can already feel a tightening in my thighs.

'I can show you some stretching exercises to help if you'd like.' He grabs his left leg with his left hand and pulls it up so it's against his backside, while trying to keep up with me. 'Come on,' he says in between hops, 'aren't you going to join me?'

I shake my head and giggle as he loses his balance. Soft sand catches him as he lands heavily on his side. His laugh is long, lurid … captivating.

I join in his laughter. 'Maybe after the walk would be a better time to show me how to stretch.' It's been a long time since I've laughed like it.

I hold out a hand to help Cooper up. His hand is strong, his skin soft. As he gets to his feet, he continues to hold my hand, making eye contact with me. I pull away. My chest tightens.

'I haven't laughed that much since …'

'Yeah, I know,' Cooper says, brushing sand off himself. 'Me too.' A moment of sadness flashes across his face.

'I wish she was still here,' I say. 'I miss her.' But then I remember. 'Sorry, we aren't supposed to talk about her.'

'It's okay. It's just, I don't want her to be always with us, like a dark cloud, you know? That's what it was like before.'

'Before?'

'Before I decided to not let it be like that anymore.'

We walk in silence for a while.

'I can't believe her parents sent her away. It doesn't make any sense.'

Cooper shrugs. 'She told me she always wanted to go to that school in Sydney. A bunch of her old friends from when she lived in Armadale go there.'

'But now? After what she did? I can't believe her parents think it was right to disconnect her from us like they have. It's like she's gone to a different planet.'

'Maybe. I mean, if she shut us out of her life, maybe she never really cared for us.' I can hear the hurt behind his words. We walk in silence for a bit. 'But it's not all bad. Like, now I get to know you more,' Cooper says. 'I don't think we'd had many proper conversations until that day at the hospital.' He walks in front of me so I have to look at him. 'I loved how you rested your head on my shoulder when I started to lose the plot that day. It said something about the kind of person you are.'

He trips on a bit of sand and nearly falls backwards, making me laugh. Further down the beach, Hayley is continuing her antics with Harry and Joe. Joe topples into the shallow water after attempting a handstand.

Cooper follows my gaze and says, 'Good to see I'm not the only unco one.'

'Hardly.' I point to a tomato paste stain on my top. 'Casualty of lunch.'

Cooper chuckles. 'We're not so different, hey.'

Maybe we're not. But maybe he's just being nice to me.

Ellen is climbing onto Brad's back. He tenses his leg muscles and rises, with her wrapped around him. Ellen's hands rest on Brad's bare chest, her face next to his, their smiles matching in size and contentment. She's probably never had this much attention from a guy in her life; other than her dad.

'Hayley's enjoying herself,' Cooper says. She turns around and shoots a smile in Cooper's direction. Then Joe does something and she laughs so hard she's bent over in the middle. The boys are laughing along with her.

'Yep. She usually does. I think Joe's enjoying having her around.'

'He is, but he needs to be careful. Girls like Hayley aren't for the long term.'

'Is that right?'

'You know that's true, Grace. I'm not being mean, she just isn't the sort of girl you look for if you want something more … long term.'

I swallow hard. 'Hey, so, what is your business idea?' I ask.

'Business idea?' Cooper says, his eyes leaving Hayley to focus on me again.

'For when you leave school.'

'Oh, I'll probably work for my step-dad to start with. But I'd like to have my own surf shop; maybe make my own boards. I'm really into wind surfing too. I could offer lessons out of my shop.'

'I think you'd be good at that.'

'Thanks.' There's a vulnerability in his eyes.

'Hey, you could create a planet-friendly surf shop,' I say.

'Oh?'

'You know—ecofriendly, minimising the environmental footprint of the surfer. You could sell products made from natural materials and stock companies that don't use slave labour. Surfers would be into that.'

He chuckles. 'Thanks, Grace. I'll keep that in mind. I think

I'd need a passionate partner to help with it, though. Have you got plans for after school?'

I lift my chin. 'I'm going to be a theatre nurse.'

'Oh? Nursing doesn't pay much.' His face turns melancholy. 'And think of all the money you could be earning while you're studying at uni. It takes years and years to make that up, not to mention how much you have to pay the government back for the privilege of a "higher education".'

I square my shoulders. 'Yeah, but I don't want to end up like my mum. She's a waitress and it hardly pays anything. It took her ages to find a place that would hire her. Nursing is a secure job.'

'Fair bit of responsibility to go with it too,' Cooper adds.

I shrug. 'I don't mind. I want to be able to help people.'

'Good on you, Grace. The world needs people like you.'

My shoulders relax. 'Maybe. I just know that I want my life to be different to my mum's. When Dad moved out, Mum was left with basically nothing. I never want to be that vulnerable, that reliant on someone else.'

Cooper puts his hand on my upper arm for a few seconds. 'Or you could be sure to put your trust in the right kind of guy.'

I chuckle. He doesn't.

Chapter 8

Monday morning starts off with a trip to the career advisor's office. Mrs MacGregor enters the room with a waft of strong coffee and spicy perfume. A cream manila folder is open in her hand. She closes the door behind her. Despite Cooper doubting my career goal, I'm excited for my Set Plan meeting—the day when I decide the pathway for the next few years of my life. Year 11. Year 12. The transition to university and to the rest of my life. I'm one of the last to do it because I couldn't organise a time for Mum to come to the meeting.

'Grace, thank you for being punctual. I see your mum has signed the Set Plan forms. She wasn't able to come in for an interview, though, was she?'

'Mum works at night so sleeps a lot during the day. Makes it hard.'

'Is she a nurse?' Mrs MacGregor sits down at the small stationary-cluttered desk between us.

'Waitress.'

'Oh. I thought maybe, since you put down that you wanted to study nursing—'

'Nope. She works at Harry's Thai.'

'But surely, Grace, if she's waitressing she could have given us a small amount of her time—'

'No. Mum works every afternoon except Tuesdays.'

Mrs MacGregor gives me a condescending glare. 'She could have come in on Tuesday.' She flicks through a large black diary. 'I can still set up a meeting.'

'She's really busy, Mrs MacGregor. She has a routine and she doesn't like to adjust it. She sleeps in, does the grocery shopping and falls asleep watching *Follow That Dream*.'

'*Follow That Dream*?'

'Gordon Douglas. 1962.'

Mrs MacGregor raises a quizzical brow.

'It's a movie. Do you know who Elvis Presley was?'

'Of course.' Mrs MacGregor gives me a smile—not the filled-with-sympathy-yet-slightly-amused smile I would have expected, but rather one filled with a strange kind of sadness, the kind I'd drowned in when Jesse died. 'I remember; your mother could be the president of the Elvis Presley fan club, from what I hear. Tell me, I understand Lisa Marie is named after Elvis' daughter, and Graceland is the name of his mansion. But I never understood where Jesse came into the—'

I stand up. 'Are we done here? Cause this is sounding less and less about my Set Plan.'

Mrs MacGregor flaps her arms about. 'Sit down, sit down, please.'

I sit down but rest my butt on the edge of the chair.

'Alright. Sorry, Graceland. What did your mum think of your Set Plan?'

'It is just *Grace* and we didn't talk about it. She just asked where to sign.' This was not how I imagined my Set Plan meeting would go.

A sigh bursts from between the woman's tense lips. 'You were asked to talk it over with your parents first. I know Lisa Marie doesn't intend to study once she's finished school next term, so when you're the first in your family planning on going to uni it helps to—'

'Yeah, well, clearly we didn't have that conversation. Mum's life-schedule doesn't leave much time for family dinners.'

'Have you spoken to Lisa Marie about your plans then?'

'No?'

'Being in Year 12, Lisa Marie may be able to offer you some additional insight into your goals and how you might achieve them.'

I laugh, not because it's funny, but because the whole idea of

Lisa Marie being able to give advice on any part of my schooling, other than my social life, is preposterous.

Mrs MacGregor shuffles the papers on her desk and glances at the clock ticking heavily on the wall. 'And what about your dad? Did you talk to him about it?'

I cough as I mis-swallow the saliva that rushes into my mouth.

'It says here he wants to be informed about what's happening with you at school.'

I roll my eyes. 'I don't know why it would say that.'

'What does he do?'

'Doesn't it tell you all this on your computer?' My question is met with silence. So, I vomit out the story of the father I haven't seen since I was nine years old. 'The man lives on the Gold Coast after running away from the life—my life—he considered to be so horrible, so despicable, that he couldn't stand to stay for a second longer. He literally described us as a stench in his wide, hairy nostrils. I have no idea what his current job is because I haven't spoken to him since he rang to tell us his skank of a girlfriend is pregnant.'

'Grace. I don't think—'

'She's only twenty-three years old. You don't think she deserves to be called a skank?'

Mrs MacGregor stares at me.

'Look. It's my life, okay? My future. I'll sort out the details closer to the time. But I'm going to finish Year 12. I'm going to go to university. I'm going to make sure that my life turns out better than anyone else's in my family has so far. Can we get on with it?'

Mrs MacGregor makes a rough, rolling sound in her throat and ends it with a cough. 'Right. Good idea.' She adjusts the glasses resting on the edge of her pointed nose before pulling out a piece of paper from the pile. 'Let's start with this then.'

She places the paper in front of me. A quick glance tells me it's my Science report from first semester.

'What about it?'

Mrs MacGregor leans over and points to the Term One Biodiversity unit.

'Yep, it's an E grade, if that's what you're pointing out.'

'And, down here it says you barely achieved a Pass overall for Science last semester.'

I shrug. 'So?'

'Well, you need Science to do nursing. In particular, you need Biology, and Term One's failed unit was foundational to the genetics unit, which you're studying this term.'

'Yeah, but we're talking about next year. Next year, I'll work harder.'

Mrs MacGregor shifts in her seat. 'Grace, it's not just next year. You will need at least a passing grade for this term's genetics unit to get into Biology next year.'

'What do you mean, I need it to get into Biology? If I put Bio down, that's what I'm doing.'

'Well, this is part of what the Set Plan is all about. So far, you haven't shown us that you are capable of passing Year 11 Biology, given that you're barely managing to pass Year 10 …'

'Are you saying the school might not let me do Biology next year?'

'Yes, Grace, that is exactly what I am saying.'

'But that's ridiculous, of course I can pass. Who do I need to prove it to? Mr Van Hayden?'

'Well, all of us, Grace. Mr Reyl, myself, and, yes, Mr Van Hayden will also have a say.'

A blanket of dread drapes itself across my shoulders, making my arms heavy to lift. I narrow my eyes. 'What do I need to do?'

'You need to pull your grades up overall in Science this semester.' Mrs MacGregor opens a drawer and pulls out a colourful folder. She hands it to me. *University of the Sunshine Coast* is headlined across the front. 'And, in particular, you must do well in this unit you've just started in Science. I can tell you definitively that if you fail it, you can say goodbye to studying Biology next year, and any chance

45

of getting into nursing at university without having to do some sort of bridging course first.'

I look at the folder in my hands. 'Why USC? I had always planned to go to the University of Queensland with Mikaela.'

'Well, cost, for one; Brisbane is an expensive place to live. Whereas living at home and going to USC would be much more affordable.' She coughs a little. 'You also don't need quite so high marks to get in.'

I hug the folder and go to stand when Mrs MacGregor says, 'Grace. You've always been a fairly determined kind of person. I think if you put your mind to it, you can do anything. But I do have my concerns. Do you have a plan B, in case you don't get into university?'

'No', I say. 'Nursing's all I've ever wanted to do, since I was little. Since—'

'Since Jesse passed away?' Mrs MacGregor's face suggests that she completely understands. As if she could ever do that. As if anyone could ever do that.

My eyes instinctively narrow. 'I've always wanted to do nursing. It's nothing to do with that.'

'Okay.' Mrs MacGregor stands and walks to the door, pointing to the folder in my hand. 'Perhaps you should put that up on your bedroom wall as a bit of motivation to get you through the semester.'

Whatever. But I say, 'Sure. Thanks, Mrs MacGregor.'

My future closes the door behind me.

I walk out and into Jack Oskar, who bumps my shoulder as he walks toward the door I've just exited from. 'Hey, watch it,' I say.

A woman beside him, I'm guessing his mum, asks him to apologise.

He doesn't turn back, but I hear a mumbled, 'Sorry'. He knocks on the closed door.

Saliva fills my mouth. Jack. Science. The group project that I now *must* pass. I run to the bathrooms in time to revisit the smoothie I had for breakfast. And I leave the University of the Sunshine Coast folder on the toilet floor.

Chapter 9

Hayley, Nikki and Ellen are at the back of our history class when I walk in and take a seat next to them. I do my best to empty my mind of the Set Plan meeting with Mrs MacGregor, and of Jack Oskar.

'What are we doing?' I ask.

No one responds. Ellen shrugs and smiles. Mrs Higgins is up the front, talking ecstatically about something to do with World War II—though I only know this because it's written across the top of the whiteboard. Hayley and Nikki are busy looking at their phones under the table.

Ellen stops taking notes as Mrs. Higgins breaks into something she called the *Horst Wessel* song. She sounds like she's crying, rather than singing. Ellen opens her pencil case and pulls out a tiny tin of mints, offering one to me with raised eyebrows. 'You okay?'

I shake my head, clenching my fists to stop my eyes from forging any tears. I take a mint. 'No, so not okay.' I indicate Hayley and Nikki, who are now whispering like a couple of second-graders who've put a fake spider on the teacher's chair. 'What's going on with them?'

Ellen shrugs. 'Spilling the tea; something about a party tonight. How'd your Set Plan meeting go?'

Hopelessness fills my mind again. 'Shit, actually.'

Ellen frowns. 'Grace.'

'Sorry. My Set Plan meeting did not go well, Miss Ellen.'

Mrs Higgins is calling my name from the front of the class. 'Are you here to socialise, Miss McKay, or are you here to learn some history?'

Heat rises to my face. I almost say 'socialise', but then think better of it and raise my shoulders instead. Hayley and Nikki are still whispering. Mrs Higgins doesn't notice, or doesn't seem to care, that they're not giving her the attention she is demanding from me.

'Well, perhaps you could enlighten us all with your opinion.'

'Sorry, miss,' I say. 'I was in my Set Plan meeting, so I've only just got here.' Hayley and Nikki stop talking and watch me with great amusement.

Mrs Higgins frowns. 'Yes, I am aware of that. All the more reason for why you should come in and start catching up on what you missed, not getting further behind by chatting with your friends.'

I open my mouth to counter-argue, but Mrs Higgins' face stops me. 'Yes, miss,' I say. 'Sorry.'

I turn to Ellen. 'See, I told you not all teachers like me. Mrs Higgins has had it in for me from day one.'

'Maybe she doesn't know about Jesse.'

I frown. 'Having a dead brother doesn't bring with it the perks everyone seems to think it should.'

Mrs Higgins interrupts again. 'Miss McKay. If you are seriously going to continue talking to Ellen in my class, then I will demand your opinion on this aspect of the Holocaust.'

I still have no idea what she is talking about.

'Hitler, Grace. We're discussing how during the Second World War he tried to create what he thought to be the perfect race of human beings—the Aryan master race.'

I shrug. 'So?'

'Well, to be a part of this perfect race you had to have blue eyes and blonde hair. So, you'd fail. Your skull and nose also needed to be of a particular size.'

'Sounds like an idiot.' There are a few chuckles from around the classroom.

'And he issued a decree saying anyone with any sort of deformity or disability should be executed. Including babies. They were taken from their mothers at birth and murdered.'

'And what, you want to know if I agree with him? Who would?'

'Some people today do.'

I roll my eyes. 'Yeah sure.'

'Some people, Grace, believe all expectant mothers should be tested to see if their unborn child has Down syndrome, and if they do, they believe they should be made to have an abortion.' I freeze. I can't move any part of my body. It's as though a wedge of ice has been driven into my heart and it's frozen every limb and muscle. 'Sounds a bit like Hitler, doesn't it? He gassed people with Down syndrome, schizophrenia, dementia, people who were paralysed.' She's raising her voice. 'Anyone considered a "burden" on society was sent to the gas chamber, and their ashes were sent to their families with some made-up story about how they died. Are people who would demand the abortion of an unborn child identified as possibly having Down syndrome any different to Adolf Hitler?'

The ice in my heart is replaced by burning that races through my chest. 'Yes,' I say, staring hard at my teacher and matching the ferocity in her voice. 'Yes, maybe disabled people should be aborted. They take up everyone's time and energy and attention, and once they've made sure you love them, *they go and die*. It would be better if they were never born.'

Mrs Higgins' eyes are intensely wide and her whole face is frozen. A burst of energy charges into my thighs, launching my chair to the floor behind me. I run from the classroom, while Mrs Higgins doesn't say anything. I hear the door close behind me as I collapse onto the top of the steps. My arms ache with the weight of what I said, my body exhausted from the adrenaline still flowing through my veins.

It's not long before Ellen joins me. 'Grace, are you okay?'

I wrap my arms around my stomach. 'She was pushing and pushing. She wouldn't shut up.'

'Well, you got her to. I don't think the poor woman will speak again for a week.'

I chuckle. 'Good. She deserves it.'

'Were you serious about what you were saying then, about wishing Jesse had never been born?'

I wipe a wayward tear from my face and grit my teeth. 'It was nothing to do with him. I needed her to shut up. To stop talking about that stuff.'

'She was totally harsh on you.' Ellen smiles with the warmth of a freshly-baked jam donut, exuding sweetness from between her pink-tinted lips. 'Especially since you just came from your Set Plan meeting. What happened in there? You seemed pretty stressed about it.'

'I'll be fine. Just gotta pass Science this term.' I shake my head and add with a layer of sarcasm, 'Nothing I can't do.'

'And that group you've been put in ...'

'Exactly.'

Ellen puts her hand on mine. 'If you need any help, I'll do whatever I can, okay?'

The bell rings and Nikki and Hayley are the first to exit the classroom.

Hayley is laughing so hard she has tears rolling down her face. 'That was the absolute best, Grace! You're a legend.'

Nikki grabs my hand and pulls me up, out of the way, as the rest of the class streams down the stairwell. 'Are you okay, Grace?' Nikki wraps her arm around me, her brown eyes sincere in their questioning. 'I've never seen you like that before.'

I wipe hot tears from under my eyes. 'Sure. My Set Plan meeting didn't go so well, and then, you know, Mrs Higgins was really getting into me.'

'Nothing new about that,' Nikki says. 'She drives us all crazy.'

'Mrs MacGregor told Grace she needs to pass Science this term,' Ellen says.

'And pass it well,' I add.

'I've the perfect solution for that.' Hayley waves her phone around in front of us. 'Ethan Riley is throwing an eighteenth party for himself this weekend and we're all invited.'

'How did you manage that?'

Hayley raises her eyebrows and cracks a smile that Dorothy's Wicked Witch of the West would be proud of. 'How do you think? Cooper Dally, of course. Cooper and Ethan are practically brothers.'

'And?' I ask.

'*And*, Cooper's invited us to come along as his special guests. Look for yourselves on Facebook—he's created an event and invited all four of us.' Hayley scrunches up her face and runs on the spot with her fists clenched. 'Looks like the rest of our high school lives are about to get a reboot.'

Chapter 10

Ethan's party comes way too quickly for my liking. Although Nikki and Hayley are bursting out of their skin with excitement, I'm petrified of the whole thing—from who will be there, to what kinds of things everyone will be doing, and how I'll be expected to act through it all.

Hayley's sister, Hannah, has offered to drive us to the Party. Her car rattles up my driveway around half past eight. Hayley greets me with a kiss on my left cheek.

'Sorry about the smell,' she says as she climbs into the front. I swipe a layer of burger wrappers off the backseat and discover what Hayley was referring to. It's a mix of off food and cigarette smoke.

'It's milk.' Hannah says as she drags on her cigarette. She drops a couple of words Ellen would cover her ears at, then adds dramatically, 'It'll never come out. I'll be stuck with this bloody scrap of unruly steel until it dies and then who knows how I'll get myself and you lot round to your parties.'

Hannah takes off up the road, narrowly missing a car that's driving the other way. She swears again and laughs nervously.

'Course, if I write the car off, I won't have to worry about how I'm going to transport your sorry asses around. I'll be up there with Mum partying away, and you guys will be left here on your own to fend for yourselves!' Hannah laughs so hard she snorts as if she's been drinking.

'Shut up and drive carefully, would you?' Hayley yells over the music. 'I'd rather you not join Mum yet, at least not until I've finished high school or got a driver's licence of my own.'

I vaguely remember hearing that Hayley's mum died when Hayley was little. Her dad moved to Los Angeles around the time Hayley moved schools, and the girls chose to stay here so Hannah could go to university.

We pick up Nikki next and head straight to the party. Ellen isn't allowed to go to parties, unless it's mine or Nikki's. Her parents are super conservative, which we're sorry about for Ellen, but are really jealous of for us.

Ethan Riley's place is in the nice part of town. A cream-carpeted staircase winding up to a second storey greets us at the front door. A clichéd, giant chandelier hangs from the ceiling's expanse. A wide corridor runs beside the staircase, drawing us in the direction of music and voices. People gather in small groups, drinks in their hands, too absorbed in their own conversations to notice an insignificant group of teenage girls walking into the house.

I grab Nikki's hand. She looks lovely tonight, with her blonde hair falling softly around her shoulders, partially covering her soft pink tank top. 'I'm not sure we should do this,' I say. 'I'm nervous.'

'Of what?' Hayley asks.

'These aren't the type of people we'd normally hang out with.'

'What do you mean, Grace?' Hayley asks, her eyes narrowed, her hand on her hip. 'You don't usually hang out with anyone else.'

'What if someone tries something on one of us?'

'We'll look out for each other,' Nikki says.

'You mean, I'll look out for you two,' I say.

Hayley laughs. 'Thanks, Gracie. You're the best.'

'We won't stay long,' Nikki adds. 'Just an hour or two, okay? If one of us starts acting weird, you get us out of here. No arguments, no questions. Okay?'

Hayley groans. 'You guys are hopeless.'

But Nikki makes Hayley agree to the plan, and we continue our walk toward the noise.

The hallway erupts into an enormous, sparkling silver kitchen, where an entire glass partition has been pulled back so it's seamless to the outside deck. Out there, a lengthy table is burdened with platters, glasses and bowls of chips, and under the table are multiple lidless Eskies. Most people seem to be outside. Screams and continuous laughter are coming from a pool somewhere off the deck.

'Are you sure it's okay we're here?' I ask Hayley. 'Everyone's heaps older than us.'

Hayley shrugs. She waves frantically, her hand stretching up as high as it can go. I see the tip of her bike shorts beneath her dress. 'There's Cooper.'

We follow Hayley out onto the deck, where a warm breeze twirls the tiny fairy lights hanging from the pergola. She walks up to Cooper and throws her arms around him.

'Thanks for inviting us,' she calls loudly, but I can barely hear her over the music.

Cooper holds my gaze for a number of seconds. He motions toward the end of the deck. We head down some stairs to a flat, neatly-mowed grass area. It's quieter down here. Cooper joins us on the grass, three beers in hand.

Hayley nudges Cooper as he hands her a stubby. 'Can you take my top off for me please?'

He turns to give Hayley his full attention. 'Anytime, babe.'

She raises her eyebrows and thrusts the beer back into his chest.

'Oh, you mean your bottle top?' He cracks his mouth so it's just a half-smile.

Hayley leans in to him. 'Whichever you'd prefer.'

I shake my head. The girl is extreme.

Cooper hands me a beer too.

'Oh, thanks,' I say, 'but I don't drink.'

Cooper tips his head to the side. 'Really? Not at all?'

'Not at all.'

'I thought people died if they didn't at least drink water.'

My cheeks warm. 'I mean alcohol.'

Cooper smirks. 'No kidding.' He's swaying a little as he talks.

Hayley raises her beer. 'Cheers.' She clinks her bottle against Cooper's.

I roll my eyes at Nikki, who giggles.

'I'm going to see if I can find something a bit softer to drink.' I head back up the stairs, leaving Nikki to watch Cooper and Hayley's ridiculous flirting, my chest tight. I struggle to hold back the tears. It's ridiculous; Cooper is not mine. Seeing him flirting with Hayley shouldn't be bothering me. Thinking I would have even the slightest chance with someone like Cooper Dally is crazy.

All the Eskies are filled with beer, except for one designated for wine. I head into the kitchen and pour myself a glass of water. I'm about to go back out to the deck when I see Brad sitting in the corner on his own. There are two chairs, so I ask if I can join him.

'Sure.' The music isn't as loud inside, but it's still not that easy to talk.

Brad moves in, indicating he wants to tell me something. I meet him halfway. His breath is warm and sweet as it brushes the side of my face. 'I saw you, Nikki and Hayley come in. Is Ellen coming?'

I shake my head. 'She's not allowed to go to parties. Her parents have said maybe once she's seventeen.' Brad seems disappointed. 'No dating until then, either,' I add.

He nods, as though he already knew that, then frowns thoughtfully. 'Why is that, do you reckon?'

'I dunno. Seems crazy, since seventeen is when everyone will be able to drive.'

'I meant about the dating.'

I shrug. 'She has a heart thing. Maybe her parents are scared a boy will break it.' I grin, but Brad just nods thoughtfully.

'Is the heart condition she has serious?'

'It stops her doing stuff. Fun stuff. So, I guess it must be sort of serious. She never talks about it. We've got used to her not being able to do some things with us.'

He leans back into his chair.

'Why are you over here on your own?' I ask.

Brad picks up a beer and indicates to how it's almost empty. 'I'm trying to slow down. Cooper's off his face and if I go too, there's no one to look out for either of us.'

'I wondered if he was. He's flirting something shocking with Hayley.'

'Really?' Brad says.

'You're surprised?'

'I am. I thought he was focusing on someone else at the moment.'

'He seems pretty interested in Hayley to me.'

Brad tips his head back and takes another swig of his beer. So much for slowing down.

'Your voice is a little slurred,' I comment.

He chuckles. 'Sorry.' He leans in again, as though he's going to lower his voice, but if he meant to, he forgets by the time he speaks. 'You know, you look pretty when I'm drunk.'

I laugh nervously. 'You mean you don't like me as much when you're sober?'

'I mean, I have less power to resist seeing how pretty you are when I'm drinking.'

'Well, you're funny and very sweet when you're drunk.'

'I wish Ellen was here. None of us are allowed to even look sideways at you these days without getting our faces smashed. So, you know, I'm trying to keep my attention on Ellen. She's sweet-as.'

'What do you mean you're not allowed to? By who?'

Brad's face drops and he indicates to Cooper, who's walking into the room. 'If Cooper asks, I was asking you where Ellen was tonight. Okay?'

I stare at him dumbly as he walks away. Cooper replaces him in the chair opposite me. 'You disappeared.'

I raise my glass. 'Took a while to find something I could drink.'

'So, what's with the "I don't drink" thing?'

I tap my glass of water. 'Only alcohol. My mum drinks a fair bit. It's not pleasant.'

'Sure. But half the kids here would say that. And look at them.' There's barely a body in the room without a bottle of something in their hand.

I run my hand through my hair. 'Okay, well, there's not a single adult in my life who isn't either drunk or sobering up so they can go stock up to get drunk again. And they all live completely miserable lives. Then there's Nikki, who gets tipsy just by smelling alcohol, and is a bit over-the-top with everything when she's drunk. I decided the world was going to be a better, safer place for me and my friends if I didn't drink. I didn't like the taste that much, so it was easy not to.'

Cooper gives me a slow nod. 'Heavy.' He puts his hand in mine. 'I don't think I could do that. Drinking helps me forget.'

'Forget what?'

He shrugs. 'Everything.' He pauses. It seems to me Cooper wouldn't have much in his life he'd want to forget. Except maybe Mikaela. 'It helps me to relax. People are funnier when they're drunk.'

'Yeah, well, I don't need to get drunk to have fun. Or to be funny.'

'Really?' His lips purse together and he gets a faraway look in his eyes. 'Wanna go for a walk?'

I try to hide any surprise on my face but can't stop my chest from growing warm. 'What, like, just the two of us?'

'Sure. Why not?'

'Where to?'

'I dunno, down the street? I have this sudden desire to get you alone.' Cooper tightens his grip on my hand and pulls me up out of my chair.

'Hang on,' I say. 'I can't. I have to look out for Hayley and Nikki.'

'They're alright.'

'Yeah but they're drinking. I'm looking out for them.'

'Sure.' His hand is still holding mine. 'Another noble cause. I respect that, Grace McKay.' He gestures to the deck. 'Come dance with me instead?'

I can see Hayley slow dancing with someone. It looks like Brad's older brother, Justin. Cooper keeps my hand in his and leads me outside.

I stand opposite Cooper and sway to the music. 'Ethan's house is so beautiful. It's like one of those display homes you see in TV ads and stuff.'

'You like this kind of house?' Cooper asks.

'It reminds me of a mansion in the States I've seen pictures of. I can only dream of living in a house like this one day.'

'Well,' Cooper says, grabbing me by the hand and flicking his feet around in some crazy dance moves, 'owning a place like this is in my game plan.' He raises his eyebrows. 'Wanna join me?'

I chew on my lip.

I watch Cooper as he continues to dance, interacting with others around him, yet keeping his focus on me the whole time. I'm not much of a dancer, so I sway and move my feet from side to side as he dances around me.

But as the music changes pace, Cooper tries to pull me in close.

'We could do great things together, Grace,' he slurs. He wraps my arms around his neck and places his hands firmly on my hips. I sway to the music as Cooper runs his hands up and down my back, his lips moving beside my ear again, but I tune him out.

I let go of Cooper and throw my head back, my hands reaching out to the stars. The music surges through my body, filling it with hope for what might still be, of what my life could become—new and different, unique to the legacy my family wants to pass on to me.

Even without Mikaela Harper in my world.

I break out of Cooper's grasp and spin. I spin and spin and spin until my feet fall over themselves and I crash into people and I laugh until someone catches me and I open my eyes and see Jack. Except it's not Jack, it's Brad. But then it's not Brad, it's Nikki, and she's pulling me out of the crowd and down the corridor and back out the front door toward home.

Chapter 11

The weekend is filled with a hundred messages about Cooper Dally and the way he was dancing with me on Friday night. Nikki and Hayley are ecstatic that we'd been at the party but are totally embarrassed by my strange behaviour. They say everyone was looking at me; I'd stopped the whole party and injured a couple of Ethan's friends with my erratic dancing. But it doesn't stop the girls going on and on about what other parties we could be invited to in the weeks to come.

By Monday morning I'm over it and ready for a new week, one where passing Science is back to number one priority. I sit in front of my bedroom wall, reading over and over my favourite inspo quotes. I picture myself, books resting in the cradle of my arm, standing in front of a university building. I walk up the steps toward the large closed doors. I remind myself I can do it, that I can be anything, achieve anything. I choose a quote from the wall, about how success is just a whole lot of little bits of effort repeated every day, and write it up the inside of my arm.

First up is HPE. On the way to class, Cooper falls in-step beside me. 'Hey, Grace. HPE. Cross-country practice,' he says.

I chuckle. 'Yeah. Joy.'

'You're not into it?'

'There's only one thing I dislike more than HPE—running.'

Cooper bounces as he walks along. 'I guess it's good we're all different. Otherwise we'd end up wanting to all have the same jobs and stuff.'

'I guess so.'

'I got you something.' He hands me a parcel in brown wrapping paper, a yellow ribbon around the outside.

'Why?'

He shrugs. 'I saw it and thought of you.'

I unwrap the parcel. It's a glass drink bottle. There's a big pink heart in the middle, with a heart-beat line running through it. Above the heart, it says, 'Cute enough to stop your heart', then under the heart it says, 'skilled enough to start it again.'

I run a finger across the curve on my lips. 'Oh, that is sweet.'

'Cute, huh? Technically it's for an actual nurse. But it reminded me of our conversation the other day and, yeah, I thought you might like it.'

'I love it, Cooper. Thank you.'

'Well, I'd say enjoy the run, but …'

'I'll enjoy the walk instead.' I chuckle. He runs off. I pop the paper in the bin and detour past the drinking taps to fill up the bottle on the way. I tie the yellow ribbon around my wrist.

I'm happy walking the cross-country course on my own; Ellen isn't allowed to participate in most HPE activities with her heart thingy, and it turns out Hayley is just as good at keeping up with the boys as she is at chasing them. Nikki isn't at school today. I pull out my phone, take a selfie with my new water bottle, and Snapchat it to her saying, 'How cute is this?'

She replies with five open-mouthed emojis, then adds:

Cooper? Really? <3

She finishes the text with a few green emojis to a photo of herself propped up in bed.

I adjust my walking pace so it's in time to the music streaming through my earphones, shuffling my feet a little and dancing my hands around my body like I'd seen some of the girls do at Ethan's party. I close my eyes and drop my head back so far I almost lose my hat, allowing the sun to shine down onto my face.

But then something brushes my leg. I open my eyes to see someone curled up into a ball; I can tell it's a boy from the hairy legs sticking out, but his head is pressing hard into his thighs so I can't see who it is.

'Are you okay?' I ask, bending down a little. No response. 'Hey, you,' I say more loudly, 'are you okay?'

There is a grunt from within the ball. The ball rocks and hums.

Tapping the ball with my drink bottle gets no response, but the humming becomes a little more rhythmic.

'Look, what's the matter? Do you need help?'

'I don't know,' replies a muffled voice.

'Well, I don't know what is going on with you, but you look really weird out here in the middle of the schoolyard with no one else around.'

Jack's face peeks out from within the ball. 'Are they gone?'

The school ground is empty. 'There's no one here.'

Jack's face ventures further out from the ball. 'So, they're gone?'

'Who's gone?'

Jack keeps rocking, back and forth, back and forth, his hands over his head. 'Just, people.'

'Well, there's no one here, so I guess so.'

Jack unwinds and picks himself up off the ground. He's still kind of rocking on his feet. He keeps one hand on his head and uses the other to wipe the bits of grass sticking to his shorts, but very little comes off.

'Do you need to go to sick bay or something?'

Jack keeps looking around. 'I don't know.'

'What happened to you?'

'I don't know.'

'Did you fall over or something?'

Jack hums again, his head in his hands.

'I think I should take you to sick bay.'

I start walking, but Jack stands there. 'Are you coming?'

He frowns. I put my hand out, and he flinches.

'I'm going to take you to the office. You're acting really bizarre.'

Jack ignores my hand and starts to walk in the direction of the office. Every part of his body moves as he is walking. It's like he can't control himself properly. He looks at my cheek as though he can't find my eyes, and smiles, but it's as if he can't even control his facial muscles properly—his mouth is wide on one side and flat on the other.

'Thank you for helping me, Graceland,' he mumbles. His lips over-exaggerate every word.

'I'm not doing much, just taking you to the office.'

'You stopped. It's nice to know you haven't completely changed.'

'What's that supposed to mean?'

Jack shrugs. 'You used to be much nicer.'

'What do mean "used to"? When?'

'When we were in Year 7. You were nice to me back then.'

'I don't remember.'

'On my first day of school, you said hi to me. You asked what school I was from and if I knew anyone else here.'

'I did?'

'You used to let me talk to you back then about Jesse. Jesse your brother. He was my friend. I miss him.'

A memory flickers like an old movie across my mind and I see Jesse as he runs around the coffee table, and I'm telling him to stop. I'm angry, but I don't need to be. I speak harshly, but I don't need to. He stops; his eyes are frightened. He leaves the house to sit in his little blue chair in the front yard. In his hand is the smooth, flat battery he would swallow, that would take his life, while I watch TV, grateful for the peace now that he is not inside with me.

I force my eyes open and gasp for air. 'I don't like to remember, Jack. It's better, easier, to forget. People change.'

'Usually people become nicer, not meaner.'

'Maybe in your world. Not in mine.'

He looks like he's going to say something, but I open the door to the office and he closes his mouth. Then I turn and walk away, putting my headphones back in, thanking God that I'm not anything like Jack Oskar.

When I finally get to the end of the cross-country course, most of the class have gone off to the bubblers and to get changed for next period. It isn't long after that people start getting called into the assistant principal's office. I have no idea why, until I get pulled out of Science too.

Mr Reyl has a teacher's voice that flips your stomach upside down and round and round whether you're in trouble or not. I fill my heart with defiant courage and stand tall as he calls my name from behind his desk. He doesn't look at me when I walk in. He's scanning some loose-leaf paper and making notes in the margin.

He glances up from behind his glasses. 'Take a seat please, Miss McKay.' I consider for a moment whether to obey, then choose to move to the carpet-padded chair, draping my arms over the armrests. He continues making notes for a few more minutes. I know this trick. He's making me sweat. He's making me think of all the possible reasons I may have been called to sit in this chair in this office. He's building the suspense so I'll be easier to break. He's dealt with me before; I won't give anything away without a fight.

'Do you know why you're here, Miss McKay?'

I shake my head. 'No, sir.' He gets real antsy if you don't call him 'sir'.

He holds up the papers in his hand. 'You brought Jack Oskar into the office earlier. Why?'

'Because he was having some kind of episode. He was lying on the ground making funny noises. I thought he might have had, like, a brain aneurysm or something.'

He pinches his forehead with his thumb and middle finger. 'That's a little dramatic, don't you think, Miss McKay?'

I shrug. 'He was acting weird.'

'And you've never seen him in a situation like that before?'

I shrug, and then shake my head.

'You've been in most of Jack's classes since Year 7. I find it a little difficult to believe you, Miss McKay.'

I hate it how he always uses my full name. 'I didn't really think about it, sir. I brought him to sick bay in case there was something wrong with him.'

'Did he say anything to you about why he was acting the way he was?'

Shaking my head seems my best response again.

'Answer my question, please, Miss McKay.'

'No, sir.'

'No? Jack didn't say anything to you about other students in the class?'

'I don't really remember if he said anything.'

Mr Reyl sifts through the papers, his eyes scanning left to right as he moves from one page to the next. 'I've spoken to a number of people already. Not only about today's incident in HPE, but also about what happened to Jack the other week during recess.' He gives me the death stare. 'Perhaps you could shed some additional light on what happened then for me.'

I involuntarily swallow. 'Not really, sir. If something happened, I wasn't around for it. I talked to him on the way to Science that morning, that was all.'

'And you hadn't heard any talk about what might have been going to happen to Jack after you spoke to him?'

'No? I don't understand; why would I have?'

Mr Reyl writes notes down the side of the page. The silence in the room pounds against the walls of my mind.

'Why can't you ask Jack what happened?'

'Jack doesn't like to talk. I think he feels it will get him in more trouble.'

'Well, I'm not the person to be talking to, either.'

Mr Reyl leans forward from behind his desk. 'You understand, Miss McKay, that it is everyone's responsibility to protect those who need our protection, don't you?'

I close my eyes and push back the pain rising in my chest. Jesse is running around me, laughing, his little face alive with innocence as I tell him to be careful, not to run around the lounge room. I push the pain back down, refusing to feel it, refusing to let it get in. My chest is so tight that I'm having trouble breathing.

'You helped Jack Oskar today,' Mr Reyl says. 'I hope that would be how you would act in other situations as well.'

'I guess so, sir.'

'You guess so?'

'No one else was around today. I had to help him.'

'No one else was around to help him on Thursday, either.'

'I don't know what happened to Jack on Thursday. I didn't see anything.'

'Okay, Graceland,' Mr Reyl says. 'I believe you. I hope you will continue to look out for Jack into the future as well. Can I be sure of that?'

I stand up. 'Can I go now?'

I don't wait for an answer, I turn and head out, closing the door behind me. I run out of the office and down the steps leading out into the school yard. I want to run and run and run and get away from this place and my memories of Jesse. And from Jack Oskar who should be able to look after himself and not need my help, not need to be protected—and Jesse, who should have been like that too.

'How did things go with Mr Reyl?' Ellen asks when I eventually return to class. 'What did he want you for?'

'Something to do with Jack. I think he's trying to work out what happened when he hurt himself a couple of weeks ago.'

'Oh? I didn't realise they were still investigating that.'

'Yeah. Something also happened in HPE this morning. Jack was acting weird, curled up on the ground in a ball, so I took him to the office.'

'What do you mean he was acting weird?'

'Scared. Like, really scared. And he was asking if they were gone.'

'Who were gone?'

I shrug. 'You don't think it could have been the boy band, do you?'

'They're in that HPE class, aren't they?'

'Yes, but no one else was around when I found Jack. I don't remember Cooper or the boys having a thing against Jack in the past—why would any of them start now?'

'Showing off for Hayley, maybe? Didn't Joe have a go at Jack that day around when Hayley had started?'

'True,' I shake my head. 'But then Cooper stood up for Jack when they were teasing him in class the other week. It doesn't make sense for Cooper, at least, to have been involved.'

There is doubt in her eyes. 'I hope you're right, Grace.'

Chapter 12

In Form the next day, I slump into my chair and try to tune out the murmurings of everyone around me. I'm not mentally prepared to face the world today, and I'm determined to make it wait. I didn't sleep well last night, with thoughts of the science project running over and over in my mind. I'd spent a couple of hours during the night reading and rereading my quotes wall, but not even that had helped.

The stress of passing Science, the need for my life to be different to Mum's, to everyone in my family, is taking over everything.

I pull out my phone, putting my head down closer to my lap so no one's in doubt about whether I want to talk. But as I swipe my phone to open Snapchat, Miss Krensky makes mention that Cooper is away. It forces me into the real world.

'Cooper is having a day off as a consequence for his behaviour of late.' The class erupts into quiet chatter. 'I hope no one follows his poor decision-making.'

I almost jump out of my chair in surprise. Cooper? Really?

Jack has his head down, headphones over his ears.

'Coop's an innocent man, miss,' Harry says. The room goes quiet. Harry hardly ever speaks. 'A victim of circumstance in a world more concerned with finding an answer than with finding the truth.'

Miss Krensky frowns. 'Mr Reyl is very thorough in his investigations. There needed to be a clear example set that Cooper's treatment of certain students lately is not okay.'

Pain races from my shoulders up into my head. I can't believe

Cooper would hurt Jack. I shake my head. 'It can't be true,' I whisper.

Hayley is laughing at something on her phone. Nikki suggests I open Snapchat.

I turn my attention back to my phone and open Snapchat, where Cooper has uploaded a story of himself standing on the beach, his shirt off, a goofy smile on his face. The caption says, *Thank you, education system.*

'Look at that body,' Hayley says, climbing into the seat beside me. I strain my eyes to catch Hayley's facial expression without moving my head. Her tongue moves over her lips like she's just finished downing her favourite juice. 'They don't come much more perfect than that.'

'Mmm, mmm,' Nikki mumbles from the seat in front of us. 'Who needs surf lifesavers when you've got that on your beach.'

The girls giggle. I show Ellen the picture on my phone.

'Oh,' Ellen says. 'Wow.' She pinches my phone's screen to zoom in on Cooper's chest.

I laugh and pull my phone away. 'No perving, Ellen. It's not in your nature.'

Ellen falls back into her seat. 'I hate not being allowed to have my phone at school.'

'I'll screenshot it and send it to you,' Hayley says. 'That way, you won't totally miss out.' Her phone clicks as she takes the screenshot.

'He'll get notification of that,' I say.

'So?' Hayley says, raising her index finger to her lips. 'He can know.' She winks at us.

'Surely he hasn't been suspended for what happened to Jack.'

The girls all mumble, but only Ellen responds clearly. 'It does seem to be pretty likely, Grace.'

'It just seems out of character for him,' I say. 'Don't you think?'

Ellen shrugs. Hayley and Nikki have moved on to another conversation.

Jack has barely moved the entire time in Form, his face glued to the iPad sitting on his lap. Mr Reyl had said to look out for Jack;

perhaps, when he called me into the office, he already knew it was Cooper who'd done it.

Brad slides into the seat next to me in Maths. 'Mind if I sit with you?'

'Not at all,' I say. I'm a bit short of friends in Maths; I usually sit on my own.

Brad pulls out his maths book and opens to the page he's working from. It's two pages behind where I'm up to.

'I saw you were pretty stressed when Van Hayden announced our groups in Science,' he says. 'Are you feeling any better about it?'

'Don't remind me.' I place my head in my hands for a moment. 'He's put me with the absolute lowest of the low for the project. I'm convinced he wants to see me fail and ruin my chances of getting into Biology next year.'

'Maybe they're not as bad as you think.'

'Look at you, being *Mr Positive* all of a sudden.' I rub my forehead with my hand, trying to prevent the stress headache that is building. 'Is it true that Cooper's not at school because he did stuff to Jack?'

Brad shrugs. 'Not my place to say. I know he's not a big fan of the guy, but he's also trying the whole kindness thing at the moment. It's a nice change, actually.'

'So, it's more likely Mr Reyl got it wrong this time?'

'A case of the usual suspect, perhaps. Mr Reyl's got a bit of a thing about Cooper; I don't think he likes him much. I ran with Coop during HPE yesterday and didn't see him do anything to Jack.' He gives me a half-smile. I put my head down to start working, when he says, 'Hey, maybe I can help with the Science problem. I could tap into the school database and pull up the report cards of those guys from last semester? So you can know what you're in for.'

'You can do that?'

Brad shrugs. 'Easily. It's the least I can do.'

'I didn't know you were into techy stuff like that.'

The corners of his mouth are twitching. 'Let's just say I used to be.'

'What, in your previous life?'

'Sort of.' He fiddles with the zip on my pencil case. 'You might say I started fresh when I moved schools.'

'I've never heard you talk about your old school.'

'I don't much.' He looks at me with a spark in his eyes. 'But it was probably good I left when I did. Things were starting to heat up in the kitchen, if you know what I mean.'

I laugh. 'No, I don't, actually.'

'I mean, people were starting to find things out. About me. I'm not like that now, though. I've changed. But I'd do it, if you want me to, as long as you promise to not tell anyone. Ever.'

'Sure.' I nod. 'But, why? You don't owe me anything.'

He looks away. 'I'd like to help make things a little easier for you, that's all.'

'Well, thanks. At least I'd know what I was dealing with.'

Brad nods. 'When it comes to Science, anyway.'

I go to ask what he means by that when he adds, 'I'll get into the database during lunch when things are a bit quieter and text you the screenshots later today. It's no trouble. Like I said, I'm happy to help out a friend. It'll be fun to do a little hacking again.' He picks up his calculator and concentrates on a problem on his page.

I pull out my phone and find a Snapchat from Cooper. He's sent me a couple throughout the morning, but in this one he's in a surf shop, holding a pair of bikinis up to himself with the caption, *Suit me much?* I'm trying my hardest to be mad at him, in case it's true about Jack, but I can't help but giggle. My heart wants him to be innocent.

In English at the end of the day, instead of answering the scene questions about *Romeo and Juliet*, I sit next to Nikki to tell her what Cooper's been up to. 'He's sent you all those Snapchats just today? I haven't had any from him.'

'He's sent me about twenty all up. This is his latest one.' I open Snapchat. The screen fills with Cooper swiping a thick layer of sunscreen across his chest. It catches the bottom of his face, so we can see how straight and perfectly white his teeth are. The text says, *If only I had someone to be suspended with.*

'Grace. Far out. Has he said anything else like that during the day?'

'No. The rest have been photos—more of him on the beach, him licking an ice cream … his abs …'

'Hold up, he sent you a photo of him licking an ice cream?' Nikki laughs out loud.

'Shh, I don't want Hayley to know.'

Nikki chuckles. 'Oh, yeah. Man, she'd be rotten at you.'

'Probably.'

'What are you going to do about it?'

'About what?'

'This.' Nikki points to the phone screen. 'Are you going to, you know, flirt back?'

'I'm trying hard to stay mad at him because of what he might have done to Jack.'

'Grace, I figured he was interested after the way he hogged you at the beach that day, but if you want him, you need to let him know you're keen. Forget Jack Oskar. Imagine if you were Cooper Dally's?'

I shake my head. 'He's flirting, and not just with me. How about him and Hayley at Ethan's party? They were sickening, their flirting was so obvious.'

'Yeah, and then you left to get a drink.'

'Why, what happened then?'

'Hayley kept flirting, but it was like Cooper became a brick wall. He basically ignored her. That's why she ended up with Justin.'

'Why would he only flirt with Hayley while I was around?'

'To get you jealous. To gauge your reaction. Who knows.'

I shake my head. 'What does he see in me?'

Nikki clicks her fingers. 'What's not to like, girl? You are beautiful. And Cooper Dally is all over it.'

A little piece of hope creeps across my face, curving my lips. 'No, he's only teasing me, using me to get to Hayley.'

Nikki chuckles. 'You keep telling yourself that if you want. But he won't hang around forever.'

I turn off my phone as Hayley returns to her seat next to me. 'What are you two so chatty about?'

'Nothing,' I say. 'Just looking at stuff.'

'Really? Like what?' Hayley grabs my phone and puts in my password.

'Hey, abuse of the privilege,' I say, but she's already in my phone, opening different apps. There's nothing there to see.

Hayley glares at me. 'Yeah, well, I won't tell you about the Snapchat I got from Cooper earlier today then.' She flicks her hair, but the waves fall back in place.

I raise my eyebrows at Nikki, but say to Hayley, 'You got a Snapchat from Cooper?'

'Maybe,' Hayley says. 'Did you?'

'Another one of him at the beach. That's what I was showing Nic.'

'You should have screenshotted it so I could see it too.' Hayley pulls her phone out of her pocket. 'He sent me a video.' She opens her photos where there is a series of screenshots of Cooper doing a handstand half in the water. 'He's such an idiot. Look at how close his arms are; there's no way he would have stayed in that position for long. His phone fell over at the end of the video so I couldn't even see his exit.'

I put my head down. Nikki jabs me in the ribs, reminding me this is really happening. To me.

Chapter 13

I purposely miss the bus and walk home from school that afternoon, despite the distance. My head is swirling with thoughts of Cooper Dally, and his latest love interest. Me. Maybe, anyway.

Back when Mikaela had been at school, Cooper only had eyes for her. He'd been besotted from the day she walked onto the school grounds. He'd chased her for more than a year before she agreed to defy her parents and go out with him. And now he's chasing me—Grace McKay. Flat-chested, pale-skinned, cashless, dry-haired me.

As I turn the corner towards my house, I can hear yelling coming from behind the front door. The grass crunches under my feet as I cut across the lawn.

Through the wire door, I can hear Lisa Marie screaming. 'I don't care. I've been offered the job and I'm going to take it.'

Tom's blue sports car pulls up out the front, a rhythmic base booming from inside, as my mother's voice rings out from somewhere within the house. 'And what, you think I care what you do? Drop out of school then! And you can go find somewhere else to live and see how you get on in this world. But when it all falls apart and your hours get cut because you've turned eighteen and cost too much to employ, don't come crying to me.'

Tom joins me on the verandah. He's wearing baggy pants and his dreadlocks are up in a pony tail.

'Hey hey, Memphis Grace.' He puts his hand up to high-five me, but I ignore it and roll my eyes.

'You're dressed up. Something special on tonight?'

He chuckles. 'Your sister is always worth a little extra effort.'

I roll my eyes again and point to the door, where heavy footsteps are approaching. 'I think World War III is breaking out in there.'

We both stare at the screen door as my mother's lecturing voice filters down the hallway; Lisa Marie's silhouette appears and yells, 'I'm not you, Mum! This is my life, not yours. Tom will look after me. We'll look after each other.' Lisa Marie picks up the bag at her feet and walks out the front door. She kisses Tom and looks at me. 'You missed the bus.'

I shrug. 'I wanted to walk.'

'You ready, babe?' Tom asks.

Next thing I know, Lisa Marie's jumping in the passenger side of Tom's car and they're disappearing down the street.

I don't go inside the house. Mum's in there, banging around in the kitchen like she's Gordon Ramsay. Tuesday's her day off, and I don't think I can handle her raging, let alone another run of Elvis movies. I need time to think. Lisa Marie not finishing Year 12 seems crazy; she only has a month or two of school left.

With nowhere to go, and tired feet from the walk home, I sit out in the little blue chair we've had in our front yard since forever. Dad bought it for Jesse for his birthday when he was little because he loved sitting out the front of the house, and it stopped him from wandering off so much. I run my hand over the wooden arms, noting how the weather is ageing it, peeling back the blue paint.

The neighbours all knew Jesse by name; they'd stop to say hello whenever he sat out here. And Jesse knew all of them too. The whole street would look out for him; they knew who he belonged to, and they'd bring him home when he'd go too far down the street.

I flick open Snapchat and take a photo of myself pouting and add it to my story. I immediately get a reply from Cooper.

Hey, babe. You k?

I type back.

I'm ok. Just got some news. Struggling to process it.

He Snaps himself with a serious, almost a little sad, face.

Wanna hang out?

Stay cool, Grace. Stay cool.

Maybe. You got something in mind?

I'm going to a mate's place. Come with? It's a small party, a few guys I know out of school. I can show you off to them.

That's cute. My heartbeat quickens.

When?

I'll come get you. We can grab something to eat first.

My fingers are trembling.

Sounds great. I'll text you my address.

No need. See you soon

I sneak around the back of the house. Fortunately, I've left my bedroom window open and it doesn't take much to break in. I throw my uniform onto the floor and quickly grab some clothes before Mum hears me. Footsteps approach. I leave the house via the same window, somehow managing to get dressed as I cross the backyard, and return to Jesse's blue chair to await Cooper's arrival.

Cooper and his mum drive up in a red convertible. I climb into the back seat. It smells like plastic with a hint of eucalyptus and the engine is so quiet you can hardly tell it's running. Cooper removes the L-plates from the car and climbs into the backseat with me.

'Mum's a bit funny about me driving with non-family in the car. She's worried I'll kill someone.'

'Not until I have their parents' permission, Cooper. And stop telling everyone I think you're going to kill someone. It makes me look like a bad mother.'

Cooper laughs.

The woman turns around. 'I assume you're Grace. You can call me Patty.' She turns the radio on, loud enough that Cooper and I can talk without her hearing us.

'Nice car,' I say.

Cooper rubs his hand along the leather seat. 'Yeah, sure is. Picked it out myself.'

My eyes widen. 'This is yours?'

'My seventeenth is coming up. Technically I have to wait until then to call it my own. Mum was keen for me to learn to drive in my own car.'

He places his hand on mine and electricity sparks in my heart as though it needed restarting. I pull my hand away. I can't until I know for sure. 'Cooper, I need to know something.'

He stretches his fingers. 'Anything.'

'Jack Oskar. Did you get suspended because you did something to him?'

A vein pops out in his neck and for a moment it looks like he's mad. But then he says, 'I used to be different, Grace. I've changed. You must have noticed that.'

I frown. 'So, you did hurt Jack?'

'Sort of.'

I cross my arms.

'Look, the boys and I, we got into him a bit the other week, after he was talking to you on the way to Science. It bugged me and I took it too far. I didn't mean for him to get hurt, but he fell over and scraped all up the side of his face. I apologised to him afterwards.

You can ask him yourself.'

I nod slowly. 'And yesterday in HPE?'

'I honestly don't know what Reyl was going on about with that. Whatever happened, it wasn't me. I ran the course with the boys. I don't even remember seeing Jack.'

His story matches with what Brad had said.

'I figure my suspension yesterday was my past catching up with me. And I was happy to take the punishment. I deserved it, if not for what happened with Jack, then for some of the crappy stuff I've done. But I'm a new guy. Trust me?'

Cooper is oozing sincerity. Whatever happened to Jack yesterday in HPE, it wasn't Cooper. And he's right, Cooper has seemed different the past week. Perhaps it wasn't fair to judge him on whatever had happened with Jack. If Cooper is really changing, then it isn't fair to single out that moment, especially without knowing for sure what happened. Perhaps Cooper gave him a push and Jack fell over. He isn't exactly known for his coordination. He's so awkward and he does seem to get particularly weird when Cooper is around.

'Okay,' I say. I take Cooper's hand. 'I'll trust you. I just don't like it when people pick on others, especially someone like Jack.' I wrap my arm around his, his biceps thick, muscles tight. 'I had a brother a bit like Jack,' I whisper, swallowing hard. 'He died a few years ago.'

Cooper squeezes my hand and puts his head against mine. 'Oh yeah. What was his name again?'

'Jesse.'

The sky is turning pink and the air is cooling down. The hills are windy, but they give amazing views of the ocean. There's only the occasional die-hard dog walker on the street. Despite the view, I'm glad to live on a flatter side of town, where walking anywhere is less likely to take a life.

The car slows and Cooper's mum turns the music down.

'Do you mind if we go here?' Cooper asks, as we pull up out the front of a row of takeaway restaurants. 'I know it's not much, but it's around the corner from my mate's place. It means Mum won't have to come back to drive us there.'

'It's great,' I say. 'I can't afford much else, anyway.' *In fact, I can barely afford this.*

Cooper pulls me out of the car. 'No need for you to worry about that. My shout.'

I go to thank Patty for driving us around, but she's already taken off. Cooper says, 'It's a pretty crappy place for a first date, though.'

I raise my eyebrows. *This is a date?*

'So, let's not consider it a date, okay?' he says. 'Then I can make it up to you with a proper first date another time.'

'We can have a great first date no matter where we are,' I say. 'It's who you're with that makes it good.'

Cooper's eyes light up. 'You are something special, Grace McKay. Why did it take me so long to notice you?'

There's a screaming in my head. I think it's excitement. But I can't help the small voice that creeps in: *Cooper didn't notice you because you were always next to Mikaela.*

We sit down, side by side, in a red leathered booth with our burgers. Out of his backpack, Cooper pulls a small parcel wrapped in brown paper and a soft green ribbon.

'What's this?' I ask.

He shrugs. 'A peace treaty. I figured you might have been upset about the whole Jack thing. So, I saw this today and thought you might like it.'

I frown. 'Really?' I tug on the ribbon so it falls off. The paper unwraps. There is a pair of light green bikinis in there. The top is a high-neck halter, the bottoms are simple briefs. 'Oh wow,' I say. My breath catches. 'They're gorgeous.'

Cooper seems to be enjoying my reaction. 'I got green to match your eyes,' he says.

'They're beautiful. I can't accept them though.'

'Sure, you can,' he says. He reaches out and tucks a wayward piece of hair, or maybe it was only imagined, off the side of my face. His hand is soft and gentle across my cheek. He leans in. 'You'll look great in them, Grace. There's so much untapped beauty in you.' Then he leans back as though snapped out of a trance. 'And they're Australian-made from start to finish, completely ethical all-natural fibres. I made sure I wasn't getting you anything that might go against your values.'

I chuckle. 'That's awesome, though I can't afford to care as much as I'd like about that sort of thing.' I glance at the tags. There is a black mark through the price. 'I'm still not sure I can accept them.'

'Well, they'll do nothing for me. I'd have needed a bigger size for a start.'

I hold the top up to my chest.

'Yep, I thought as much,' he says. 'They're going to look amazing on you.'

He reaches over and takes my hand.

I put my head down and say, 'Are you sure you're ready for this?'

'For what?'

'Dating again. It's only been—what? Two months since…'

'Come on, Grace. Moving on. This is all part of the decision … the plan.'

I try to gauge his sincerity. 'What, am I part of that decision?'

'You. Me. A fresh start. New goals. New reasons to get up in the morning. And you're one very awesome reason to get up each day.'

As we walk through the backstreets to Cooper's mate's place, I look down at our entwined hands. This must be what people mean when they say they can't see which fingers are his and which are their own.

A few determined stars shine above us, but the moon reveals some thicker clouds moving in. There's a smell of rain lingering in the air.

'So,' Cooper says, 'are you going to tell me what upset you so much this afternoon?'

Am I? I nod slowly. 'When I came home from school today, my mum and my sister—you know Lisa Marie?'

'I do,' he says. 'The second most beautiful girl at school.'

I frown and then giggle. 'Oh, right,' I say. 'Sure.'

'What about her?'

'She and Mum were having a huge fight.'

'What were they fighting about?'

'I don't know. But I think maybe it was something to do with her boyfriend because she …' I pause. I don't know if I want to tell Cooper that Lisa Marie is dropping out of school, since it hasn't actually happened yet. She could still change her mind.

'What?'

'I got the feeling she's planning on moving in with him.'

'I don't see why parents get so upset about that kind of thing. I know Tom; he's a top bloke. At least she'll still be local. You won't have to go far to visit, like I do with my brother on the Gold Coast.'

'Yeah, well, Tom annoys me. He's way too chill. And he has a stupid nickname he calls me all the time.'

'I tell you what.' There's excitement in his voice. 'What about if we hang out at the shops Saturday morning? I'll spoil you. There's nothing like shopping to turn a negative situation into an awesome one. It'll help make you feel better about it all.'

'You like shopping?'

'I do when I have something, or someone, to shop for.'

I can't help but wonder what exactly spoiling me would look like, but given the bikinis I've just been given, I suspect it's something I should be excited about. 'Sounds great. I'd love that.'

Mikaela's family is pretty well off, so if Cooper did this kind of thing for her, Mikaela probably wouldn't have thought much of it. But as I look down at my old jeans and the same crop top that I wore to Maroochy Beach, I can't help but allow myself to feel fairly delighted about the idea of being spoilt by Cooper Dally.

We come to an enormous tree, a trunk so thick I couldn't wrap my arms around it. Red lollypop flowers droop generously from its branches. Cooper reaches up and picks one to give to me. I lift it to my nose, but its smell isn't strong enough to contend with Cooper's aftershave. He leans me against the tree, the rough wood prickling my back. Cooper is so close and he smells so good. His eyes are soft and tender as hair rustles against his forehead in the light breeze.

'You know, you really are the most beautiful girl in the school.'

The shy smile I try to conceal bursts onto my face. 'Come on, Cooper. Exaggerating, much?'

Cooper leans in, his face so close the stubble on his chin is brushing my cheek. 'I mean it. And I want you all to myself, Grace McKay.' My heart pounds. He's watching my lips. 'In fact, I'm determined to make you my own.'

I close my eyes and allow him to move in; our lips gently touch. I run my hands across his chest and over his shoulders. He moves his hand around to the back of my head, pulling me in closer, pressing his body up against me. He's so close, so tight, I struggle to breathe. I try to pull back, but I can't. I put my hands on his chest and gently apply pressure. He gets the hint and pulls back.

'Sorry,' he says. 'You had me there. I could barely contain myself.'

I giggle nervously. 'I noticed.'

He moves in again, running his lips over my cheek so I can barely feel them, and kisses me gently on the lips. 'So—' his lips are so close I can still feel them against my own, '—can we make it official?'

This must be what it means to have your breath stolen away. I can barely speak. 'Official?'

His eyes are still on my lips, his mouth wide with his smile. 'That you're mine and no one else's. You and me together.' Cooper leans back in and kisses me again. 'You're going to, like, perfect me, Grace McKay.'

I laugh. 'I'm not sure if that's really sweet or really creepy.'

'Let's go for sweet, then. So, is it a yes? Will you be mine?'

I widen my eyes. 'Yeah.'

He kisses me quickly, grabs my hand and starts to run, pulling me along behind him. I laugh. 'What are you doing?'

'Paul's house is around this corner. I can't wait to introduce you to the world as my girlfriend.'

Chapter 14

The next day when I get to school everyone is already talking about how Cooper Dally has a new girlfriend. When I see Nikki, she greets me with a kiss to the cheek and whispers, 'Is it you?'

I nod.

'Hayley?'

'I don't know how she'll react when I tell her.'

It turns out I don't need to. By the time she gets to school, she already knows. She comes right up to me. 'Is it true?'

I don't know whether to apologise or tell her to suck it up. She doesn't look as upset as I expected her to.

'Well,' she says, 'don't think I hate you for it. I mean, I would have liked it if it was me, but whatevs. I'm just glad it was one of us.'

It turns out Ellen is more upset at me than Hayley.

'What are you thinking?' she asks.

'What do you mean?'

'You're Cooper Dally's girlfriend. What do you think he's going to expect from you?'

I shake my head. 'I don't know. Not being with any other guys? Not much is going to change there.'

'That's not what I mean.'

I figure she's probably talking about sex. My heart races. 'Well, he's not getting that much from me,' I promise her. 'Not until I'm sure he's the one. He's kissed me. That's it.'

Ellen shakes her head. 'I didn't even realise you liked him in that way. Not seriously, anyway.'

'I never believed it was even an option.' I press my hands into my chest. 'But he's the whole package. Gorgeous. Rich. Sweet-as. And he knows just about everyone.'

'You hardly know him.'

'I'm *getting* to know him.'

'And it's only been, what, two months since he and Mikaela broke up?' Ellen's hands are on her hips. 'And she was your best friend. It doesn't feel right.'

'Why is this such a big deal, Ellen?'

'I think there's more to Cooper than you know about. You should talk to Mikaela. Cooper Dally isn't the kind of guy you mess with.'

I laugh. 'Ellen, come on. You're being melodramatic.'

'Am I? When was the last time you tried to call Mikaela? You should do more to find out why she left.'

'Why, what do you know that the rest of us don't?'

She shrugs. 'Mikaela and I used to talk sometimes. She wasn't as happy with Cooper as she let on.'

My heart drops to my feet. 'What do you mean? She loved him.'

'It's not my place to say anything. But, it's been a while. She might answer her phone now if you give her a call.'

I cross my arms. 'I've given up trying to contact her. She knows where I am. If she wants to be in touch, she can contact me.'

'I know you were hurt by what she did. But imagine what she's been through. She deserves more than for us to give up on her so soon. And you should talk to her if you're going through with the whole Cooper thing.'

'Okay,' I say. 'I'll think about it.' But I don't have any intention of talking to Mikaela Harper about Cooper Dally, even if I can get hold of her.

We're about to head into Form when Cooper comes up and puts his arm around me. 'Here she is!' he announces loudly. 'My leading lady, the beautiful Grace McKay.'

I glance at Ellen, who gives a sad smile.

Cooper keeps his arm around me and we walk into class together. I see Jack sitting at his desk near the door, watching me. As we walk past, Cooper says to Jack, 'Too bad, mate. She's taken now.'

Jack drops his eyes to the floor and rubs his hands together firmly, like he's super-stressed or something.

'Why'd you say that?' I ask.

'Because Jack Oskar has been in love with you since day one back in Year 7.' Cooper laughs heartily. 'Don't tell me you're the only person in Year 10 who doesn't know that.'

Jack is rocking in his chair, his thumbs still pushing with great strength into his other hand. He glances up at me, but quickly looks away again. And I can't help but feel a little bit sorry for the guy.

And then I remember Science.

'Okay everyone, hurry up and take your seats in your groups, please.' Mr Van Hayden opens the science lab door and we shuffle in after him. A few people mill around the teacher because they have forgotten who is in their group, including Seb. Ellen sits in her group near me. Hayley is up the back. She's in a group with Joe and is drawing a floral pattern up his arm with a black fineliner, while he whispers to her. Whatever he's saying is making her smile.

Cooper raises his hand. 'Hey, Mr Van. Any chance we could swap around our groups a bit?'

Mr Van Hayden seems unimpressed. 'Are we in Grade 3, Mr Dally?

'Hey, reset, sir,' Cooper says indignantly. 'I'm just not sure you've got the most up-to-date information about what's happening, you know, socially, in the class, that's all.'

'Social movements will continue to happen once you leave school and go out into the workplace.' Mr Van Hayden walks around the classroom, handing out a worksheet. 'Whether you strongly dislike a work colleague or they have recently broken your heart, Mr Dally, will make little difference to your boss.' The class laughs. 'If you are placed in a project group then, you will need to put your differences aside and get the job done. It is no different now.'

Cooper mouths what looks like the words, 'I tried', to me.

I mouth back, 'Thanks.' It's sweet that he was trying to get the groups changed.

So, this is my group. Seb has earphones in and is banging his fingers on his legs like he's doing a drum solo. Jack is staring out into the garden, rocking back and forth. Latisha is sketching someone, who I think is probably Mr Van Hayden; I can't even imagine what sort of person sketches their teacher. This group's a nightmare. The three reports Brad printed off for me burn in my pocket. Seb at least got a couple of Bs for his results last semester, but Jack and Latisha were, like me, barely passing. I close my eyes so tightly it makes me dizzy. If I make myself sick enough times in Science, maybe Mr Van would give me a sympathy passing grade. There is certainly no way I'm going to be able to lead this group through to a pass on my own.

I pick up the sheet to read what we're supposed to be doing for the lesson: choosing an area of genetics for the research project. I read the sheet out to everyone. No one responds. 'Okay, so we need to work out what our options are, right?'

Latisha says, 'We could brainstorm ideas. Like, one idea is we could create an ad, like for TV or something.' She talks with her hands, flashing long fingernails that are cream against her dark skin.

Relief. 'Good idea, Latisha. Let's just go with that. Jack, any ideas for a topic?'

He looks at the ceiling. 'Too many to choose from.'

'Right, well, how can we work around that?'

His eyes move erratically. 'We could research the different areas of genetics and come up with one topic each. Then choose from them.'

I stare at him for a moment, my mouth slightly open. 'Good,

Jack. Everyone happy to do Jack's suggestion of researching different topics first?'

I swat Seb on the arm. He takes an earphone out of one ear and says, 'Take it easy, sister.'

'I am not your sister. Did you hear what I said?'

'You're not my sister?'

'Before that, you idiot.'

'Settle. Man, you are one uptight lady. I heard what Jack said. We gotta research the genetics and come up with a topic. No stress. Peace and calm.'

Latisha's laptop is flat so she moves closer to a powerpoint. Seb asks to go to the bathroom. Jack and I are left sitting alone.

'Are you able to do the research on your own?' I ask.

Jack's eyes rest on the knot in my school tie. 'Yes. Maybe.'

Mr Van Hayden is watching me.

'Can I help you get started? I could write a few key words down that you could type into Google.'

Jack looks like he shakes his head, then glances over to the group where Cooper sits, and starts rocking.

'You don't need me to, or you don't want me to?'

Jack looks at Cooper's group again. 'I don't know.'

I move closer to Jack. His rocking becomes more vigorous. He's almost lifting the chair legs off the ground. I ask, 'Why are you doing that? What's the matter?'

Jack puts his hands over his ears and starts saying something quietly over and over under his breath.

I go over to Mr Van Hayden. 'Something's going on with Jack, Mr Van.'

'What did you say to him?'

'I asked him if he needed some help to get started. Then I moved closer to him.'

Mr Van Hayden goes over to the phone and calls someone. He talks to Jack, who nods, but keeps rocking. Mr Van Hayden takes

Jack by the arm and leads him out of the classroom, coming back in alone a few minutes later. He indicates for me to join him outside the classroom, closes the door and leans against it.

'Where's Jack gone?' I ask.

'I asked the Teacher Aide to take him for a walk.'

'Why?'

'Sometimes he needs to take a break from being around people, when he gets upset like that.'

'I don't know what happened; I was just asking if he wanted some help.'

Mr Van Hayden rubs his chin. 'I admit, I'm not very good at understanding why Jack reacts to things, either.'

'Maybe it's the noisy classroom?'

'Maybe. But I think, too, doing things like group work are especially difficult for him. There's a lot more to it than that, but he can get overwhelmed by things quickly.'

'I know the feeling. I know Jack has autism but Latisha can barely work in a group. I'm doubtful about Seb as well.'

'Grace, it's different for Jack. Think about Jesse; he looked like everyone else but his brain worked differently to yours and mine. And yet he wasn't so different—there were things he was good at and things he struggled with, just like everyone else.' Mr Van Hayden is one of the few teachers at school who had known Jesse. He knew how beautiful he was, how kind and funny and wonderful he had been.

'Jesse wasn't like everyone else,' I say. 'The doctor could tell from the moment he saw him that he had Down syndrome.'

'You're right, Grace. He was better than everyone else.' Mr Van Hayden gets a faraway look on his face. 'Remember how he used to sit out the front of your house and say hello to everyone who walked by? He loved people so much. He had so much time for everyone. It amazed me how he knew everyone's names, and people would tell him things that no one else knew. It was a gift he had.'

'They trusted him because he was simple.'

'They trusted him because he cared and took the time to listen, and he'd remember and ask them about their problems again the next time he saw them.' Mr Van pauses, the wrinkles on his forehead suggesting the importance of what he was about to tell me. 'Mrs Higgins told me about what you said in her history class.'

I raise my eyebrows. 'So?'

'She said you suggested people with disabilities are unable to contribute anything worthwhile to society.'

'It's true, isn't it?'

'Do you really believe Jesse's life meant nothing? That he didn't achieve anything in his short time here?'

'No, how could he?'

'Grace, hundreds of people came to his funeral.'

'Whatever. Can I go back into class now?'

'Grace, I've never told anyone this before.' He lowers his voice to just above a whisper. 'My wife left me six years ago.'

'I know that, sir. Can I—'

He ignores me. 'When I moved into your street, I didn't know if I even wanted to continue living, I was that distressed. In an effort to pull myself out of the dark depression I was in, I started walking every afternoon. And I got to know Jesse, as he sat out the front of your house. He always remembered my name. He'd always ask how I was going. He'd ask when I'd last spoken to my children, if my wife was speaking to me yet, if I was taking care of myself. Not like that, of course, but in his own way. I could tell him anything, and he wouldn't judge me. He'd look at me and say something like, "That's too bad," or "It shouldn't be that way," or my personal favourite, "Things will get better one day".' Mr Van chuckled. 'He got me through that time. He was an amazing young man.'

I swallow back my tears and harden my heart. 'And then he died.' Reminding people Jesse is dead is my go-to when I don't want to talk about what we're talking about. Shuts them up every time.

'Yes, Grace.' Mr Van Hayden's face drops and I think for a moment he is actually going to cry. 'You know, Grace, Jesse had strengths. He found things he was good at and focused on them. It's the same with Jack. And Latisha and Seb. You need to work with their strengths. That's why I put Jack with you because I thought you'd be able to work with him. Help him.'

Anger is bubbling in my chest like a kettle about to switch off. 'You know how much I need to pass Science this semester, sir. This is hardly the time for some social experiment where you get me to work a miracle on the others in my group.'

Mr Van Hayden opens the classroom door and goes to walk in, but then adds, 'Who says it's them who need the miracle?'

My whole body is shaking uncontrollably as Mr Van Hayden leads me back into class. I want to run away, to find something to punch, somewhere to crawl into and never come out of again. Cooper catches me looking at him and blows me a kiss. I run my finger across my lips as though I caught it. I force any thoughts of Jesse well into the back of my mind where he belongs. I'm not like Mikaela; I'm stronger than she was and I won't choose to give up. Focusing on Cooper is a better way to spend my energy. I steady my hands before slipping him a note asking if I can hang out with him after school. He reads the note, and yells out, 'Woo-hoo!'

I take it that means yes.

Chapter 15

Cooper leads me through the school parking lot to his mum's car. She's sitting in the front seat with P!nk blaring from the speakers. Her head is down as she scrolls through something on her phone. Cooper indicates for me to get in the back, where a kid, probably about Grade 7, is playing on an iPad. I slide onto the back seat of the dark grey Audi and say hello but am ignored. Cooper's never mentioned he also has a younger brother, let alone one that goes to our school.

'Hey, Mum,' Cooper says. She throws her phone into the cup holder. 'Remember Grace?'

Cooper's mum glances in the rear-view mirror and turns the music down. 'Yeah. Hi, love.' She looks at Cooper. 'Is she staying for dinner?'

Cooper shrugs. 'We haven't planned that far ahead, Mum.'

'Let me know when you've decided.' She looks into the rear-view mirror again. 'You've let your mum know you're coming to ours, I assume?'

I hold my phone up and Patty turns the music back up again. I open the Messenger app, and toy with the phone screen for a bit. Mum will be on her way to work soon and won't know whether I come home from school or not. Lisa Marie might notice I'm not on the bus, if she even went to school today, but she's unlikely to care. I click the phone off. If someone gets worried, they know how to contact me.

We drive up streets around the area Ethan Riley lives, and I almost laugh as we pull into the driveway of a white house with four fat pillars linking two storeys. It's so big it's almost ridiculous. Images of Elvis' Graceland mansion immediately come to mind. The driveway wraps around the side of the house and ends in a double garage where there's room for another equally large car.

I follow Cooper into an open-plan living area that's the size of my house. The couches, curtains, rugs and accessories are all creams and browns. A large wooden table with ten white leather chairs lines the centre of the room, dividing two living areas. There's an oversized TV in front of one set of couches. On the other side, the central focus is a large window looking down over other houses and the sea in the distance. Cooper throws his shoes into a hallway cupboard. I follow suit, shuffling them against a wall near the front door. My big toe sticks out of my sock, so I quickly remove them too, and shove them into my shoes.

There are a few dishes in the kitchen sink, but otherwise, Cooper's house is immaculate. Double doors off to the side of the room reveal a bulky wooden desk that has papers all over it. A flat computer screen rises up out of the mess. 'Mum works from home,' Cooper says as I stare into the room. 'Do you want a drink?'

'Sure. Thanks. What does she do?'

A strange look comes over Cooper's face. 'What, Mum?'

I nod.

'Oh, I dunno,' he says. 'She's a business manager or something. She's on the phone all the time.'

'From home?'

Cooper shrugs. 'Yeah. Sometimes she has to go to Brisbane or Sydney. Stuff like that. But it's Gary who makes the real money.'

Cooper hands me a tall glass of red juice. He picks up a thin glass bottle and adds clear liquid to his drink. He gestures to me. 'I'm guessing you don't want some?'

'What is it?'

'Just something to loosen me up a bit.'

I shake my head. Cooper leads me out of the room and down a long hallway, past a room with a cinema-sized screen and rows of chairs set up like a theatre. It smells like spring as we walk past it. We go up a set of stairs to a landing that contains more couches arranged in a semi-circle around a large screen TV. The cream carpet is soft under my feet. Cooper puts his half-empty glass down among the numerous remotes and game controllers that are spread across the coffee table.

'I have a few ways of relaxing after school. Do you have a preference?'

I put my glass next to Cooper's and sit beside him. 'I'm not into gaming.'

'Or alcohol—' he indicates to the glasses sitting side by side, '—another of my favourite things.'

I screw up my nose.

He presses a few buttons on the TV remote and a video clip with Jon Pardi comes on. A drone voice is singing about a girl on a dance floor.

I laugh awkwardly. 'Country music?'

'You're not a fan?'

'I don't mind Keith Urban.'

'Well, we must have something, other than Mikaela Harper and a few classes at school, in common. Let's see if we can find something we both like doing.'

He leans over and kisses me. I close my mouth, lightly kiss him back, and mutter, 'You have a nice house.'

Cooper shrugs. 'I guess so.'

He moves in and kisses me again, a little harder. He's trying to open my mouth with his lips, but I'm not responding. He pulls back and frowns. 'What do you want to do then?'

'I don't know, maybe we should get to know each other a little bit?'

'What do you think I was trying to do?'

I rub my aching neck and shoulder. 'I'm way too tense.'

Cooper moves behind me. 'How about I give you a massage then?'

'That would be awesome.' I relax back into the couch.

He kisses my neck as he moves into position behind me. 'You are tense.'

'I know,' I say. 'This science project is stressing me out so bad. I can't believe Van Hayden put me in that group. He knows I have to pass this term. It's like he looked for who would be the most likely to make me fail and put me with them.' I wince as Cooper pinches the skin on the top of my shoulders. 'I never did anything to him.'

'You wagged a couple of his classes last year,' Cooper says. 'I remember. I was with you.'

I giggle. 'Oh, yeah, I'd forgotten that. Good times.'

'Except you were with that wiener, Mark.'

'That wiener was your mate back then, remember.' Mark is in one of the other classes now. I can't remember the last time I even remember seeing him at school.

'Yeah, he was one of my mates. Until he stabbed me in the back.'

'You really aren't into the forgiveness thing, are you?'

'Why would I be?'

I chuckle but stop when I realise he's deadly serious. 'He was my first boyfriend, you know. My first and only, until now.'

Cooper smirks. 'Your first time was with Marky Mark, huh? What a disappointment for you.'

'Actually, we didn't even kiss, not really. Just a couple of pecks, that was about it. It was a bit weird, now that I think about it.'

'No way!' Cooper's shock doesn't seem to match my revelation. 'What?'

Cooper smacks his hand against his forehead. 'Mark used to come to school with all sorts of stories about what he was getting up to with you, like on weekends and stuff.'

'What?' My hand flies up to cover my mouth. 'He was making stuff up about us?'

Cooper stands up and sits back down, like he's not sure what to do with the news. Tears burn my eyes. 'Why would he do something like that?'

He holds my hands. 'You don't need to worry about him now. You're with me and there will be no storytelling. I don't need to do anything to try and boost my reputation.'

I lean in to kiss him, this time a little more passionately.

'You know,' Cooper says, rubbing his thumb gently along the side of my face. 'I could do something about the Science problem.'

I search Cooper's eyes. 'What do you mean?'

'Well, I could organise for Jack to be kept away from school for a while.'

'How? What do you mean?' I sit back and cross my arms. 'You don't mean hurting him. We've talked about this.'

'Of course not,' Cooper said. 'I was thinking more, something like his family winning a trip somewhere. An instant win, but they have to take the trip in the next two weeks.'

I chuckle. 'Oh, okay. Well, it sounds expensive.'

He shrugs. 'You'd be worth it.'

I spin around so Cooper and I are face to face on the couch. I allowed myself to laugh with him. 'And how would you organise something like that?'.

Cooper closes his eyes and kisses me again. 'I know people.'

I burst out laughing. Cooper opens his eyes, his smile taking up half his face. 'You have a beautiful laugh. Your eyes light up like Christmas lights.'

I laugh again. 'Are you trying to be romantic?'

'How am I doing?'

'Not too bad. Your simile wasn't brilliant though.'

'Well, there aren't a lot of green things to compare your eyes to. You know, green tree frogs are cute and all, but …'

'You've obviously been thinking about this for a while.'

'Well, you know. When a girl is worth the effort.'

I kiss him again. Cooper puts his hand gently on my face and moves it through my hair, running his fingers around to the back of my head so my face presses harder into his. His free hand is resting gently on my hip.

There is a strange sensation on the side of my face and an unpleasant smell wafts around me. I open one eye and see Cooper's younger brother staring at me from only centimetres away. I let out a scream and jump backwards.

'Sam!' Cooper flies off the couch, yelling obscenities at his sibling. He swings his arms around madly, picks him up by the back of the shirt and throws him through an adjoining doorway. He follows him into the room and shuts the door, appearing again a minute later. I stare at Cooper as he casually walks over to the couch and picks up his drink as though nothing has happened. 'Sorry about that. Sam's a piece of work. Sometimes he needs to be reminded of his place.' He finishes off the rest of his juice. 'You'd better drink that. If it had been knocked onto the carpet, Mum would have thrown your ass out onto the street.' He laughs. 'And mine for that matter.'

I swallow the rest of the juice. 'What did you say to him?'

Cooper shrugs. 'I know how to make a threat. And Sam's been hanging around me long enough to know that I can carry them out as well.'

'What do you mean, hanging around?'

'Sam's my step-brother. Mum and Gary got married about three years ago. My older brother, Mitch, left home when Mum and Gary made it official. Gary and Mitch couldn't stand each other.'

'My parents aren't together anymore, either,' I say. 'Dad lives on the Gold Coast with his teenage wife. She already had a kid and now she's pregnant with Dad's. Or she might have already had it. Lisa Marie and I don't see him anymore.'

'No one knows where my dad is. Seriously. Like, he could be dead for all we know. Seems we've found something else in common after all—our dead-beat dads.' Cooper looks me over. 'Are you keen to do something this Saturday night?'

'Yeah, of course.'

Cooper takes my hand. 'I was hoping you might say that. I've got something in mind I think you'll love.'

'Oh, what's that?'

'You'll find out. Keep it free. And see if the other girls would like to do something too. I think it's time for us to shake this town up a bit.'

Chapter 16

I pull down the miniskirt Hayley's lent me so it's halfway down my thighs. Nikki grabs it and slides it back up. 'You're Cooper Dally's girlfriend now. You need to dress the part.' She takes the white shirt Cooper bought me on our shopping spree that morning and ties the bottom of it into a knot, showing off my midriff. 'You should get a belly-button piercing,' Nikki says. 'It would look awesome with what you're wearing.'

Ellen frowns and pulls my skirt back down. 'She doesn't have to dress differently because of Cooper. That's stupid.'

I jump away from them both. 'Hands off both of you.' I look in the mirror, my hair pulled up into a messy bun on the top of my head. Nikki's foundation is barely visible across my nose, but it hides my freckles. My eyelashes are heavy each time I blink. I do look different, but not in a bad way.

Cooper pulls up out the front of my house in his convertible at half past eight, just as we're heading out the door. He meets us halfway up the front path; Ellen and Nikki rush past and climb into the car. Cooper grabs my arm and draws me close. 'Don't I get a proper hello?'

I'm not exactly sure what he means, but before I have the chance to say anything, he pulls me in and kisses me. I run my hand along his face, his cheeks rough with stubble which kind of turns me on a bit.

As we pull away his face erupts, showing off perfect, white teeth in the moonlight. 'Now that's more like it,' he says. 'But Mum's in the car, so, you know, let's not get carried away just yet.' He opens the back door for me and whispers, 'I love how you're wearing the shirt I got you.'

I slide into the back seat next to Ellen; P!nk is blasting from the speakers again. Patty says something in our direction, but I can't hear. The volume is a bit over the top, but at least Patty and Cooper don't share his love for country music.

Hayley is waiting for us on the corner of the streets that Cooper said we'd meet on. Brad and Joe are with her. I can't help but notice Brad's blue jeans hug in all the right places, and the white shirt that's tucked in to them accentuates his slim build.

Cooper holds my hand as he helps me out of the car. Ellen and Nikki tumble out after me.

'I'll be by at 11.30 to pick you all up,' Patty yells over her music.

Brad rushes over and wraps Ellen in a bear hug. 'I didn't know you could come out tonight!'

'I told Mum I'm staying over at Grace's,' she says.

'Which is true. She is,' I add.

'I just didn't mention the going-out part.' Ellen looks super-guilty.

'Wow, you look a bit of alright tonight, Grace,' Joe says.

Heat is rising to my cheeks. Brad jabs Joe in the ribs.

'That's okay, boys,' Cooper says, holding up his hand. 'Appreciation where appreciation is due. My Grace is looking particularly good.'

Brad whispers something in Ellen's ear and her cheeks colour to clash with her strawberry red hair.

'So, what's this place you've kept us all in suspense over?' Hayley asks.

Cooper points to the tavern a few doors down. His eyes are alive and he is still wearing the massive smile he had after he kissed me.

'A pub?' Hayley says. 'Are you kidding?'

Cooper raises his finger. 'Not just any pub,' he says. 'Come with me. You won't be disappointed.'

We walk a few hundred metres to the tavern and enter through a side door. There is a narrow hallway with paint chipping off the ceiling and minimal lighting that casts strange shadows on the walls. The musty air makes me cough. He taps a couple of times on a heavy wooden door and waits.

'Are you kidding me?' Hayley asks. She has her hands on her hips and a don't-mess-with-me expression on her face.

The door opens a crack and a face pops around the corner.

'Mitch!' Cooper pushes through the door and greets a taller, older version of himself. 'Good to have you back in town.'

Mitch grins. 'Hey hey, little bro. Nice to have you drop in. And bring some additional company with you.'

Cooper introduces us all to his brother, leaving me until last, and Mitch greets me like he knows who I am. He looks me up and down. 'Nice.' I know it's a compliment, but it feels like the compliment is more for Cooper than for me.

Cooper grabs my hand and pushes past Mitch, mumbling for him to keep his eyes to himself. The lights are dimmed low and a live jazz band is playing smooth tunes in a corner. A full bar is stretched out against the far wall. There are about twenty people in the room, mostly sitting at small round tables with short, fat glasses in front of them. A few couples are slow dancing in front of the band. None of them take any notice of us entering the room.

Cooper indicates an empty booth. 'Mitch saved a booth for us. First round is my shout. Mitch has set it up so I'm right to buy drinks, so anything you want, I'll organise it for you.'

It doesn't take long before the number of empty glasses on the table outweigh the number of people. Even Ellen is laughing more than I've heard her do before. I worry that alcohol could do something to her heart. She and Brad snuggle together in the booth's corner. Cooper asks me if I want to dance.

'You alright?' Cooper says once we're on the dance floor. 'You seem very distracted tonight.'

I shrug. 'Fine. Just not sure what Ellen's doing. She's not

supposed to date until she's seventeen. And she probably shouldn't be drinking with that heart thing she has.'

'She's not supposed to come to nightclubs, either, I'll bet.'

I chuckle. 'Definitely not.'

I put my head on Cooper's chest and sway to the music. He smells so good. He wraps his arms tightly around me and lifts me a little off the ground to swing me around. As he gently returns me to the ground, I lift my head up to laugh and he meets my smile with a kiss. I can't help myself; my eyes drift over to Brad and Ellen. I can't see for sure, but from their body positions, I'm pretty sure they're making out.

Cooper runs his hand down to my bottom and I quickly grab it and lift it to my lower back. He repeats, and I do the same.

He asks, 'What?'

'What do you mean, *what*?'

He moves one hand so it's sitting heavily on my hip. His other is on my bare skin just under my shirt. 'You won't let me drop my hand while we're dancing?'

'We're in public. Our friends are all sitting over there.'

'Come on, Grace, as if they care. I reckon Brad's getting more action tonight than I am.' My chest tightens. 'Isn't it time we step things up a notch?'

'In terms of?'

'Well, clearly you're holding out on me. It makes me wonder if there's someone else you'd rather be with.'

I narrow my eyes and involuntarily swallow. 'What do you mean?'

'Tell me straight that there's no one here you're uncomfortable showing affection to me in front of.'

'You mean, other than the twenty strangers in the room?'

'So, there's no one else you'd rather be on the dance floor with?'

Our friends are all watching us, except Ellen and Brad. 'What, Cooper? What are you talking about?'

'You've been staring at Ellen and Brad all evening. You sure it's Ellen you're concerned about?'

I have no idea what to say. I stand there with my mouth open, shaking my head.

Cooper clicks his tongue, his eyes ablaze. 'I'm going to get another drink.'

I throw my hands up in the air and head to the bathroom. In the tiny room, a single fluoro light flickers against white tiles. I put my hands on the yellow-stained sink and take a few deep breaths.

Hayley is the first to burst into the room. 'Wow, Grace. What was that between you and Cooper?'

Nikki and Ellen tumble in after her. I can barely move.

I splash some cold water on my eyes to try and stop any tears from leaking out. 'I honestly don't know. Cooper was being weird. I think he was accusing me of liking Brad or something.'

Ellen gasps. 'Do you?' Her blue eyes plead at me.

'No.' I grab some paper towel and clear the mascara smudged under my eyes. 'I mean, sure, he's adorable.' I smile at Ellen. 'But clearly, his attention is all over someone else.'

Ellen's cheeks colour.

'Yeah, what's with you two tonight?' Hayley says. 'It's like you've got your own little private function happening there.'

Ellen giggles. 'Nothing's happened yet. But we have so much in common. We like the same books, the same sorts of movies, we even follow a couple of the same YouTubers.'

Hayley drops a hip and frowns. 'You mean you've just been *talking* this whole time?'

Ellen bites her lip as it curves into a smile.

Hayley slaps herself on the forehead. 'Grace, you've got to clear this up with Cooper. You're our only chance to stay hanging out with the boy band.'

'Yeah,' Nikki adds. 'If you can't hold on to Cooper for more than a week, the group will disband again, like we did after Mikaela left.'

'But hang on, Cooper was being a jerk,' I say.

'Sort it out. Please,' Nikki adds. 'For the first time ever, I've got Joe talking about something other than soccer; he might be interested. And then there's Ellen and Brad. We're just getting started.'

I roll my eyes. 'Whatevs.'

The girls follow me out of the bathroom and Hayley pushes me down toward the end of the bar, where Cooper is sitting. His hands are wrapped around a beer with a thick white top.

'Hey.' I sit opposite him. The girls disappear around the corner, back into the booth. I squirm a little, uncomfortable about how alone I am with Cooper, but not really sure why. 'I don't get what happened with us just now.'

He has a strange expression on his face. 'Tell me it isn't true.'

I put my hand on his. 'There isn't anything with Brad, I promise. I shouldn't have reacted like I did; with all the pressure of school at the moment ...'

'I don't see why school is such an issue for you. You keep freaking out about Science, what does it matter anyway? It's only Year 10.'

'Because I really want to do something with my life; I have goals, things I want to do after school. You've seen the area of town I live in. You know some of what my family is like. I want more for my life.'

'And you will have more. I'll make sure of that.' He's looking around the room, his eyes darting from person to person as though he's looking for someone. His eyes settle on me momentarily. 'Stick with me and I'll make sure you get everything you want in life.'

Cooper motions to the bartender and whispers to him.

'Cooper?' His eyes still have that strange glaze over them. 'What did you order?'

Cooper frowns. 'I'm getting enough for you too. Don't worry.'

'I don't do drugs. I don't want you to either.'

He stands up and leans in so he's right in my face. 'My girlfriend doesn't tell me what I can and can't do, Grace.'

He grabs a package from the bartender and thanks him.

I step backwards. 'I don't like what that stuff does to people. I want you as you are, not whacked out on drugs.'

He sits back at the bar. 'Go somewhere else then. I don't want you hanging around me if you're going to be like that.'

My jaw drops. 'If you're going to take drugs, I don't want to stay here.'

He grits his teeth. 'Maybe you should go and hang out at church then, instead.'

'What are you talking about? I have no idea what I've done wrong, Cooper. You're acting really weird.'

'I'm acting weird? You're the one pulling back all the time.' He swings around to face me. His eyes are dark, sad. 'What's with that? When I pick you up you're all over me, but now we're here, you're holding out on me. I mean, come on, Grace. It feels like you're driving forty in a one hundred zone.'

'Maybe you're with the wrong girl. I don't know what you thought, but I'm not going to get high and start sleeping with you because you say some nice things and buy me a bikini.'

'Well, what the hell are you doing kissing me like you did when I picked you up then?'

I search his face. He's dead serious. 'Cooper, I kissed you, I just—'

'It was more than that, Grace. You know it was.' He swings around on the bar stool and puts his knees either side of my legs. 'You're worrying about stuff and that's stopping you from living life. We don't need to worry about all that school crap. I'll look after you now.'

'But I want to make something of myself. And I certainly don't want to end up like Lisa Marie.'

'From what Tom says, Lisa Marie knows how to live life.' He tries to nuzzle into my neck, but it feels weird. 'And she knows how to keep her man happy.'

'My sister—' I grit my teeth and pull back, '—is dropping out of school and moving in with Tom, exactly like my mum did when she was her age. I'm not going to make the same mistakes.'

'Who's to say it's a mistake? If Tom and Lisa Marie are happy, why shouldn't they move in together? Tom's got a good job. He'll look after your sister.'

I shake my head. 'I've had enough. I'm going home.'

Cooper raises his hand and slaps me across the face. Air races to my lungs as I stumble off the bar stool. I hold my cheek, my eyes wide. 'What the hell do you think you're doing?'

Cooper gets off his bar stool, his eyes wide. 'Shit, Grace. I'm sorry, I didn't mean to do that.' He grabs my face, his hand over my own, and kisses my cheek multiple times. 'I lost it for a sec. I'm so sorry.'

Still holding my cheek, tears stinging my eyes, I run to the exit.

'Grace,' Cooper calls. He's coming after me, but some random guy grabs him and is yelling at him.

Cooper's brother, Mitch, stands in the doorway so I can't get through. 'Hey. Don't take that personally. Cooper's always been a bit aggressive when he's been on the African Black.'

'He's already taken something tonight?'

'He popped a few pills when he first came in. I'm surprised he didn't slip you some. He's usually pretty generous.'

I manoeuvre around Mitch and head down the passageway and onto the street. It's quiet for a Saturday night. I run down the street and around the corner, hoping no one has followed me. Leaning heavily on the white brick wall behind me, I pull out my phone, but have to wipe my eyes to be able to read that it's only 10pm. I open my contacts and stare at the screen. If only I had more friends who could drive! Mum will still be at work. I call Lisa Marie's mobile but she doesn't pick up. I hear voices coming; I can't face my friends. I can't tell them what Cooper just did to me. The heat on my cheek burns, but so does my whole face, with the embarrassment of what Cooper had done. I take off again, running around the next corner and down an alleyway into another street until I come to a park. There's a small wooden cubbyhouse as part of the climbing equipment; I crawl into it, hugging my knees up to my face. I put my head down and sob.

My heart is thumping in my chest, but I can't tell if that's from the running or my heart breaking. I thump my fists into my knees. I can't believe Cooper did that to me. I hold my cheek, still warm from where his hand landed.

Flashes of our time together race across my mind. How gentle he was with me when he taught me to surf. Buying me lunch that day. The drink bottle. Our first kiss under the flowering tree. The way he insisted he was trying to change, and that he wanted to be a better person because of me.

But then there's the other stuff—the thing with Sam, and Jack, not to mention how he acted tonight, high and half drunk. That wasn't the Cooper I wanted to be with.

'Hello,' I hear a voice outside the doorway. 'Are you okay? Do you need some help?'

I peek out the door. My heart sinks into my stomach. It's Jack Oskar.

Chapter 17

'Jack? What are you doing here?' I ask.

There is silence for a moment. 'Graceland?'

I groan. 'Why do you have to call me by my full name?'

He squats down into the cubby's doorway. 'I'm sorry, I just forget. Whenever I think about you, I think about you as Graceland. I like your name. It's difficult to stop calling you Graceland when that is what I always call you in my head.' He is quiet for a moment. 'Why are you in this cubby?'

I laugh softly. 'Because my life is sh—,' I pause, then say, 'a complete disaster. I want to go back to being four-years-old. Life was easy back then.'

'Jesse was born when you were four.'

'Yes, Jack, he was.'

'You were going to swear then, weren't you?'

I laugh again. 'Yes.'

'You never used to swear.' There is silence again for a moment. 'You look like you have been crying.'

'I have.'

'Mum said I should see if I can help you. We saw you run into the cubby. But I didn't know it was you, Gracela ... Grace.'

'Your mum is here?'

'She is in the car.'

'Why are you driving around so late?'

'I am getting more confident to drive at night.' He pauses, then adds, 'and I have been out. Mum came to pick me up.'

'Oh,' I say. I go to get out of the cubby, but Jack doesn't move.

'Can I get out, then, please?'

He moves to the side and says, 'We could take you home, if you want.'

There is only one car in the street. It's still running and I can see a woman sitting in the front passenger seat. What other option do I have?

'Thanks,' I say, 'that would be great.'

Jack opens the back door of the little green car for me and I notice the plates on display in the car's windows.

'You have your Ps already, Jack?'

'Yes. I'm a year older than most people in our class. I don't drive on my own yet, though.'

I laugh. 'Why not?'

'Because Mum says I'm not ready. I can have trouble when there is lots of traffic or when cars beep their horns at me.'

'But she let you go for your licence?'

He shrugs. 'I booked in for them on my own. She didn't know about it until afterwards.'

'You telling me you're a bit of a rebel, Jack Oskar?'

He looks at the ground, his cheeks glowing. 'I got into trouble for it. It was the wrong thing to do.'

'But you passed.'

He smiles a little within his embarrassment. 'Yes, I did.'

He opens the door and closes it behind me, then climbs into the driver's seat. 'Mum, this is Gracela … I mean Grace. I know her from school.'

His mum reaches around and shakes my hand. 'Pleased to meet you. Oh, look at you. Here, I have some tissues in the glove box.'

'Thanks,' I say. I clean up the makeup Nikki had so carefully applied earlier that night in the rear-view mirror. Jack is watching me.

Mrs Oskar says, 'Is this the Graceland you were talking about?'

'Yes.'

'You've been talking about me, Jack?' I ask.

'He says you're Jesse's big sister.'

'I am.'

'I can see the resemblance.' She looks me up and down. 'Jack needs a good grade in Biology this semester,' his mum says. 'He said you're the team leader in his project group at school.'

'I am.'

A worried look flickers across her face.

'It's okay, Mrs Oskar. I haven't been drinking. You can smell my breath if you want.'

She shakes her head. 'It's fine. Even if you have, it's none of our business.'

I try to pull down my skirt that has ridden up my thighs. 'Why aren't you driving off yet, Jack?' I ask.

'You haven't put your seatbelt on,' he replies. I put it on, but he still doesn't drive off.

'I've put it on now.'

Jack nods.

'And?'

'I don't know where you live.'

'Oh, right.' I pause to stifle a giggle. 'Turn left up here.'

Jack pulls away from the curb just as Hayley and Nikki run into the street. I put my head down so they can't see me and open my phone. I text Nikki to let her know I've found my own way home.

When I get to school on Monday morning the girls are super angry. I'd been silent on social media all Sunday, using the time to think things through—like Cooper and how I'd managed to get myself in the situation I was in.

At first, the girls walk past me without saying a thing. When I ask them why they're ignoring me, Ellen is the first to voice her anger. 'I was supposed to be at your house Saturday night, Grace. I left my overnight bag there and everything. I had to sleep at Nikki's and explain why it was her dad dropping me home without my gear on Sunday morning.' She puts her head down. 'You know I'm supposed to avoid stressful situations with my heart condition.'

I vaguely recall seeing a strange bag when I'd picked up my school uniform off the bedroom floor that morning. 'Sorry, Ellen. I totally forgot. What did you tell your parents?'

'What do you think? I lied to them. I told Mum we'd had a huge fight and that Nikki's dad had come and picked us up in the middle of the night. Don't be surprised if you get a mouthful from my mum the next time you see her.'

'I'm sorry, Ellen. It didn't even enter my head.' I turn to Nikki. 'Thanks for taking her in.'

'Where'd you even go, Grace?' Nikki asks. 'We were worried sick about you, until you sent that text. Hayley saw something happen with you and Cooper. But then you left us all there. You ran off.'

'Cooper was being a complete jerk. His brother told me he'd been taking drugs while we were there without us even knowing.'

The girls all look from person to person.

'What, you mean you all knew?'

'He was offering them around to everyone. We assumed you knew too.'

'No, I didn't. Did any of you take some?'

'Just Hayley.'

Hayley frames her face with her hands as a gesture of innocence.

'It's okay,' Nikki says. 'We looked after her after you left.'

'Is that supposed to make me feel bad?'

'Maybe.'

Ellen touches my hand. 'What happened with Cooper? You were supposed to be sorting things out with him.'

'I told you he was being a jerk,' I say. 'And then he slapped me in the face when I said I wanted to go home.'

'What?' Ellen stood up.

'He didn't!' Nikki cried.

I hold my hand to my cheek momentarily, the sting still so real it's like I can feel it again.

'What, did he, like, leave a mark?' Hayley asks.

'Why does that even matter?' Ellen and Nikki say at the same time.

'Well, how hard was it?' Hayley studies my face. 'I can't see anything now.'

'It was hard enough.'

'It's not okay that he did that to you,' Ellen says.

'Thanks, Ellen,' I say, glaring at Hayley. I give Ellen a light hug.

'You should tell someone, Grace,' Ellen says. 'Like a teacher— or your mum?'

'I agree, Grace,' says Nikki.

I shake my head. 'It's okay. I don't want him to get in any more trouble than he already is with me.'

'How did he react when you broke up with him, then?' Nikki asks.

'Well, I haven't,' I say.

The girls all look at me, Nikki's mouth is hanging open.

'You're still going out with him?' Ellen asks.

I nod. 'I mean, it was totally not okay, and I'm really mad at him for it. But, you know, he's not usually like that. I think it was the drugs.'

Ellen shakes her head. 'I'm not happy about it, Grace.'

'I'm not happy about it, either,' Nikki says. 'But maybe Grace is right. Perhaps it was a one off. Mikaela never said anything about him doing that to her.'

'I agree,' Hayley says. 'If you love him, you'll let it go and move on.'

We all glare at Hayley.

'What?' she says.

I touch Ellen on the arm. 'I am really sorry about you sleeping over on Saturday night,' I say. 'I can't believe I forgot. I guess I got caught up in the whole Cooper thing.'

'It's okay,' Ellen says. 'Just don't expect me to ever be allowed to sleep over at your place again.'

Nikki taps me on the arm. 'Look out. Here comes Cooper.'

My heart leaps into my throat and I feel sick. 'I'm not talking to him,' I say. I reach out for Ellen's hand. 'Don't leave me with him.'

Cooper walks up and hands me a bunch of red roses, tied together with a blue ribbon.

Hayley says, 'Oh, how sweet.'

Cooper ignores her.

'Grace,' he says, 'can we talk, please?' The girls all hold their positions in the circle. 'I won't be long. I have some things to say to Grace. Please.' He's making that sweet, innocent face with big, sad eyes—the one he makes when he's trying to get away with something. It works on the girls. I give each of them a death stare as they walk away, while trying to hold on to Ellen's hand. She mouths 'sorry' as she lets go.

'Let's sit over here,' Cooper says. He guides me into an area where there is seating among a bunch of overhanging bushes.

He sits down. I don't.

'Come on, Grace. Can't you tell I'm trying to apologise to you?'

I narrow my eyes. 'For what?'

Cooper droops his shoulders. 'I was a complete jerk on Saturday night. I'm sorry for everything. For the way I treated you, for what I said to you. And especially for hitting you. That was totally not on. I can't believe I did that to you.'

The bell rings and the school grounds go quiet.

I sit down beside him. 'You scared me, Cooper. Really scared me.'

Tears form in his eyes. 'I can't believe I acted like that. I've never, ever hit a girl before. I don't know what happened. I threw the rest of the package down the toilet; I wouldn't even let Mitch take it. It was rubbish. There must have been something mixed in with it.'

'You didn't just scare me when you hit me, Cooper. You were talking like all you want from me is sex. Like, you're not hanging out with me because you like hanging out with me, but because you want something from me.'

'That's so not true. You're the most amazing girl ever. You're funny and kind and you're passionate about stuff. I love hanging out with you.'

'You told me to trust you. How can I do that now?'

'I can't tell you I don't want sex, Grace. You're, like, the most beautiful girl ever. But if it means I get to spend time with you and hang out with you, I'm cool to wait. I wasn't thinking straight Saturday night. I wasn't myself.'

'I could tell.'

He holds my hand in his. 'Please, Grace. Can we start over again?'

I hope like crazy I'm not completely senseless when I say, 'If we're going to be together, you have to promise me no drugs, okay? The drinking I can handle. You're kinda a bit over the top when you're drunk, but you can also be super sweet. But the drugs, I can't handle. I can't be around you if you're doing that.'

Cooper leans in close. 'So, you forgive me?'

I lean forward to meet him and kiss him. 'I guess I do.'

Footsteps approach and suddenly Miss Krensky is standing in front of us, hands on her hips. 'You two. Form. Now.'

Giggling, we run upstairs to Form hand in hand. As he takes his seat next to Brad, I slide in next to Ellen, placing the bunch of flowers on the desk in front of me. The other girls look at my roses admiringly.

I'm pretty confident that things will be okay with Cooper now. Science is on again after HPE and standing up to Cooper makes me feel like I can do anything. Like, I can get things organised with my project group. I can put the weekend behind me and move on. It's time to get myself into Year 11 Biology, and back on track to changing my stars.

Chapter 18

In HPE the following week it's drizzling and so we spend the lesson in the hall playing volleyball. Ellen is coming to HPE for a bit—volleyball is one of the few activities she's able to join in with us. Hayley is sitting out on account of her bandaged hand.

'What happened to Hayley anyway?' Cooper says in between serves.

'She smashed her hand up working on Hannah's car on the weekend,' Nikki says.

'She was working on her sister's car?' Cooper asks.

'Yeah, she was changing the car's oil, or changing brake pads, maybe? I don't know, something went wrong, something slipped.' Nikki shrugs. 'She did tell me.'

'What the heck is she doing changing anything on a car?' Cooper asks. 'That's what mechanics are for.'

'Her dad made both the girls do a course on how to look after a car before he went overseas,' Nikki says. 'He refuses to pay for servicing for Hannah's car, saying the girls have to learn to do it themselves.'

Cooper doubles over he's laughing so hard. 'I can't imagine Hayley doing that. You'd reckon she'd be terrified she'll break a nail.'

'I dunno,' I say. 'I would have liked it if my dad had been around to teach me some things like that. It's a way of saving money. Mum's car breaks down heaps because she can't afford the regular servicing.'

Cooper pulls me into a hug. 'Stick with me and you'll never have to even look under the bonnet of a car.'

'Yeah well,' Nikki says, picking something out from under a fingernail. 'Secretly, I think there's a lot less money in the family than Hayley likes to let on. We went shopping the other week and I'm sure she wasn't paying for half the stuff she got.'

'Really?' I say. 'Hayley?'

'She's a lot more insecure than she lets on, Grace,' Nikki says. 'I think some stuff happened at her last school. She barely had any friends and from stuff I've heard, the teachers tried to get her dad to get testing done on her.'

'Why?'

'I dunno. Because no one liked her and stuff.'

'Well,' I say, wrapping my arms around Cooper, 'she sure was keen to get in your good books, Cooper.'

'She has got good taste,' Cooper chuckles, giving me a light kiss.

'She knew what she needed to do to be liked when she came back to school here,' I add.

Brad serves an ace over the net to the other team. Every time we score, Cooper high-fives the boys and kisses me on the lips. Eventually the teacher notices and goes off at him, but it doesn't stop him from walking around with his chest out and head high. I notice a couple of times Jack, who's also sitting out, is watching Cooper's every move.

'Things seem to be going okay with you and Cooper,' Ellen says, as we go for a drink break.

'Yeah. He was extra nice to me all last week. And we went to Café Glass for brunch on Saturday. Have you been there?'

She shakes her head.

'It was so nice. We sat and talked for hours. Mostly about surfing,' I laugh. 'But I sure could get used to it.'

'"It" being talking about surfing or having brunch?'

'Everything. Hanging out with Cooper is a whole different way of life.'

'And Science?'

I shrug. 'We're getting there. Small steps of progress.'

Ellen taps my water bottle. 'Yeah, well, don't lose sight of the real goal, okay?'

By the time we get to Science, I'm determined to make our group project work. Taking Mr Van Hayden's advice on board, I get them to write down their strengths. Latisha's is drawing. Seb's is making music. Mine is being organised and I'm pretty good with keeping notes in class. We decide to make a TV advertisement creating awareness for a couple of genetic disorders, with Latisha doing the diagrams and Seb creating a catchy jingle for the ad. But Jack's a problem. He says he doesn't have any strengths. I decide to spend the rest of the lesson working on finding something Jack can contribute.

We head up the back of the classroom, but as soon as we sit down, Jack rocks again. 'Jack,' I say. 'Don't start the rocking thing again. You have to keep leaving class, and I need you to stay and work with me.'

Jack rocks back and forth, his eyes focused on a point at the front of the classroom. 'I'm not supposed to talk to you.' He looks in Cooper's direction.

'But you spoke to me on Saturday night, last week, remember? You even drove me home. Why do things suddenly change once we get to Science?'

Jack moves in the chair as though there are tacks on it. 'Cooper was not there.'

I scan the classroom; Cooper is watching me. 'What, you mean you will talk to me when Cooper is not around? What does Cooper have to do with anything?'

Jack looks at the ceiling and almost stands up he's moving around so much on his chair. 'I'm not allowed to say.'

'What has Cooper said to you?'

Jack shrugs. He settles down in his seat a bit, but his hands are still rubbing each other like crazy under the table.

'Well, Jack, I'm telling you that it is fine for you to talk to me, even if Cooper is around, okay?'

Jack looks down to his hands, then up at the ceiling. He's moving his mouth as though he's trying to say something, but no words are coming out.

'Wait here,' I say.

I walk over to Cooper. 'Hey. Did you say something to Jack about him not being allowed to talk to me?'

Cooper gets his big, innocent eyes happening, and pouts. 'Maybe. But only because I knew Jack likes you. I was setting some boundaries, reminding him of his place, that's all.'

'We're in the same Science group, Cooper. How are we supposed to work together if he thinks he's not allowed to talk to me?'

'I didn't mean all the time. Of course, in class would be okay. Besides, I said that to him before I knew you were working in the same group.'

'You mean, before we'd even got together?'

Cooper chuckles. 'Grace, sometimes a guy has to work behind the scenes to make things happen. Jack has had a crush on you since forever. I was just, you know, eliminating any potential competition. Not that Jack Oskar was ever in the race.'

'Well, you need to tell Jack it's okay to talk to me again. He won't talk to me any time you're around.'

Cooper looks past me and calls out across the room, 'All good, Jack-o! Talk away.' He puts his thumb up and gives a cheesy smile. He looks at me. 'Better?'

'Thanks.'

I walk back to my seat next to Jack. 'Cooper has said that it's fine for you to talk to me, Jack. Okay?'

Jack keeps looking over at Cooper's group. 'Okay, Graceland.'

Cooper gives Jack the thumbs up again. Then blows me a kiss.

'Jack, I know it's difficult for you, but I need you to call me

Grace, please. I don't like my full name.'

'But why?' He stops looking in Cooper's direction and focuses his attention on my left cheek. 'It's pretty.' Jack's smile is lopsided, making it a bit cheeky.

'Do you know what Graceland is?'

'Your name,' he says.

'Yes. But do you know what else it is?'

'Yes. It's the name of Elvis Presley's mansion in Memphis, Tennessee.' Jack keeps his smile. 'His daughter owns it now.'

'Then you can understand why I don't like it?'

'No.'

'It's the name of someone's house, Jack. That's what Graceland means to the world. I'm named after a house. On purpose. My mum is obsessed with Elvis Presley. And you can imagine what they say when they find out my sister's name is Lisa Marie.'

'Lisa Marie Presley is Elvis Presley's daughter.'

'That's right.'

'And Jesse was his twin brother.'

'You know that?' I say.

'He died.'

'Most people know Elvis is dead. Except for those conspirators who think he faked his death and he's living it up somewhere.'

Jack tilts his head to the side. 'I meant Jesse. He died.'

My face twitches a little. Usually I'm the one to say that. 'Harsh,' I say.

Jack frowns. 'Elvis' brother, Jesse. Not your brother Jesse. But he did die, too.'

'Oh,' I chuckle. 'Yes, Jack. That's right. Elvis' brother died at birth or something.'

'Elvis' twin brother died before he was born, then Elvis was born after him. Elvis was the only person in the world to know Jesse before he died. Your Jesse died when he was eight years old. You knew him. So did I.'

We sit in silence for a moment.

'Jack, sometimes it makes me sad to talk about my brother.'

'It's been four years since Jesse, your brother, died.'

'It still hurts me—' I put my hand over my chest, '—in here, whenever I think of him.'

Jack puts his hand to his chest, too. 'But it's okay to think about him in short little bursts, when you don't have to think about it too much, about how he's not here anymore.'

That is right. 'How do you know things about Elvis Presley?' I ask. 'Like, not many people know Elvis had a twin brother.'

Jack looks at the ceiling. He's holding his breath.

I look at the same spot on the ceiling. 'You know, it's weird having a name that is connected with someone who was alive so long ago.'

'Elvis would have died before your mum was born.'

'He did. Her grandma loved Elvis. And she was super close to her grandma 'cause her own mum wasn't around much. Maybe that's why she likes him so much; it's a comfort thing.'

'Maybe. That's what I do too,' Jack says.

'What do you mean?'

'I like to do the same things over and over. It makes me comfortable and clears my head and helps me to think more plainly.'

'That's cool. I wonder how we can use that to help you learn in Science?'

Jack looks to the ceiling. Then at me. Then at his hands. 'I don't know.'

'Alright. Well, we'll think about that some more. In the meantime, we have to put together this portfolio of learning for each of us to go with our project. Maybe you could be in charge of collecting the work that everyone in our group has done. You know, check it over, make sure everyone has done the different parts.'

Jack nods.

'And you still have to do some of the work yourself, you

understand that?'

He nods again.

'Okay, well that's a start.'

'That's a start.'

The bell rings and I gather up my belongings and, joining Ellen, we head out to recess. There's a bit of a commotion behind us and I turn around to see Jack scrambling on the concrete path for his laptop and pencil case, which has split open and the contents are all over the ground. Joe and Hayley are sniggering as they walk around him.

I confront Cooper as he goes to walk past, too. 'Cooper. Did one of you do something to Jack?'

Cooper raises his hands in innocence. 'I didn't. Did you, boys?'

The guys all shake their heads and mumble a bunch of 'no's.

'I think he tripped,' Brad says.

'Well, you shouldn't have been laughing,' I say. 'It's mean.'

'What's with her?' Joe says as the boys walk away.

'She's okay,' Cooper says. 'Just a bit sensitive. Science is stressing her out.'

'I thought things were okay between you and Cooper again,' Nikki says.

'They are,' I say. 'I'm just not sure if there's still some stuff going on between Cooper and Jack.'

'Remember us, won't you?' Hayley says as she joins us. 'Think of all the great parties we're getting invited to. That could stop, if you and Cooper break up—over someone like *Jack*.'

I shake my head. 'I'm not breaking up with Cooper. And even if I was, I'm not going to stay with him so we have something to do on weekends, Hayley.'

'Some friend,' Hayley says.

'I could say the same thing to you.'

Hayley walks off and Ellen steps into her place beside me. 'She's being a cow, Grace. Don't worry about her. I don't think things will change between me and Brad if you and Cooper break up, so maybe that will be enough for you all to still be invited to stuff.'

'Thanks, Ellen. I really like Cooper—there's just some things that aren't quite fitting in the puzzle. Like why Jack seems genuinely afraid of him.' We head toward the lockers and I stand in front of mine. Mikaela's stands empty beside it. I miss her. I wish she were here. We could have talked about everything that had happened, and she would have known what to do.

I fiddle with my locker number, momentarily forgotten as I aimlessly move the numbers around. Ellen unlocks her locker on the other side of me. 'The twenty-first of August, isn't it?' she says, peeking around from behind.

I chuckle. 'Thanks.' I set the numbers into position, and then shove my laptop and books into the box. 'So,' I say, as we head off to lunch. 'You and Brad are getting pretty serious?'

Ellen's cheeks colour a little. 'He's happy to wait until my birthday before we make anything official, but yeah, I think we're getting pretty serious. Nothing like you and Cooper, but serious in our own kind of way.'

I'm happy for her. It seems everything is all coming together.

Chapter 19

I get home from school the next day and Mum's standing in the kitchen, staring out the window into our barren backyard. The lawn needs mowing, which is really just weeds because the grass is all dead. A rusty set of swings stand as a reminder that children once lived here.

'Hi, Mum,' I say.

She jumps a little and turns around to indicate a huge thing of flowers on the kitchen bench behind her. There's a pink teddy with it. 'What's with this?'

'No idea,' I say. 'Who are they for?'

'Says on this card they're for you, from someone called Cooper.' I can't stop the blood from rushing to my cheeks. 'Who is he?' Mum asks.

I walk over to the table and pick up the teddy, a purple bow tied around its neck. It's so soft. Mum has her hands on her hips.

I forgot I hadn't said anything to her about Cooper yet. 'Ah. He's my boyfriend?'

'Since when?'

Lisa Marie walks into the room. 'A few weeks, isn't it, Grace?'

'Something like that.'

Mum runs a finger over one of the petals. 'It's an awfully expensive present when it's not an anniversary or something.'

I shrug. 'Something happened in one of our classes. I guess this is his way of saying sorry.'

'Man, must have been a big fight,' Lisa Marie says. 'You're not sleeping with him, are you?'

'I don't see how that is any of your business,' I say. 'And since when do you still live here? I thought you were moving out.'

'Tom and I are waiting to find the right apartment. I hear you've been out partying a fair bit.'

I roll my eyes. 'Like you can talk.'

'Actually, I haven't.'

'What—not since you got all adult and decided to drop out of high school?'

'Shut up.' Lisa Marie turns to Mum. 'Cooper Dally has a lot of money. He knows just about everyone worth knowing on the East Coast of Australia. And, from what I've heard, he's pretty generous with those he chooses to hang around with. Haven't you noticed the new clothes Grace has been wearing?'

'He can also be a jerk,' I add, putting my hand to my face.

Mum picks up the card. 'Sometimes you have to take a bit of crap to get to where you want to go, Grace. Sounds like this guy might do a lot to help you.'

'He may also give me mental health issues.'

'Just make sure he's your Holly. And not an Aleshia,' Mum says.

'What?'

Lisa Marie laughs. 'She's talking about *Follow That Dream*, Grace.'

I roll my eyes. 'Seriously, Mum.'

Lisa Marie casts a strange look at Mum before saying, 'Come on, Priscilla. Looks like Graceland needs a bit more educating about your movies.'

'Don't call me Priscilla,' Mum says. 'It's disrespectful.' Her eyes are serious. Mum turns to me. 'Holly is the girl right in front of Toby's nose, and she's totally in love with him. Aleshia comes along and tries to woo him with her charm and worldly ways. You can guess who Toby ends up with.'

'Holly?'

'Of course he does,' Mum says. 'That's the way the world should work. The right girl should end up with the right guy. Elvis deserved to get the girl who truly loved him.'

'Except it's a movie, Mum,' Lisa Marie says. 'If circumstances have taught us anything, it's that life doesn't end up all happily ever after like it does in the movies.'

'You deserve a happily ever after,' Mum says, as she runs her hand down the side of my face. 'You're wearing makeup.'

I choose not to tell her Cooper bought it for me. 'A bit.'

'The card says he wants to take you to a party tonight. Are you planning on going?'

I shrug.

'At least call him to thank him for the flowers,' Mum says. 'And remember, don't be too slow to forgive, Grace. Life's too short.' She gets a faraway look in her eyes. 'Perhaps I'll watch *Follow That Dream* and shop later. Are you girls right to find yourselves something for dinner?'

I almost laugh. Why would tonight be any different? But I say, 'Sure, Mum.' I take a selfie of myself with the flowers and, ignoring Lisa Marie's bemused look, walk down to my bedroom.

I throw myself on my bed and hit the play button on the Bluetooth speaker beside me. I open Snapchat, write, 'Nice move', on the selfie and send the photo.

He rings me straight away. 'You got my apology then?'

'It's sweet. Thanks.'

'I got the vibe you weren't too happy with the whole Jack thing.'

'You sensed correctly. I'm not sure what's going on between you and Jack, but I need it to end. I'm going to fail Science at this rate.'

'It's done. Finished. Did you find the chocolate? One of the roses is not what it seems ...'

'I didn't. I'd better find it before Lisa Marie does. You spoil me.'

'I've told you before, you're worth it.' He pauses. 'So, will you come out with me tonight? It's just a few of the boys getting together with their girls. Brad's trying to get Ellen to come along.'

'There's no way Ellen will be allowed.'

'But, still. Come on. It's going to be lame if you don't come.'

'It's Tuesday so Mum's home. I'll have to ask her if I can go out.'

'Do you reckon she'll say yes?'

'I don't think I've ever asked her if I can go out before. What time are you thinking? I'll have to cook myself dinner beforehand.'

'Don't. I'll organise dinner. I'll be round to pick you up at eight.'

Cooper's mum arrives right on time. Fortunately, Mum's left to do the shopping by then and I don't have to do any embarrassing introductions.

As Cooper walks up my driveway, I leave the house and catch him eyeing me up. He cracks a half smile; clearly the high-waisted jeans and halter-neck top meet his approval. He wraps his arms around me and kisses me. 'Damn, I'm a lucky guy. Are those the jeans I got you? They go well with that old top of yours.' He indicates my house with a flick of his head. 'Are you going to invite me into your house one day?'

'Probably not.' I laugh, but I'm deadly serious.

He leads me to his car. This time there's no roof. 'It's a nice evening. I thought we'd ride with the top down.'

I'm glad I've got my hair up in a ponytail.

Patty greets me by name. 'You know, I'd like to meet your mother one day.'

'Yeah, sorry,' I say. 'Mum's not usually home in the evenings.'

'It's just Cooper's birthday is fast approaching. The more driving hours he can do, the sooner he can go for his licence and I can get my life back.'

Patty turns the music up. I reckon I know P!nk's songs better than she does now.

Cooper's mates live pretty close by. 'Text me when you're wanting to come home,' Patty says as she pulls up out the front of a small, brown-bricked building.

I shiver as we're left alone in the dark street.

'Sorry, are you cold?' Cooper asks.

'No. It's just not the usual neighbourhood you'd hang out in.'

Cooper chuckles. 'You're right there. But these guys are cool. You'll see.'

'I thought we were going to eat first?'

Cooper holds up a bag. 'I thought I'd go one better and cook for you.'

The wire gate groans as Cooper opens it onto a shattered concrete path. My chest tightens. 'Are you sure this is a good idea?'

'There's nothing to worry about. Matt and Hamish are uni students, so they're broke half the time, but they're good blokes.'

'How do you know so many people who go to uni?'

'My family moved around heaps when I was a kid, so I'm older than most of the guys in our year level. These guys are closer to my age than Brad and Joe are.'

We walk into the house without knocking. There's a group of five other guys sitting on couches in a dimly lit room. A pedestal fan swings fresh air across my face. Cooper walks around the room greeting them all by name and with weird handshakes. He then introduces me. A series of acknowledgments are mumbled in my direction.

'Grace and I thought we'd cook something up. I brought plenty of food for us all.'

There's more mumbles and nods of approval as we head into a cluttered, but clean kitchen. Cooper's pulling extra things out of the fridge. I jump up onto the bench and pop some tunes on my phone. I watch him move around the kitchen to the music like Jamie Oliver.

'Where'd you learn to cook?' I ask, as he throws a few ingredients in a bowl and mixes them together to create a creamy dip.

'My real dad's a chef. We used to cook together all the time before he went weird on us. And Mum's not much of a cook, so I do a fair bit at home.' He hands me a few carrots. 'Can you slice them nice and thin for me? I'll cook up some chicken and other bits and pieces.'

I grab a knife and start slicing. 'You know,' I say, 'you knowing your way around a kitchen like this is pretty hot.'

He stands in front of me, a wooden spoon in his hand, and I wrap my legs around his torso as we sway in time to the music and kiss. 'Yeah, well, remember that later when there's opportunity for more than just this.'

He finishes cooking and tells me to help myself. 'Better you eat now before the guys get into it. They forget to eat sometimes, so they don't leave much behind when they do.'

We take the remaining food into the lounge room and put it on the coffee table. There's now another guy and a girl in the room but Cooper doesn't acknowledge they're there. The boys are smoking something that doesn't smell like cigarettes, and when they offer some to Cooper he says, 'Nah, Grace has me on a health kick.' There's an awkward silence. Cooper turns to me and says, 'Come on. I'll show you around the rest of the house.'

I get up and follow Cooper but have no idea why he'd be showing me around such a boxy little house. He takes me past the kitchen, down a little hallway and opens a door into a bedroom.

He beckons me in. 'Cooper, I'm not comfortable being in some strange guy's room.'

Cooper sits down on the bed. 'This was my room.'

'Huh?' I put my head into the room and look around. It reminds me of my own bedroom, but it has a double bed. The one bedside table, and tiny cupboard in the corner, have been badly painted white. In the far corner there's a tall pile of books on the floor.

He holds out his hand. 'Come in. Hamish won't mind. I want to tell you a story.'

'What kind of story?'

'The story of where I've come from.' I walk in and take Cooper's hand. With me standing in the room, and Cooper's legs hanging off the bed, there isn't much room for anything else.

'This house, it used to be my place. Before Mum remarried, when we were still living with Dad.' He looks nostalgically around the room. 'Crazy, hey, that my mates have since moved in here.'

I join Cooper on the bed. 'This place is tiny. Your whole family lived here?'

'Mitch and I shared this room. Mum and Dad's room was on the other side of that wall. One bathroom. Two bedrooms.'

'Wow. A bit different to where you live now.'

Cooper laughs. 'Yeah. Crazy, hey. It was tough for Mum. Dad wasn't the easiest guy to live with.' Cooper lies back on the bed. 'I remember staring up at that ceiling, trying to go to sleep, while listening to Mum and Dad arguing in the kitchen.' He holds his breath. 'I'm determined to never go back to living like this. Me or my future family.'

I lie back on the bed and stare at the ceiling, imagining him as a little boy going through all that. I place my hand on Cooper's face and lean in to kiss him. We lie face to face, drinking each other in as he tells me stories of his childhood, of what life was like for him as a scared little boy living under this roof.

'You see, Grace,' he coos into my ear, 'I get you. I know where you're from and I remember what it's like. I know what it's like to want more in life. I'll take care of you. I'll give you the life you want.'

Cooper's hand moves up my body. He rests it on my stomach, then goes a little higher. I frown but let him.

'You're so beautiful, Grace.'

He kisses me and I allow his hand to wander. He smells so good. His back muscles are strong, his biceps thick and tense. My heart beats faster; his lips are so soft as they move around my neck and across my cheek to find my mouth again.

Cooper moves in closer; his face millimetres from mine. 'Your skin is soft. I don't think you know just how beautiful you are.'

I giggle.

His eyes are alive as he looks into mine. 'I've been watching you, the way you talk to people, the way you care for our friends.' He moves his body so there is no space between us. 'I want to be one of the people you care that much about.'

I smile. 'You're already one of the people I care about, Cooper.'

He's nodding, his face moving against my own. 'You do, don't you? You do care about me.' I can feel him smiling as he kisses me. 'I care about you too. I know you've had a tough life. I can give you so much more, so much of what you want.' His hand moves around to my back to play with the fastening of my bra. 'Of what we both want.'

I shake my head. He's still fiddling with my bra. I pull back. 'Hang on,' I say.

'There aren't many people in this world who care about me. Not really care. I need someone who will love me. And I know you want that, too.'

He moves his body so it is almost on top of me. I get my hands between us and push up, but he's too heavy.

'Cooper, stop,' I say.

'Come on Grace. Just relax.'

'No,' I say again.

'Yes, babe. This is what we both want.'

'No, Cooper,' I say more forcefully. 'I'm telling you – no.'

He pulls back, his eyebrows down, his lips clenched. 'What?'

'I'm not ready for this.'

'Not ready to show me how much you care?'

'I can show you that in other ways. I'm not ready to sleep with you. It's too soon.'

Cooper sits up and runs his hands through his hair. He breathes out hard. 'How long, Grace? How long am I going to have to wait?'

I sit up next to him and shake my head. 'I don't know. What kind of question is that?'

He stands up. 'So much for caring for me.'

'That's hardly fair,' I say. 'This is not what I want. Not yet. I'm not saying never, it's just too soon. We don't really know each other.'

'We'd know each other better if you hadn't stopped us just now.' His voice is salty. Almost sulky.

I grab my jacket. 'I'm going home.'

Cooper follows me. 'Wait, don't go. Come on, let's hang out a while longer.'

'You're being a jerk,' I say as I head out the front door.

'Grace, I'm sorry. I thought if we had a good go of it, you'd be up for it.' I'm a good few steps ahead of him but struggling to maintain the pace.

'You're such a gentleman,' I say.

'Well, that's what happened with Mikaela.'

I stop walking and turn to face him. 'What do you mean?'

'Mikaela wasn't so keen at first either, but then she came around. We were making out one time and she was keen to keep going. So, we did. I thought you were the same.'

'You and Mikaela slept together?'

'Yeah. A number of times.'

'She never told me.'

Cooper raises his eyebrows. 'Girls are a bit different like that. Boys like to talk. Girls, not so much.'

'That's so not true. If Mikaela had slept with you, she would have told us.'

'Well, clearly, that's not the case.'

Cooper takes my hand. 'Come on, I'll call my mum and get you home.'

I pull my hand back and pull my phone out of my pocket. I stand under a small tree, toying with my phone, and consider walking home. A few large drops of rain fall. What would Lisa Marie be up to at the moment?

'Come on, Grace. I really am sorry. Let me get you home.' His eyes are sad.

I wipe the mascara that I feel smudged under my eyes. I sigh deeply and nod.

We sit in the gutter and wait for Cooper's mum. 'Grace, you're the best thing that's happened to me in a long time.'

I pick up a brown leaf and begin pulling it apart. 'I'm still not sure how to take you sometimes. You can be the most sweet and amazing guy one minute, and the next, I'm wondering who the heck you are.'

He's got his head down. Drops of rain are falling through the branches, but I'm sure some of the dots on the ground are tears.

'I want so badly to be the guy you can say you love. If I can just have another try, I'll prove to you that I can do it.' He looks at me with a shiny face. 'Kindness, remember? Happiness and kindness. That's what we're going for.'

Patty arrives. The car ride is silent, other than P!nk's tunes trying to revive the mood.

I go home and do the only sensible thing there is to do. I ring Mikaela.

Chapter 20

I tap on Mikaela's face in my contacts and it asks if I want to call. I hesitate for a moment. It's late, and a school night. I don't know if she has access to her phone during the week at her boarding school, let alone know if she'll answer if she sees it's me. I push call. It rings and a sleepy-sounding Mikaela answers the phone.

'Hey, Mikaela,' I say. 'How are you?'

There's a pause for a moment. 'Grace?'

'Yeah, it's me. Thanks for answering. Can you talk?'

'Hang on.' There's some shuffling and then a door closing. 'Grace, what are you doing?'

'I needed to talk to you. You answered.'

'I had to stop it ringing before it woke my roommate.'

'Right. But still, you could have ghosted me. Sorry for calling you in the middle of the night.'

'My roommate is a heavy sleeper.'

'You know,' I say, 'I tried hard to contact you, after what happened.'

'You rang to tell me that?'

I swallow. 'You never responded.' Silence. 'You disappeared without telling me why.' Silence again. 'Mikaela? You still there?'

'Grace, it's the middle of the night. What do you want?'

'I'm sorry for not trying harder.'

'That's what you've rung to say?'

'Actually, I wanted to talk to you about something else.'

Neither of us speak for a hundred years.

'What?'

'I've started dating someone. Cooper.'

I hear Mikaela suck in air.

'I know that's awkward. Sorry.'

'It's fine. Fine.'

'Okay, well, it's just, Cooper and I had a fight tonight and he told me you two were sleeping together. I said if that were the case you would have told us.'

'What does it matter if we did?'

'He's putting the pressure on, you know?'

Silence.

'Are you okay? You still there?'

Her voice is pretty quiet. 'You're digging up stuff I'm trying to forget.'

'So, is it true then?'

'Look, Grace.' Mikaela's voice is unsteady. 'Cooper and I, we'd been together forever. He'd been on at me for ages, saying how much he loved me and that he wanted to be with me for the rest of our lives. He was persuasive. Romantic, even. He took me to this house he'd lived in when his dad had been around. He cooked a meal for me while his mates were passed out in the lounge room and then showed me his old bedroom. Gave me the sob story. I fell for it.'

I quietly repeat a series of swear words over and over to settle myself down. Into the phone, I say, 'What do you mean, you fell for it?'

'He knew exactly what he was doing that night, Grace. He was sucking me in with stories of his parents fighting and how terrible his childhood had been. But then, before we went all the way, I wanted to stop. I said I didn't want to do it and tried to stop him. But he kept telling me he loved me, and that if I loved him too, I would want it. I was so confused. He convinced me it was what I had to do if I wanted to show him I really loved him. The ironic thing is, afterwards, just being around him was making me sick.'

'Are you telling me—'

'My counsellor tells me it will empower me to tell the story, to use the word rape, but it still doesn't sit well with me. I made him think one thing and then changed my mind. I don't know if it was really rape or not.'

'Shit. Mikaela, I'm so sorry.'

'The worst part was when I found out later that it wasn't even his old house. He'd never lived there. He made the story up to get me into the bedroom, to make me feel sorry for him.'

A hand reaches out through the phone and punches me in the stomach, winding me.

'I can't tell you what to do, Grace, but you need to think seriously about whether being with someone like Cooper is what you really want.'

I grasp for something to make more sense of all this. 'Why didn't you tell us?'

'Tell you what? How do I tell everyone that the boy I loved had done that to me? How would I have even been able to look at you all again?'

I wipe my face, wet with tears I didn't know had escaped. 'We would have supported you, Mikaela. We would have helped you.'

'Cooper was going to ruin me if I broke up with him, Grace. We slept together two more times. But I got to the point where I couldn't stand to live one more day under the dark cloud that had become my life. I just couldn't do it anymore. When my parents found me unconscious that night, and when I told them what had happened with Cooper, they cut me off from everything and everyone that ever had anything to do with Cooper Dally. Including you guys. The doctors saved my body that night, but moving me away from everyone is what saved my life. I'm happy here. I have the new start I needed.'

I run my free hand over the back of my neck. 'Why didn't you go to the police?'

'And tell them what? That I'd snuck out of my parents' home to go to a house filled with bong smoke, sat on a boy's bed, made out with him, which lead to us sleeping together?'

I swallow hard. 'If he raped you, Mik ... we would have believed you.'

Mikaela is breathing deeply on the other end of the line. 'I was naive. I was stupid. I was embarrassed and mortified and hurt—so hurt, Grace. I loved him. For the longest time, I thought we were going to be together forever.'

I get off the phone to Mikaela and cry. I cry so hard my ears ache and my jaw becomes stiff. And when my alarm goes off for school the next day, I hit the snooze button and go back to sleep.

Thursday rolls into Friday and when the weekend comes, I still can't face anyone. I'm not sure I can face anyone ever again.

Chapter 21

I've stayed off social media as a way of avoiding Cooper, of avoiding life, for four days. I can see he's sent a ton of messages, and I got an email saying my data had been topped up, which I assume was him as well. But I can't bring myself to read anything from him. It will just be more apologies. I'm surprised I didn't have another basket of flowers appear on my doorstep over the weekend.

On Monday morning, Mum comes into my room and sits on the edge of my bed. 'Graceland.'

I groan.

'Grace.'

I groan again.

She runs her hand over my head. 'I don't know what happened to you, or why you've been so miserable the last few days. But, honey, you've got to go to school. No matter how much we want someone to make the world go away, it never does. You can't stay in bed for the rest of your life.'

I shake my head. 'I can't, Mum. It's too hard.'

'It can be hard. But you're stronger than you think, Graceland. It's never too late to remember to forget about the things in your past you need to move on from.'

I get the reference. 'Mum, quoting Elvis songs doesn't always help, you know.'

'Lots of words of wisdom in some of those old songs.'

I nod. 'Well, what if you're just repeating the mistakes that someone else has already made before you?'

She stands up. 'Then change your stars, Graceland. Change course and set a different road for yourself to walk.'

Lisa Marie drives me to school. Everyone is waiting to go into Form when I arrive. Cooper is acting his usual self; prancing around and demanding I hang off his arm. I fasten myself to Ellen, but play along, anything to avoid having a confrontation with him in front of the rest of the class. The other girls are mad at me because I've had my phone off for four days and haven't told them why I'm not at school. But I give nothing away. Until I'm alone with Nikki and Ellen.

'You're acting different, Grace. Are you sure you're okay?' Ellen asks.

'Something happened with me and Cooper last week.'

'I wondered,' Ellen says. 'Brad wouldn't tell me what, but he had been making hints about stuff Cooper had said.'

'Like what?' I ask.

'Nothing much. Just bragging about stuff that he'd been doing with you, but it didn't make sense to me.'

'Yeah, well, Cooper's been trying his best to get me to go further and further with him.'

'Doesn't surprise me,' Ellen says.

'And,' I say, 'I rang Mikaela last week.'

'Really?' Nikki says. 'Why didn't you tell us earlier? How is she?'

'She's doing okay. I think she's happy at her new school. But that wasn't what we talked about.'

'What did you talk about then?' Nikki asks.

'Cooper?' Ellen asks.

I say, 'Yeah. Mostly.'

'What did she say?' Ellen leans in closely.

'Just, that I should be careful.'

'Did she talk about what happened with her and Cooper?' Ellen asks.

'Yeah, a bit. But the most confusing part is she talked about how he asked her over to this house that he used to live in with his dad and told her how poor they'd been.'

'What's confusing about that? It makes sense to me,' Nikki says. 'I've heard Cooper talk before about how his family used to live in virtual poverty.'

'Yeah,' I say. 'And it made sense to me when Cooper told me the same story last Wednesday night.'

'So?' Nikki says. 'He told you both the same story about his past. Nothing strange about that.'

'Yeah,' I say, 'except Mikaela said she found out later that it was just a story, that it wasn't true. She reckoned he'd done it to get her sympathy and get her to sleep with him.'

'And did she?' Nikki asked.

Ellen and I nod.

'You knew, Ellen?'

Ellen tilts her head; her eyes say yes.

'Why did she tell you, and not me and Grace?' There's a hint of anger in Nikki's voice.

'She was embarrassed,' Ellen says. 'I just asked the right questions at the right time.'

I add, 'She hadn't wanted to go that far, but Cooper kind of forced her.'

'No way,' Nikki says. 'And what, did he try the same thing on you?'

Tears sting my eyes. 'Yeah, he was pretty persistent.'

'Shit,' Nikki says. 'But you stopped him, right?'

Everyone's eyes are on me. 'I did. But now I don't know what to believe.'

'Mikaela wasn't exactly the most honest friend we've ever had,' Nikki says. 'If he hurt her, I can imagine her doing her best to make him look the absolute worse she can. Especially when talking to his new girlfriend.'

'Yeah, but to lie about something like that? I don't know,' I say. 'She sounded sincere, and I didn't tell her that Cooper had tried the same thing with me, so she had no reason to lie.'

'Other than making him look worse.'

'I guess so.'

'And when you asked him to stop, did he?'

'Eventually, yes,' I say. 'I was scared for a few moments, thinking he wasn't going to.'

'So why stop for you and not for Mikaela?'

I shrug. 'I don't know. But I don't think Mikaela was lying.'

'Maybe you need to confront Cooper about it,' Ellen says.

'Maybe,' I say. 'But he's not going to like it if I do.'

Chapter 22

It's tough to concentrate in class with a problem like Cooper Dally playing on your mind. I'm doing everything possible to avoid being alone with him. He's buying into the lie that everything is okay between us, though it must be killing him that I haven't responded to his messages.

The right time to confront him hasn't presented itself ... fortunately. Confronting Cooper for the truth about Mikaela is the last thing I feel like doing right now.

It doesn't help that in Science, the others have done virtually nothing on the days I was away. We go back over the plan, but it's the folio of learning I'm most concerned about. Not just because I've been away and missed some stuff, but I don't think the others are keeping up. I suggest we meet at the end of the day to go through it all, but Jack is the only one able to stay back. The two of us agree to meet in the library straight after school.

On my way to the library, Cooper catches me and asks if I want to go back to his place.

'I don't think so, Cooper. I've got to get some Science stuff done.'

'Well, at least walk me to my car?'

I agree, though I know what's coming. I don't have time to discuss Mikaela; I need to meet with Jack in the library.

'You haven't responded to my messages,' he says, his head down.

'No, I haven't read them. I put a social-media ban on myself. I needed some space.'

He nods. 'Are we okay?'

I rub my left shoulder. 'I'm confused, Cooper. I don't know what to think at the moment.'

'I stuffed up pretty bad, yeah?'

'You could say that.'

'Just tell me what I need to do to make it up to you, Grace. I'll do anything. Flowers, proper dinner dates, vow of celibacy.'

The air thins a little and I crack a tiny smile. 'Good on you.' We reach the car park. 'I just need some time to think.'

He leans in to kiss me but I move away. His eyes wilt as he gives a half-smile and heads to where his red convertible is humming in the carpark.

The library is quiet, with only a couple of Year 7 girls reading with headphones on in the corner. The librarian is busy covering books at her desk and there is the occasional rustling of papers from within a teacher's office off to the side. I've never stayed back at school after the bell before—voluntarily, at least. It's weird for the place to be so empty.

I open my laptop and a photo of me with Cooper appears on my desktop. Somehow, he's got into my laptop and changed my wallpaper.

The library walls are lined with books; a multitude of binders in random colours and sizes. A large poster shows some students breaking through the library wall about to enter into a new world behind it, with spaceships and strange animals waiting for them to enter. It reminds me of when I was a little girl and Grandpa read me *The Lion, The Witch and The Wardrobe*. I must have only been about five. After Grandpa would read it to me, he would talk about how there is another world within this world that we can escape to. Those grandparents had never visited again. He'd had such a kind voice; it was a shame he hadn't been able to pass his kindness on to my father.

I place my head in my hands for a moment and try to settle myself. There's no escaping to Narnia anymore; such worlds don't exist. Just this one, with its rules and demands and hard work and hurt and people who work more against you than for you. Like now. Surely this assignment is a case of the blind leading the blind.

The automatic doors open and close, and Jack walks into the library. He stands still for a moment before heading over to me.

'Hey,' I say.

'Has Cooper gone home?'

'Yes.'

'Are you sure?' Jack's eyes flitter around the room.

I lower my laptop screen. 'Yes. I watched him get into his car.'

Jack fidgets with his hands. 'Did you see them drive away?'

'Yes.'

'All the way out of the car park?'

'Jack.'

'Yes?'

'Cooper has gone home. It's okay.'

Jack sits in the chair opposite me.

'Don't you think it would be easier if you sat beside me?'

He looks nervously around the room again, before moving to sit beside me. He puts his head down on the table.

'Didn't you bring your laptop?'

Jack looks up in surprise, making momentary eye contact with me. 'You didn't say to. You said to bring my science stuff.' He holds up an A4 binder book.

'If we're studying, if we're working on the evidence of learning portfolios, don't you reckon you need your laptop?'

Jack seems confused.

'It's okay. We can just do everything on mine.' I fully open my laptop again.

Jack pulls out a notebook from his pocket and scribbles something down.

'What are you writing?' I ask.

'Just some notes to help me.'

I shake my head. *Whatever.* 'So, where do we start?' I type in my password and a blank document appears on the screen. Jack keeps his head down. 'I'm most concerned with how everyone is going with their learning portfolios. Did you get that email from the others letting us know where they're up to?'

Jack shrugs. 'I haven't looked at my emails today.'

'What? All day? You haven't checked your emails *all day*?'

Jack's eyes are plastered to the orange table. I can see he's fidgeting his hands beneath it. I refresh my email inbox for the hundredth time that day, but there's no email from Latisha.

'Okay. Well, from what I know, they're both behind but not too bad.'

I might as well be talking to the wall.

'What about you? Did you finish writing all the answers up from last week?'

Jack shakes his head.

'Do you at least have the answers written down for section one?'

'No,' he says.

'Well, where are you up to? How many do you have written in your science book?' I open his book but it's almost completely blank.

'None, I guess.'

'None at all?' I say, finding it difficult to keep the frustration out of my voice. 'Didn't you answer some during class?'

Jack looks up to the ceiling and seems to be holding his breath.

'Man.' My heart thumps in my chest and I grip the edge of the table. I put my head on the edge of the keyboard. The computer makes a funny noise.

'Your head is on the space bar,' Jack says. 'That's why the computer is making that noise.'

I lift my head slightly. The noise stops.

'Why did you put your head down like that?' Jack's hands go still.

I raise my head. 'I need to pass this subject. I need to do well on this assignment.'

'I know. You told me already.'

'You're not helping, Jack. You have to work with the group. You have to do the work the teacher sets. You have to check your emails. You have to come to school and go to class and you have to answer the questions!'

Jack frowns. 'I have answered the questions.'

'What do you mean? You just said you hadn't.'

'I read the questions and I answered them. But I didn't write the answers down.'

'Well, why not?'

Jack shrugs. 'I don't like writing.'

'Okay, well, how about we write down your answers now.'

Jack briefly makes eye contact again. 'Okay.'

'If you had your laptop here, you could look up the answers as I type.' I open a document with the questions in it.

'I already know the answers,' Jack says. 'I don't need to look them up.'

'Really? Well, let's start with the first question: *What is DNA?*'

Jack looks straight ahead, as though he's reading something from a screen in the back of his mind. 'DNA is the carrier of genetic information in the human body. It is what makes someone who they are, or something what it is.'

'Hang on,' I say, typing madly. 'Not so fast.'

'But to be specific, DNA is an acronym for deoxyribonucleic acid.'

I pause typing and look at Jack.

'What?' Jack looks briefly at me as I stare at him.

'Okay,' I say, beginning to type again. 'Can you spell it for me?'

Jack shakes his head. 'I know it starts with "d" "e".'

I type *DNA* into Google and a definition along with a few pictures pop up on the screen. I copy and paste the acronym definition into the document.

Jack leans in closer to the screen. 'It's only two words, deoxyribonucleic, and then acid, even though there are three letters in the acronym.'

I shake my head. What the heck's going on? 'Did you, like, memorise Wikipedia or something?'

'I like science. Especially biology. I like all sciences.'

'I can see that,' I say. 'But you don't do well on, like, tests and stuff, do you?'

He shakes his head, but then frowns. 'Why do you know that?'

I swallow hard, clasping my hands and resting them on the table in front of the laptop. 'A friend hacked into the school computer system. I know you got a D for Science on your last report.'

Jack tucks his chin down into his chest. 'That was not a nice thing to do. That is an invasion of my privacy.'

'I wasn't thinking about you when he did it. Sorry.'

I can see him frowning under his blond fringe. 'Just because you weren't thinking about me and my feelings doesn't make it right. Even if you don't know someone very well, you shouldn't do things like that to them. You should ask the person, not steal their information.'

'You're right, Jack. I'm sorry.'

Jack looks from the table to the ceiling and back to the table again. His breathing has gone weird.

'Jack, I am sorry. Will you forgive me?'

Jack closes his eyes for a moment. 'Yes, I will forgive you. But I hope you won't do anything like that again.'

'Okay, I promise. I can see it hurt you. I really am sorry.'

Jack smiles for the briefest of moments; if I'd blinked, I'd have missed it. 'I mean what I say when I say things. I forgive you. You don't need to apologise again once I have forgiven you.'

I chuckle. 'Okay.' I turn back to my computer screen. 'Let's keep going then. What about the next question: *Why do scientists call*

DNA a blueprint for someone's characteristics?

A little spark explodes in Jack's eyes. 'That's a funny question that one, because they do call it a blueprint, and it sort of is, but not just for someone, but for practically everything; it's what tells flowers to have different shades of purple, and that they should open and close with the sun. It tells a seed that it should start growing upwards once the conditions are right and that it should grow into a gum tree and not a mango tree.'

My fingers dance across the keyboard in an ungraceful flurry of activity. 'Okay, but what about for people?'

'Well, calling DNA a blueprint is kind of like an analogy because blueprints are what they use to build buildings, and DNA is what our bodies use to know the way it's supposed to build everything about us. So, it tells the body it is supposed to have two arms and two legs, and green eyes, but it also tells your body to make it so you feel it when I put my hand on your arm.' Jack's hand lands softly on my arm and stays there.

'Jack,' I say. His eyes meet with mine for a moment, but he then looks to the side, as though he's looking at my cheek, or perhaps my ear. 'You have your hand on my arm.'

Jack looks down, as though he isn't aware he's doing it. 'I was making a point.'

'Yeah, but your hand is still on my arm.'

Jack nods.

'Jack, what do you think it means when a boy puts his hand on a girl's arm?'

He frowns. 'I don't know.'

'Well, some people would think that means he likes her. That he's kind of flirting with her.'

Jack's face bursts into a dark shade of red. He immediately withdraws it and rubs his hands together under the table.

'Jack, can you look at me?' I tap just under my eye. 'Here, at my face?'

Jack shakes his head.

'Why not?'

'I have trouble looking at you.'

'Why?'

'Well,' he looks to the ceiling, 'I have trouble looking anyone in the eyes because it sends my brain crazy thinking of a thousand million things at once and I can't concentrate on anything that's being said to me.'

'And with me?'

Jack pauses, his eyes darting around the room. 'I have trouble looking at you in your whole face, not just your eyes.'

'Why?'

His eyes remain fixated in one place on the ceiling. 'Because—' his eyes are darting around again and he rocks a little, '—when I look at your face all I can think about is how soft your skin looks and how you have such little ears and how pretty your eyes are; and that makes me think about how it's amazing that you even have green eyes because your mum doesn't have green eyes and neither does your sister, and Jesse had blue eyes, but I don't know about your dad. But he must have blue eyes because green eyes are recessive to brown eyes which your mum has, but green eyes can be dominant over blue eyes and so your dad must have blue eyes, so the recessive gene could come out in you.'

I laugh. 'My dad does have blue eyes.'

Jack rocks back and forth. 'I thought he must have.'

The large clock on the library wall clicks over to half past four. 'Oh, seriously, look at the time.' I close my laptop. 'My sister will be here any minute.'

'I am going to walk home.' Jack stands up and walks toward the library door. I rush to keep up with him. As I fall into step with him, I say, 'It looks like it might rain. Lisa Marie could drop you home too.'

'I'm not allowed to get lifts with people I don't know.'

'You don't know Lisa Marie?'

'I know who she is. That doesn't mean I know her.'

'Well, I hope you make it home before it rains.'

'I hope so too. My laptop might get wet.'

'What do you mean *your laptop*?' I ask.

'My laptop is in my school bag. My school bag isn't waterproof, so my laptop might get wet.'

'Jack, where is your school bag now?'

Jack looks at me as though I'm crazy. 'It's just outside the library. You're not allowed to bring your school bag into the library.'

Chapter 23

Jack spends the week living in his own world as usual, but I start noticing other stuff about him. Like how he mouths the answers to questions the teacher asks; how he puts his earphones in his ears when the classroom gets noisy; how he goes the long way around to anything if it involves him having to walk past Cooper's locker.

I also notice that Jack has the kind of smile that you know you deserve when you get one. And I deserve a few in Science. I make a point of asking him a question and keeping the others quiet while waiting for him to get the answer out. Sometimes his words come out funny, especially if he talks for a few minutes at a time, but he always seems to have something pretty amazing to say.

Outside of stuff to do with Science, Jack doesn't talk to me.

Cooper gives me the space I asked for, even though our friends hang out together every recess and lunch. Watching him interact with everyone else reminds me of the side of Cooper I love. He's generous, funny and entertaining to be around. The way his curls fall across his forehead and his eyes light up when he's having fun make my heart ache. I want so much for him to be the kind of guy I have been in love with since the first day we met, back in Year 7, back when he fell in love with Mikaela.

When Friday rolls around again, he approaches me as we're leaving Form at the end of the day. He comes up behind me and slips something into my hand. The scent of his aftershave arrives a few seconds later.

'What's this?' I ask, looking at the square velvet box wrapped with a pink ribbon.

'You know me. I couldn't resist.' His smile stretches halfway across his face. I open the box. A silver bracelet sparkles in the sunlight. There's a single charm on it; a heart that says *Trust*.

'It's lovely,' I say. I close the box.

'You don't want to put it on?' he asks. A hint of facial hair frames the squareness of his chin. He tosses his curls around with each movement of his head. Despite how much I don't like him right now, I miss the way he is when he's being sweet.

'Cooper,' I say and raise my eyebrows. I lean back when he leans in to kiss me.

'Still too soon?'

'I don't know, Cooper.'

'Well, it's the weekend and I want to hang out with you. Let me show you how sincere I am. I miss you.'

I shake my head. 'I don't know if I'm up to going out again.'

'What if I beg?' Cooper gets down on one knee. 'What about brunch with Nikki and Joe? Nikki seems keen on Joe, but I think Joe needs some encouragement.'

'Not Brad and Ellen?'

Cooper slumps his shoulders. 'Brad's being a jerk at the moment. Saying stuff it's not his place to say.'

Butterflies tumble into my stomach. 'What's he been saying?'

'He reckons Ellen is surprised you haven't broken up with me.'

'It's not like her to say something like that.'

Cooper shrugs. 'Brad's gone weird. Ellen is changing him.'

'That could be a good thing. Ellen is a super nice person.'

'Yeah, well, she's been putting words in Brad's ear. Stuff about you ringing Mikaela to ask about me, other rubbish like that.'

The butterflies take off and fly around. 'Well, I can't believe Ellen would tell Brad that, but I did speak to Mikaela last week.'

'Why?' Cooper steps back and runs his hand through his hair.

'Because of what you told me about the two of you. I wanted to find out for myself.'

'And she answered her phone? Is she okay? What did she tell you?'

'She said it was true that the two of you had been sleeping together.'

'So, now do you trust me?' His face is a mixture of soft anger and hurt.

'I don't know,' I say. 'She says it wasn't exactly consensual.'

Cooper just stares at me for a moment. 'What do you mean?'

I lower my eyes then look up at him, desperately hoping he'll deny the charges.

Cooper runs his hands through his hair again. He paces back and forth for a bit. 'I can't believe she would say something like that.'

I bite my bottom lip. 'Is it true?'

Cooper glares at me. 'As if!' He paces again, back and forth in front of me. 'She said she loved me. She wasn't perfect, but I never thought she was a liar.'

'So, it's not true?'

Cooper comes over and takes both my hands. 'Grace, I loved Mikaela. It's a bit weird for me to talk about her like this with you. But, she was my world. I would never have done anything to hurt her.'

'Why would she say something like that then?'

'No one else knows this.' Cooper picks up a twig and snaps it. 'Mikaela and I had a huge fight the night she overdosed.'

'What did you fight about?'

'She was talking about wanting to go to boarding school. I said I wanted her to stay here with me, to get married when we finished school. But she'd been talking to her parents about boarding school and they were coming around to the idea. On the last day I saw her, I gave her a promise ring. She refused to take it, accusing me of trying to control her.'

'Mikaela always was pretty feisty.'

Cooper laughs through wet eyes. 'She sure was. One of the

things I'd loved about her. One of the things I love about you.'

We stand there, holding hands in the empty school ground. I search his eyes for any hint of a lie, for them to convince me he is only speaking the truth. There's nothing to say he isn't being totally sincere with me.

'I shouldn't be surprised Mikaela would try spreading some lies about me. Anything to take the heat off herself for leaving us all like she did. She could be a bitch when she wanted to be.'

He looks at me to gauge my reaction. I soften a little. It was true—Mikaela could be moody and take her sullenness out on everyone around her.

He rubs my hand. 'If you're up for it, I'd love to hang out with you some more again.'

I nod slowly. 'Sure. But no drugs and no parties. Just you and me hanging out. In public. And no trying to make any moves on me. We are going to take it slowly, Cooper Dally, or else.'

He squares his shoulders. 'Of course.'

Then he leans in and I let him kiss me, long, slowly, and I remember how much I adore being kissed by Cooper. Most of the time.

When we separate I look into Cooper's eyes and smile. 'I've got to work on my science project this weekend.'

'You set the rules, Grace. You set the pace. I am yours, however much of you I can have.'

I stand on my toes and kiss Cooper again. 'You can be the sweetest guy in the world when you want to be, Cooper Dally.'

He walks me to the empty carpark. 'You've missed your bus.'

I look up at the clouds. It might not rain.

Cooper pulls out his phone. 'I'll call Mum to come and get us. I was going to run home, but those clouds are looking a bit dark. My Nikes could get ruined in the rain.' He hits the call button. 'Though, if I'm going to keep driving you around like this, I really gotta get the okay from your mother, so my mum will let me drive with you in the car. It's wasted time sitting in the passenger seat.'

Chapter 24

Cooper messages me later that afternoon.

> Sorry, babe. Can we delay our plans to hang out? The fam is going to Brisbane for the weekend and wants me to come too. The four hour drive there and back will finish up my hours.

> Sure. I reply. I'll be busy working on my science project anyway.

> Maybe we could hang out Sunday night?

> Lisa Marie and I have plans to watch a movie together Sunday night. She's moving in with Tom next week. We'll just see each other at school on Monday. K?

He puts a sad face. I don't respond.

There is only so much I can do toward the science project on my own. I message Jack, Latisha and Seb about getting together. Seb never replies. Latisha says she can on Sunday afternoon and so does Jack.

> Great. I message. Where shall we meet?

> Jack: My mum is out for the day and I'm not allowed people over when no one else is at home.

Latisha: Not my place, it's outta town.

Me: Okay. What about the town library?

I get two thumbs up. The library it is.

Me: Can one of you pick me up?

Jack: I can.

Latisha says she'll meet us there. But when we pull up out the front of the library, there's a sign on the door saying the library is closed for renovations.

I groan. 'Now where will we go?'

'I guess I could cancel my meetings and stay home,' Jack's mum says.

'Or, maybe we could work at the church, in that room off to the side of where your meeting is,' Jack says.

'They've set a nursery up for the afternoon in that room,' says Mrs Oskar.

'What about your place?' Jack asks me.

'People don't come over to my place,' I say.

'Why not?'

'Jack, don't pry,' Mrs Oskar says.

'But we have people over at our place all the time. Isn't everyone like that?'

'No Jack,' his mother says. 'Not everyone is like that.'

'I do have people come over some times,' I say. 'But only close friends.'

Jack tilts his head and frowns a little.

I sigh. 'We can go to my place, it's fine.'

'Don't feel pressured by him, Grace. Is your mother at home?'

My cheeks grow warm. 'Mum's been at church this morning and usually goes to work soon after.'

'What church does your mother go to?' Mrs Oskar says.

I shrug. 'Some little one just down the road.'

'You don't ever go with her?'

I shake my head. 'I'm not into that kind of thing.'

'You should come to church with Jack one week,' she says. 'You might like our church better.'

I smile to be polite.

'Shall we message Latisha to say we're meeting at your place instead?' Jack asks.

'I'm not comfortable about you and Jack being in your house on your own,' Jack's mum says. 'Even if Latisha is there eventually.'

'We won't be alone,' I say. 'Lisa Marie, that's my older sister, she'll be home. She's packing because she's moving out.'

'Oh? Is she preparing for uni or something?'

I wince. 'No. She's moving in with her boyfriend.'

'Oh, I see,' Mrs Oskar says. 'Well, as long as your sister is at home, I think that might be best. It would be better if I can go to my meeting.'

I'm silently dying inside. How I'm going to explain my house to Jack, I don't know. I text Latisha.

Tom's car is in the driveway. I unlock the front door and we're met by familiar bass coming from under Lisa Marie's door. I don't bother letting her know I'm back.

I use my body as a shield to stop Jack from seeing into the lounge room and direct his attention to the kitchen. I clear things off the table to make room for our laptops.

'You have a messy house,' Jack says.

I laugh. 'Yes, well, Mum works long hours.'

'Isn't she just a waitress?'

'Yes, she's a waitress. She works at night and sleeps during the day.'

'You should get a house cleaner. A house cleaner would help you to keep things clean. It doesn't look very hygienic in your kitchen.'

'Jack, that isn't very nice. I know my house isn't very tidy but telling me just makes me feel bad. Or, like, embarrassed.'

'But I wasn't telling you to make you feel bad. I was giving you advice on how you could make the situation better.' Jack looks from the kitchen and back to me, confusion across his face. 'It's good advice. My mum had a house cleaner when she got sick one time. It helped a lot.'

'Okay, well, thanks.'

'We could do some cleaning now, before we get started on our assignment. That would be a nice surprise for your mum when she gets home to find the house cleaner.' Jack fills the sink with warm, soapy water.

'I don't think my mum would like you cleaning our house, Jack.'

'Why not?'

'Because it would make her feel bad that someone came over and felt the need to clean her house.'

'But it does need cleaning.' He's looking at the piles of plates, dirty glasses and mugs like they're an alien invasion.

'Yes, I know it does. Jack, come on. Let's get started on the assignment. I'm sure Latisha will be here soon.'

Jack fills the sink with dishes and some of the foam splashes onto the floor. 'The floor needs to be cleaned, too,' he says, looking down at his feet. 'But if the dishes are cleaned, that will be a start.'

I give up. I grab a tea towel and dry as he washes.

'Is your mum sick?' he asks.

'No, why?'

'Because your kitchen is messy. My kitchen was messy because Mum was sick.'

'Yeah, well, I guess you could say that my mum has had it tough lately.'

'Since Jesse died?'

'Since she was born.' I chuckle.

Jack has a blank expression on his face.

'It's a joke,' I say. 'Well, kinda. I just mean she's had a hard life, you know?'

Jack puts the last few plates in the sink. 'You know, if you soak the plates it makes it quicker and easier when you wash them.'

'Right-o,' I say. 'That'll do with the house cleaning advice. Hurry up so we can get started on the assignment.'

But Jack has other plans. He wipes down the bench. Then, before I even realise it, before I have a chance to stop him, he's gone around the corner into the lounge room. I can hear him moving around in there. I'm frozen to the spot. He walks back into the kitchen, puts a few glasses in the sink of soapy water, and goes to head back to the lounge room.

'Jack, wait,' I say.

He pauses and looks in my direction, but not at my face.

'Aren't you going to say anything?'

'About what?'

'About the lounge room.'

Jack frowns. 'No. Why would I?'

I walk into the lounge room ahead of him. The lights are dimmed, but I know what everything is and where it is placed. 'You don't think this is odd?'

Jack walks into the room behind me. 'Not really. It is very common for people who have experienced loss to express their grief in different ways. I've done a lot of research about it.'

He moves around the room as though his eyes are not seeing the wall hangings, the DVDs, the CDs, the posters, guitars or sequined outfits. He pauses at the life-size cut-out. 'This is how a lot of people remember Elvis, with his hair slicked back, his white suit covered in gold sequins. But by the time he died, he was overweight and unhealthy.' He moves to a poster of Elvis and reads aloud, 'He wasn't just a star, he was the whole damn galaxy.' Jack chuckles. 'People sure did love Elvis.'

'Some people a bit too much,' I say.

'Do you mean your mum?'

I don't bother to answer, but instead say, 'Ever since Jesse died, she's been adding to this monument to Elvis. She watches his movies over and over. It's like she's even more obsessed with him now. I don't understand it. She wasn't even born when Elvis was alive, and yet she was so obsessed with him that she named all three of us after him in some way. I reckon she jinxed Jesse by naming him after a baby who died when he was born.'

'Actually, Down syndrome is a genetic chromosome disorder, so Jesse had Down syndrome from conception; logically your mother giving him that name couldn't have anything to do with him being born with Down syndrome.'

'Yes, Jack. I know. It's just that when you lose someone you love, logic doesn't always come into it.'

Jack picks a few plates up off the floor and goes back into the kitchen. 'Your mum isn't a very tidy person. With her being sad about Jesse dying, plus working long hours, you should do more to help her out.'

'Thanks for the life tip, Jack. But seriously, butt out. Coming into my house and seeing what you've seen doesn't make you an expert on me, my life or my mother.'

'You're angry.'

'Yes, I am.' I run a hand through my hair. 'I'm trying not to be, though.'

'Why are you angry at me?' He follows me back into the kitchen.

I turn to the sink and wash the plates. The food is caked on from how long they've been sitting in the lounge room. 'You can't just come into someone's house and start cleaning up and making judgements about their lives. It's not nice. It hurts people's feelings.'

'Is that what you think I have done?'

'Yes, I think that is what you have done.' I try putting the cleaned plates onto the sink, but there's very little room left for the dishes to drain. Jack is watching me. I point to the tea towel and he gets the hint and starts drying them. 'This is why I don't like having people come to my house. My family's kind of a mess, but Mum has done the best she can. She's been through a lot, but she's also made mistakes. And I'm determined I won't make the same mistakes. I can't stand to just repeat what everyone else in my family has done with their lives. I want to be something better.'

'I'm sorry, Grace. I didn't mean to make you angry. Or sad. I don't understand when it is okay to offer people advice. Usually, what I think is very good advice upsets people. I still don't know why people take it badly.'

I finish washing the final plate. 'You do have a point though, Jack. I could do more to help my mum out.'

'You know. I think it's appropriate that you're named after Elvis's house, Graceland.'

I chuckle. 'And why's that?'

'Well, Elvis' family was really poor when he was little. His dad went to jail for a while for trying to steal money from one of his bosses. And they lived in a tiny two-room house. But Elvis ended up being rich and successful. Jesse once told me that people still go and visit Graceland, his mansion, because it reminds people that you can become whatever you want, despite what you were born into. People can change their stars. That's a bit like what you want to do, Grace.'

'That is very cool, Jack.'

'Jesse was a smart kid. He knew a lot about people. And about Elvis. He loved Elvis. He talked a lot about his sister who had the same name as Elvis' house. It was his dream to go to Graceland one day.'

'Yeah, I'd forgotten that. Mum used to joke about taking him there when he turned eighteen.' I put the last plate on the drying rack. 'You know,' I say, 'maybe it wouldn't be so terrible if you did call me Graceland sometimes. At least, maybe when there is no one else around.'

Chapter 25

'Hey, Graceland,' Lisa Marie says as I emerge from my bedroom, my hair a mess, my eyes blurry. 'You okay?'

'Tired. I had that movie replaying in my head all night. I told you we should have gone for a comedy.'

'Are you going to school today?'

'Of course,' I say. 'Why? Am I late?'

'No. I just thought, maybe, you might like a ride to school. I have an appointment before work and it's nearby.'

'Sure.'

'Don't make me late, though.'

I pull a clean shirt out of the laundry basket and try to shake the creases out. I throw my things in my bag and grab a banana. Mum is nowhere to be seen.

In Mum's car, Lisa Marie rubs her hands over the steering wheel.

'You don't drive much anymore,' I say. 'Since you and Tom got serious.'

'I don't.' Her knuckles are turning white. 'But he also pays the petrol, so, you know, there are benefits.'

Houses are dotted among the trees, parking lots and roads. What are the lives like of the people living behind those doors? Do they have to worry about how to pay for petrol?

'How's school?' Lisa Marie asks.

I shrug. 'How's work?'

'Boring. But it's okay. They're teaching me latte art. I'm getting pretty good at it.'

I chuckle. 'Cool. I'll have to come buy a coffee off you some time.'

'Yeah, cool. Hey, um … I have something to tell you.'

'Okay.'

'Grace,' her voice is serious, 'you know how I'm moving out?'

'Yeah,' I say. 'Is it tomorrow?'

'Thursday.'

I go to look out the window again, but then I notice she has a tear running down her face.

'What's the matter?' I ask.

'It's just, look, I've only just found out, so it's not the reason I'm moving out, okay?'

'What? What is it?'

I can see her swallow. 'I'm pregnant.'

I stare at her. Her words pound in my head, but not in the right order, as though they're being tossed around by an unruly sea.

'So, you and Tom, you're …'

'Starting a family, a little earlier than we'd planned, yes.' She gives a little laugh, as though it's a joke.

But it isn't.

I watch her as she drives, moving in and around the traffic, not even eighteen years old yet. 'How do you feel about it?'

She moves her head from side to side. 'I was petrified at first. When I told Tom, he was shocked, but now he's totally ecstatic. He loves kids. He's always wanted a big family. Three or four kids at least.'

'When did you find out?'

'Last week. The doc says I should wait a few more weeks before I tell anyone, just in case something happens, but I wanted you to know.'

'And Mum?'

'I'll tell her tomorrow when she's not working. I wanted to tell you first, to gauge your reaction.'

'How'd I do?'

'Pretty good. I was more worried about your reaction than

Mum's. Mum can't be too mad. After all, she got pregnant with me when she was my age.'

A wave of sadness settles over my shoulders.

When Lisa Marie drops me at school I head straight to the bathrooms. I lock myself in a cubicle, lower the seat and sit down. Lisa Marie's pregnancy shouldn't be a shock to me. I'd half expected it. But for some reason, it is. I feel numb, like my world should be changing but I know it won't. I don't need to cry, but I allow a few tears to escape before wiping them carefully and checking in my reflection to see if my mascara has run.

When I head up to Form, people are standing around talking quietly in small groups. I try to hide the sadness that seems determined to remain with me. I shouldn't be sad. I'm going to be an aunty.

As I walk up to Ellen, Nikki and Hayley, they all go quiet.

'What's up?' I say casually, though my heart is sitting at the bottom of my stomach.

No one says anything. I look at Ellen. 'Come on, spill it.'

Ellen looks at the other two girls. 'It's Jack,' she says.

'What about him?' I ask.

'Miss Krensky came past us before, on her way to a meeting. She said she'd be late to Form, that there were some things to sort out.'

'Like what?'

'Something's happened to Jack. They're having a meeting up there. Mr Reyl and Mr Van Hayden too. And some woman. Ellen reckons it's Jack's mum.'

My head spins. 'What do you reckon has happened?'

Ellen shrugs. 'There's a few theories being thrown around. One is that Jack's failing.'

'And,' Hayley says, 'the school is finally coming to their senses and realising he doesn't belong here, so they're kicking him out.'

'Hayley,' I say with narrow eyes. 'That's a horrible thing to say.'

She shrugs. 'Truth hurts.' She gets up and walks away.

Ellen puts her hand on mine. 'Don't be mad at her. She has her own things to be messed up about. Besides, Rosie said she saw a couple of policemen in the foyer.'

'And it doesn't explain why the meeting is happening now,' Nikki says, 'when Form is about to start.'

'Unless the police are here for something else,' Ellen says. 'And the meeting is just running late.'

'Or?' I say, though I don't want to hear it said.

'Or something's happened to Jack,' Ellen says. 'No one has seen him this morning.'

'Something that got the police involved,' Nikki adds.

Hayley is hanging off Joe's arm as she joins the boy band, laughing with them.

'What happened between you and Joe, Nikki?' I ask. 'I thought you two were getting involved.'

Nikki shakes her head. 'Hayley put a stop to that idea.'

'I didn't know she liked Joe,' I say.

'I don't think she does,' Nikki says. 'She's just playing him. She's playing them all; keeping her options open.'

The bell for Form rings, but no one comes for five minutes. Then Miss Krensky arrives, all apologetic.

As she's unlocking the classroom door, I ask her, 'What's going on, miss?'

Miss Krensky just mumbles for us to come inside and sit down. We all pour into the classroom. Someone turns the lights on. They flash several times, highlighting how dark the room had been. Gloomy clouds are rolling in overhead.

Miss Krensky is quieting everyone down and calling out names for the roll.

She gets to Jack's name and pauses.

'No one's seen him this morning, miss,' someone calls out.

'Yes, I am aware of that,' Miss Krensky says.

Someone else asks where he is.

'Jack is in hospital.' She pauses but her eyes are busy, like she's having a conversation with herself. 'He won't be at school for a while.'

'What happened?' Ellen asks from the seat beside me.

Miss Krensky continues marking the roll as she speaks. 'We're still piecing the puzzle together.'

'What puzzle?' I ask.

Miss Krensky holds eye contact. 'Jack was in a car accident.' She moves from face to face around the room. 'And it looks like he was targeted. Police have found his brakes were tampered with.'

Shards of ice flood into my chest and I double over onto the table, holding my stomach. Salvia fills my mouth. Someone is asking if he's okay.

'I believe he will be fine. The airbag went off, breaking a few ribs, and he broke an ankle when the car crashed into a pillar.'

'And his mum?' I ask.

'She walked away without any serious injuries.'

I glance up long enough to see Cooper looking at me intensely. I run out of the classroom and vomit over the balcony into the garden below.

Chapter 26

Miss Krensky follows me out of the classroom and places her hand on my back as I continue to expel my stomach contents. She has a couple of tissues in her hand. 'You alright, Grace?'

A stupid question. Clearly, I'm not.

'I was with Jack yesterday afternoon,' I say. 'He was at my house studying.'

'Yes, Mrs Oskar said as much,' Miss Krensky says. 'After Form, I'll get you to come down and have a chat to Mr Reyl. He'll want to know what time Jack left your place, that sort of thing.'

'Am I in trouble for something?'

'After your reaction to the news about Jack, I'm thinking not.' Her eyes are soft. 'But only if you're up to talking about it. You did just fertilize the garden for us.'

I chuckle and wipe my mouth with the tissues. 'Sorry.'

'That's okay. Looks like the sky is about to let loose. It'll clean up the mess for us.'

There is a rolling of thunder in the distance.

Once Form is over, I walk down the stairs and knock on Mr Reyl's office door. When I open it, Mrs Oskar is sitting in the carpeted chair, her eyes red and puffy. I apologise, but Mr Reyl asks me to come in. I stand awkwardly in the room.

'Grace.' He gestures to another chair and I slide over to sit gingerly on the edge of it. 'I understand you saw Jack yesterday afternoon?'

'Yes, sir. He came to my place.'

'You two were working on your science project, is that correct?'

I tilt my head. 'Sort of.'

'What do you mean, sort of?'

My face warms. 'Well, we keep getting together to work on the science project, but then we seem to end up talking and not getting a lot of work done.'

'Why's that?' Mrs Oskar asks.

I have to fight off the tears threatening to form in my eyes. 'I dunno. I guess we have interesting conversations.'

'So, you didn't orchestrate this?' Mrs Oskar asks. I can hear the anger behind her words.

'What do you mean?'

Mr Reyl puts his hand on Mrs Oskar's shoulder. 'We just weren't sure, Grace. We hoped you were genuine, that you were being a friend to Jack, and not setting him up.'

'Setting him up for what?'

Mr Reyl says quietly to Mrs Oskar, 'Do you mind if I continue this conversation with Grace on my own?'

Mrs Oskar nods and shuffles out of the room. She's talking to the receptionist as Mr Reyl closes the door.

'Jack has had some run-ins with your boyfriend, Cooper Dally, this term, has he not?'

'Well, yes, but that was a while ago now. I don't think Cooper and Jack get along very well.'

'Exactly. And you and Cooper, well, you seem to be a link between the two boys.'

'Are you saying you think Cooper tampered with Jack's car?'

'I'm saying that of all the people in the school who may have done something like this, Cooper is right up there on my list of suspects.'

'But Cooper was in Brisbane this weekend and he doesn't know the first thing about cars, other than where the petrol goes. Though, truthfully, I'm not even sure he knows that.'

'Well, I'll be interviewing him. We'll see where we go from there.'

I leave the room to where a line of students wait. Cooper is first in line. He blows me a kiss as I walk past.

'It can't have been Cooper,' Hayley is saying as I walk into English and put my books down next to Nikki's.

'How can you be so sure?' Ellen asks.

Hayley glances at me. 'I know it can't have been Cooper because I was with him last night.'

'What?' I yell, much too loudly for Miss Krensky's liking and I get a death-stare. I open my laptop and hide behind the screen. 'What do you mean you were with Cooper last night?'

'Not *with*, *with*,' Hayley says. 'Not, you know, like that. We had a study date.'

I laugh. 'You had a *study date* with Cooper?'

'Well, why not? You've been having plenty with Jack. Can't Cooper have study dates too?'

'I'm in Jack's project group for Science. We have to work together.'

'Yeah, well, Cooper's been struggling a bit with some other areas of science, so we were exploring them together. On his way home from Brisbane we were texting about genetics and stuff. He suggested I come over and study with him.'

'He was texting you on the way home from Brisbane? But he went to Brisbane to get his driving hours up.'

Hayley shrugs. 'I dunno. Maybe he decided he'd rather text me than drive.'

My chest goes tight, my lips flatten. 'Why would he text you about Science and not me?'

'Oh, well, I may have let it slip that Jack and you were round at your place studying. I guess he didn't want to interrupt.'

I lunge across the table and grab Hayley around the top of her school dress. 'Why would you tell him that?' I thrash a closed fist in her direction but she dodges. Hayley laughs as the class goes into an uproar, yelling 'Fight!' multiple times.

It lands us both back down in Mr Reyl's office.

'Really, Miss McKay,' Mr Reyl says. 'I've seen about as much of you as I want to this term.'

'Sorry, sir.'

'So, explain why you felt the need to fling yourself onto your friend and try to hit her.'

'Because she was being a bi—' I pause. 'She was trying to get me angry, I think, sir.'

'Well, she seemed to achieve her goal.'

I nod.

'Did this have anything to do with Cooper Dally and Jack Oskar?'

'Maybe,' I say.

'Maybe?'

'She told Cooper I was studying with Jack yesterday afternoon.'

'And that got you angry? You anticipated Cooper would not like that?'

'Well, yes,' I say. 'But that wasn't why I was angry.'

'Then why were you angry?'

'Because her saying something might have been the reason why Jack got hurt yesterday.'

Mr Reyl nods. 'Thank you, Grace. I think that may just be the most honest you have managed to be with me yet.'

I stand up to leave. 'I hope not, though, sir. It seems too cruel a thing for even Cooper Dally to come up with.'

Chapter 27

'Before you even ask, it wasn't me, okay, Grace?' Cooper says, his eyes wide and serious. 'Mum's made a statement to the police and everything.'

I stand in front of our Science class, waiting for Mr Van Hayden, my arms folded. 'Hayley said she told you I was studying with Jack. It does sound like something you might get angry about.'

'Then why were you studying with him?'

'We were working on our science project.' I unfold my arms and point my finger at him. 'Why were you over at Hayley's?'

'We were working on her folio thingy. She knew I'd done the section she needed help with. She was texting me about it on the way home from Brisbane.'

'Hayley needed the help?'

'Yeah. I don't know why she didn't just ask the others in her group. But I'm not a complete idiot when it comes to science. I know stuff.'

'I thought you agreed to go to Brisbane to get up driving hours.'

'I did.'

'I'm not stupid, Cooper. You can't text and drive a car at the same time.'

'I wasn't. Mum had my phone and was typing my replies for me. In the end, I said it would be easier if I just got dropped at her place. So that's what we did.'

I shake my head. 'It's hardly the actions of a committed boyfriend.'

'What do you mean? You not only studied with Jack, but you studied at *your* house. Why does Jack Oskar get invited into your place and I don't?'

I roll my eyes. 'You're kidding me, right?'

Cooper narrows his eyes. 'You think you're all so high and righteous, but what's okay for you is not okay for me?'

'Well, did you and Hayley study in her bedroom?'

My question is answered with silence.

I shake my head again. 'Jack didn't even use the bathroom, let alone see my bedroom. We never went any further than the kitchen. You tell me who is more innocent in this? Latisha was also going to be there, but didn't turn up. Hayley is still flirting with you, trying to get your attention. Jack can barely look me in the eyes.'

Cooper raises his finger in my face. 'Maybe. But just remember who you are, Grace. Watch the way you're talking to me.'

I roll my eyes at him. 'I know who *you* are, Cooper. And I know who you can be. There is definitely one Cooper Dally that I like a lot more than the other.'

Cooper goes to say something, but then Mr Van Hayden comes puffing up the stairs, mumbling about lost keys. He rushes past Cooper and me, and disappears into the crowd of students waiting to go inside. As I turn to follow him into the classroom, Cooper grabs my arm and swings me back so I'm facing him. His face softens, and he leans in to kiss me. I keep my eyes open. He pulls back. 'You're so feisty, Grace. I do love how you're willing to stand up to me.'

'It doesn't feel like it,' I say. 'I spend more time wondering why you're with me than being confident you still like me.'

Cooper chews on his bottom lip ever so slightly. His eyes are smiling. 'I more than like you, Grace. I love you. Every day you remind me that I can be a better person than I am, and why it is that I love hanging out with you.'

I have no idea how much longer I can stand to stay on Cooper's crazy roller coaster ride.

Jack's return to school the following week brings with it a new definition of the term awkward. If he was clumsy before, it's nothing compared to Jack Oskar on crutches.

'How long will you have your foot in the moon boot?' I ask.

'Six weeks. But it's nearly been one week already.'

We're sitting in the yard at recess. Nikki and Ellen wait for me to join them near our lockers.

'I'm a bit surprised you've come back to school so soon.'

'Mum made me. She says we need to let whoever did this to me know they haven't beaten me.' He fiddles with his fingers. 'That and I still need to finish the science project so I can do Biology next year.'

'We're nearly done, though,' I say. 'Last week Seb played me the jingle he put together for it, and it's actually really good. And Latisha's drawings are amazing. We just need you to do the voice-over.'

He shakes his head. 'I can't do things like that. How about I tell you what to say, and you do it?'

'But I'm already doing the section on Down syndrome. Your section is about autism. It would be better if the voice-over was someone *with* autism.'

'It's only a school project.'

'All the more reason why you should do it.'

He starts rocking. 'There's still the portfolio of learning too.' His eyes are focused on something in one of the nearby trees. 'I'm a long way behind and if one of us fails, it brings all our grades down.'

'We'll sort something out, Jack.'

He keeps looking at the tree.

'Well, I'd better go. I hope you manage okay with your crutches. If you need any help, you can ask me, okay?'

Jack says to the tree, 'Thanks, Graceland.'

Chapter 28

'I don't see why they call Down syndrome a *disorder*,' Jack says. 'Jesse was my favourite person in the whole world to hang out with.'

Mr Van Hayden has given us permission to work in the library during Science, so Jack feels more comfortable talking to me. His fear of Cooper seems to have increased again since the accident. I figure he feels more vulnerable on the crutches.

Jack and I have been working on his portfolio for over half an hour and we've both had enough. It's so long and tedious; me reading the questions and typing out Jack's answers as he talks. I close my laptop. 'Mum says it's a good school, that special school you both went to.'

'We'd moved from Victoria just so I could go to it. I was in Grade 3; Jesse was in Prep.'

'He loved going to school from the first day,' I say. 'He came home so excited and talked nonstop for like two hours and drove us all nuts. Jesse loved to talk.'

'I remember him that day. Right from the start, he was so much fun. He went around talking to everyone in the whole school. By the end of the day, just about every kid at school knew who Jesse was.'

'And he was really good at remembering names.'

'We used to call it his superpower.'

I laugh. 'That's funny.'

'Jesse used to come sit with me because I was sad. I missed my dad. I'd only just started talking and I didn't know how to talk about Dad leaving. Jesse worked that out and he would tell me different stories about dads, mostly from Elvis movies. And when he ran out of movies to talk about he'd tell me about Elvis.'

'Jesse talked to you about Elvis?'

'All the time. He used to tell me stories about Elvis's life and his favourite songs. I would listen, and Jesse would just talk and talk and talk. For hours. I didn't much like it when he tried to sing his songs, though.'

'I don't remember Jesse loving Elvis *that* much.'

'Once we had to write a story. I remember Jesse's teacher being so excited because Jesse's story was so good—she read it out to the whole school in assembly. Everyone clapped and told Jesse how proud they were of him. But I knew it was the story of *Follow That Dream*, his favourite Elvis movie. But I never told the teachers. I never told Jesse I knew, either. That was when he was in Grade 3. That was just before he died.'

'*Follow That Dream* was Jesse's favourite Elvis movie?'

'It was his favourite movie full stop! He said he would watch it during the night, with his dad, when he couldn't sleep. Jesse was a terrible sleeper.'

'I don't remember that. I don't remember my dad ever liking Elvis movies.'

'That's why it's good to talk about it.'

'Why did your family move up here? What was so good about the school?'

'I didn't talk until I was about seven,' Jack says. 'I used to rock a lot, and groan, and thrash my arms and legs around. I've seen the videos Mum took for the doctors; I was a very angry person. They didn't know my brain was working under all my noise and rocking. But then one day the words started to go together right in my head, and so I started to say them.'

'And?'

'Mum was telling everyone that I was smart. That I said smart things. She started to teach me to read and she reckoned I was picking it up fast, which I was. And she took me to a different speech specialist, one who didn't know I had delayed speech. That lady helped me to put the words together even quicker and clearer. And then Mum found out about this school that helps kids like me go into normal high schools. So, she packed us up and moved up here. But Dad stayed in Victoria.'

'What kind of smart things did you say?'

'I would remember stuff. She would read to me, like books on planets, and I would tell her about it later. Then after a while I'd say things she didn't even remember telling or reading to me. She'd get me to watch documentaries on YouTube when she couldn't answer my questions anymore.'

'Is that why you know so much about science?'

Jack nods. 'But I still don't read very well. It takes me longer to learn something if I have to read about it. I learn quicker when people tell me stuff, or if I can watch things like documentaries.'

'And so, do you think, if you learn better by hearing or watching things, that you would be better at telling someone what you know, rather than by writing it down?'

'That's what they used to do at Special School. But they always want things written here.'

'And that's why you don't do very well.'

'I didn't talk until I was seven. Most people begin when they're one or two years old. I didn't even write my first word until I had moved up here. Everyone else has a big head start on me.'

'Well, I have an idea.' I jump up and hand Jack his crutches. 'Come on, let's go and talk to Mr Van Hayden.'

'I'm not sure exactly what you're proposing, Grace,' Mr Van Hayden says from the front of the science room. Everyone else has left to go to recess, so his voice bounces off the walls as he talks.

'What I mean, sir, is rather than Jack having to hand in a portfolio of his learning, that maybe you could just sit and talk to him about it.

He knows heaps, much more than anyone else in the class.'

Mr Van Hayden runs his fingers across his mouth. 'I appreciate the sentiment, and even the reason behind it, Grace. But the portfolio is evidence of learning. I can hardly keep a conversation with Jack in my filing cabinet now, can I?'

I look at Jack. 'What if I videoed you talking to Mr Van Hayden?' I look back at my teacher. 'That could be kept as evidence, couldn't it?'

Mr Van Hayden nods, but looks at Jack. 'Tell me, Jack, how do you feel about that?'

Jack shrugs.

'Jack, come on,' I say.

He looks up at the ceiling and down again. His fingers are rubbing hard against his hand.

Mr Van Hayden says, 'Tell me, Jack. For any given gene, what determines which DNA strand serves as the template strand?'

Jack looks at him, then at me.

'Jack, you know this!' I say. 'I know you know. Why are you doing this?'

Jack starts rocking.

'I think you're stressing him, Grace.'

'Am I, Jack?'

He nods, but only slightly.

'You go to recess, Jack. I'll catch you later, okay?'

Jack leaves the room and I collapse into a stool. 'What am I supposed to do? He knows so much, but I can't sit and type up everything he says. It takes too long. I've got my own portfolio to work on.'

'Think again, Grace. I'm sure you can come up with another way of showing just how much Jack knows about this topic.'

'He's awesome when he's just sitting talking to me,' I say.

Mr Van Hayden raises his eyebrows. 'Like I said, I'm sure you can come up with something.'

I slowly raise my hand to my mouth. 'I think I have an idea.'

Chapter 29

I ask Jack to meet me in the library after school later that week. I've already talked to the librarian about setting up a camera, so it looks like it's just randomly sitting on the bench waiting to be returned. She agrees to start recording when Jack arrives.

When Jack struggles in on his crutches, his backpack on his back, I direct him to our usual place. He sits beside me without me asking him to. He pulls out his laptop, which I hadn't told him specifically to bring. Jack glances over at the librarian.

'It's okay, Jack,' she says. 'I haven't forgotten. You are allowed your backpack in the library while on crutches.'

Jack looks intently at his laptop screen. He places an earpiece in one ear. The computer is highlighting words and I realise it must be reading an article out to him. On my laptop, I bring up the next lot of questions he's supposed to have already answered for the portfolio.

'Jack,' I say. 'Are we ready to go with the next lot of questions?'

He muffles some sort of response.

'Jack.'

He frowns but doesn't look up.

'What are you even reading about?'

'Prairie voles.'

'What the heck are prairie voles?'

He taps the space bar. 'Voles are a type of rodent. I watched a documentary on them when I was nine. I only just remembered them when Mr Van Hayden was talking about DNA affecting our personalities.'

'And what do voles have to do with anything?'

'Some scientists believe there is a repetition in a string of their micro-satellite DNA that influences them so they are monogamous.'

'They're what?'

'They are faithful to their partner. They have longer strings in their DNA that make them spend more time with their mate and with their offspring. Because they have more receptors, they have a greater release of vasopressin, dopamine and oxytocin into their brain when they're with their mate.'

That's way too many long scientific words in one sentence. 'I don't get it.'

'There's something in their DNA that causes them to get good feelings from being with their family. And so, they want to stay.'

'Stay where?'

'With their family; they raise their offspring together. And they look after each other. They comfort each other when they're hurt or have been mistreated. They find a partner and stick with them for life.'

'Sounds better than most humans. They're more likely to use you up and spit you out.'

'That's why you should wait and not have sex until you're married.'

I burst out laughing. 'Good grief, Jack. Are you serious?' But clearly, Jack's very serious. 'No one waits anymore, Jack.'

'Some people do.'

'Like who?'

'Me.' Jack is not rocking. He's not even fidgeting with his hands. 'I will not even kiss a girl until I think I will most probably ask her to marry me.'

'I can't imagine anyone waiting to be sure with me. You have to sleep with them eventually, or they break up with you.'

'That's not true for everyone, Graceland.'

'Do you really think DNA impacts whether someone stays with their family or leaves?'

'I think staying is a choice. Like being happy and staying in love are choices. People make the choice to love or to stop loving.'

'But, you think it's in someone's DNA—some people are more likely to get divorced? There should be a blood test you can take for that.'

'Well, regardless of our DNA, people still make the choice to stay or to leave. But maybe it takes a lot more dopamine and oxytocin for some humans to make the choice to stay.'

'I don't think any amount of dopamine or oxy-whatever was going to make my dad choose to stay.' I have my head down, but Jack's gaze burrows into my soul.

'Some humans do choose to stay together for life.'

I lift my head slightly. 'My dad's grandparents stayed together. They got married when Granny was only nineteen years old. Grandpa died after a stroke when they'd been married for fifty years. Dad says Granny died of a broken heart a few months later.'

'I'm going to be like that,' he says. 'I will meet someone, marry them and never leave them.'

We sit in silence for a moment.

'Cooper has been trying to get me to sleep with him.'

Jack looks at me for the longest time he has ever looked at me. 'Have you?'

I laugh, but Jack's face is full of concern. 'No, I haven't.'

His face relaxes. 'I want my girlfriend to wait, too.'

I chuckle. 'Yeah, well, good luck with that.'

He rocks a little.

'You know, most people wouldn't ask a question like that, about whether they're sleeping with their boyfriend.'

Jack stops rocking. 'I hear the boys saying stuff like that all the time. They're always talking about who has slept with who.'

'Really? And how do you know this?'

He shrugs. 'The boys think I'm stupid. They just talk around me like I can't understand what they're saying. I try to learn how to talk from listening to them.'

I laugh. 'They're hardly the role models you want to learn from, Jack.'

'That's what Mum says too, but I can't learn to talk like a teenager by hanging around adults all the time.'

'Is that why you talk proper, like an adult?'

A smile flashes across his face. 'No. I talk proper because it sounds better.'

'Jack Oskar, did you just smile?'

Jack frowns. 'I smile.'

'When? I rarely see you smile.'

'I smile when I'm at home.'

'Really? And what makes you smile at home?'

He fiddles with his fingers and looks at his usual spot on the ceiling. 'You.'

'Me?' I laugh. 'But I've never been to your house.'

He rocks harder. 'I think about you when I'm at home.'

'Why don't I make you smile when I'm around you then?'

Jack rocks so hard he can't look at his spot on the ceiling.

'It's okay, we don't have to talk about it.'

His rocking eases.

My phone buzzes in my pocket and I pull it out to see a Snapchat from Cooper. 'It's Cooper. He's throwing a massive party tomorrow night and he's ridiculously excited about it. Look, he's sent me a photo of his fridge all stocked up.'

Jack rocks again, just ever so slightly. His eyes are darting around the room. 'Are you going to the party?'

'He's throwing a party because it's his birthday. I can't not go.'

'Why not?'

'Well, I guess because he's still my boyfriend.'

Jack's fiddling with his hands. 'You shouldn't have to do anything you don't want to do.'

'Maybe, in some other life, that's the case. But I feel like lately all I ever do are things I don't want to do.' Jack doesn't respond. 'Cooper doesn't do things in halves; there'll be lots of people there. You could come along. No one would notice an extra person.'

'They'd notice me,' he says.

'You could come anyway.'

'That would be one way to end my life, I guess. But, I'm not ready to die yet, at least not *death by Cooper Dally*.'

Chapter 30

Nikki asks me to hang out at her place Saturday afternoon, which suits me fine, since it means we'll arrive at Cooper's party together. Cooper has been all sweetness and kindness to me in the lead-up to his party. But, I'm still nervous. I long for him to be more of the guy I thought he was.

I'm terrified of what it will mean for me if he's not.

Nikki and I sit on her double bed listening to music while we put fake nails on each other.

My phone buzzes in my pocket. I pull it out. 'Cooper's putting up photos on Instagram. He and the boy band are almost done setting up.'

'How's it looking?'

'Amazing.' I show her some photos. 'There seems to be a red theme happening.'

'Didn't Cooper tell you that? Red and black.'

I pull out of my bag a lovely light blue dress I got at an op shop. 'No, he didn't.' I try to brush some wrinkles out. There is a sheer fabric that flows over the top of the dress. 'I guess I'll stand out tonight, then.'

'You're not wearing that again, are you?' Nikki's voice sounds both amused and disgusted.

I look at her blankly. 'Again?'

'You wear that dress every time you have a special occasion to go to.'

I hold it up against myself. 'It's the nicest dress I have.'

Nikki gives me a cheeky look. 'Not anymore.'

I raise quizzical brows. She hands me a parcel—brown wrapping paper tied with a red ribbon.

'Cooper. He asked me to pass it on to you for tonight.'

I tug on the red ribbon and the package falls open. Inside is a red strapless dress. I hold it up to myself. It falls to my knees at the front but touches the floor at the back. A thick silver band sparkles in the centre.

'Wow,' Nikki says. 'Now that's a dress.'

I sigh deeply.

'You don't like it?'

'Of course. It's the most beautiful dress I've seen.'

'But?'

'I feel like this is another way Cooper tries to control me.'

'You think Cooper is controlling?' Nikki asks.

'You don't?'

She shrugs.

I pull the ball I've been making with all the other Cooper ribbons out of my handbag and begin adding the red ribbon to it.

'What's with all the ribbons?'

'They're from the gifts Cooper has given me. He wraps them with a different coloured ribbon each time.'

'That's sweet. We should put them up into your hair tonight.'

'What? No, that's silly.'

Nikki starts knotting the ribbons all together. 'Let me try.'

She clips the tied ribbons to my hair and begins braiding them in, until they are all pulled together into a bun on the top of my head. The red ribbon stands out the most. 'It looks adorable, Grace.'

It does look pretty awesome.

'Okay, but I think it's kind of corny.'

'No one else will know. But, Cooper might.'

I put the dress up to my body again and turn around in front of the mirror.

'You know, Grace, lately it seems like you're not so into Cooper.'

I chuckle. 'Is that right?'

'Well, you're avoiding Cooper at school—and he says he's having trouble getting you on your own. You're coming up with excuses all the time for why you can't hang out with him.'

'They are legitimate reasons.' I drape the dress back on the bed and join Nikki on the couch in her bay window.

She hands me bright red nail polish. 'Do you think what Mikaela said is true?'

I swipe the polish across my thumbnail. 'Truthfully, I have no idea. When Mikaela told me about it, I was convinced. When I spoke to Cooper about it, he was convincing too. Mikaela's story would be easier to believe if she'd told us about it at the time.'

'I agree. I can't believe she wouldn't have told us.'

'But, knowing Cooper as I do now, I can also see it as something he would do.'

'Really?'

'You don't see him like I do. He's aggressive when he's high, super-flirty when he's been drinking. He has a terrible temper. He's pretty good at making promises and breaking them. And so, when I put all that together, it's difficult to know if the Cooper I love is the real Cooper, or just someone he's pretending to be.'

'You'd prefer someone else? Someone like Jack Oskar, perhaps?'

I shake my head. 'You guys are out to make my friendship with him something more than it is.'

'Well, he's had a crush on you since forever.'

'I don't believe that. He liked me because I was nice to him on our first day at high school. He's innocent like that. I think that even if he did like a girl in that way, he wouldn't know what to do with those feelings.'

'You're saying that even if he did like you in that way, that he's unaware of it?'

'Sort of, yes.'

Nikki laughs. 'Boys aren't like that, Grace. Surely you know that by now.'

'But Jack's different.'

'You can say that again.'

'It's a sweet difference. He sees the world differently. Not because he's simple or anything, because he's not. He just chooses to see everything and everyone at their best. He reminds me of Jesse like that. He sees all the things that you do wrong, but it's like he also sees, at the same time, how you're so much better than that.'

'Hang on, are you telling me you're going to break up with Cooper?'

'No.' I rub my hands up and down my arms. 'Not tonight, anyway. I'm just doubting if I love him—I thought I did—and I think I should know that for sure by now. Don't you?'

'I don't know. Three months isn't that long.'

I move back in front of the mirror.

'Why don't you try the dress on.' Nikki hands me it. 'It might help remind you of the side of Cooper you love.'

I slip out of my jeans and t-shirt and step into the dress. Nikki pulls the zip up the back. 'Wow, Grace.' Nikki adjusts the bun on my head. 'You look sensational.'

The mirror agrees. The dress hugs where it should and falls to streamline everything else. Cooper has proven, once again, he can shop for me better than I can shop for myself.

'My shoes won't go with it.' The pale-blue high heels I brought with me look exactly what they are—cheap.

'Yeah, you need silver shoes. Can't believe Cooper didn't think of that.'

'He hasn't bought me shoes before—he wouldn't know my size.'

She rummages around a box at the bottom of her wardrobe. 'I have a pair you can borrow.' She emerges, holding up a pair of silver stilettos.

'Are you kidding me? I can't wear them. I won't be able to walk around without falling over.'

'You'll be fine. Put them on and have a practice.'

I slip Nikki's shoes on and walk awkwardly round the room. I'm better than I thought I'd be, but it doesn't stop Nikki from laughing at me. I stop in front of the mirror and run my hands down my dress. Three months ago, I had worn op-shop shorts and hand-me-down t-shirts and been somewhat happy with that. I hadn't owned foundation and didn't even know what a beauty blender was. Tears form in my eyes.

'I'm not convinced Cooper loves me. He seems to enjoy making me into something I'm not.'

'Yeah, I can tell. He must hate you if he spoils you the way he does.' She removes the price tags from the dress.

'Does it say the price?'

Nikki shakes her head. 'Come on, Cinderella. Let's get you to the ball.'

Chapter 31

The music inside Cooper's house vibrates against the front door. I pause, my hand resting on the handle. Nikki's looking at me expectantly, but I can't put into words the dread that's flowing throughout my body. I don't want to go in. I don't want to face what is behind this door.

Nikki puts her hand on mine on the doorhandle, but I stop her from opening it. 'I need a moment, Nik. I can't go in just yet. You go in. I'll be there in a minute, okay?'

Nikki disappears through the door and I walk back down the path to the street. I take a few deep breaths to try and stop my heart from racing. Then I feel my phone vibrating.

It's Mikaela.

'Hi, Grace,' she says. 'How are you?'

I don't even know how to answer that. 'Um, okay, I guess. Cooper's hosting a party. You caught me as I was about to walk in.'

'I figured as much,' she says. 'It's his birthday, after all.'

There's an awkward silence for a few seconds.

'How are things going with the two of you?'

'You're ringing to ask me that now?' After all this time?

She clears her throat. 'I should have called sooner. I know. I'm sorry.'

'It's okay. I get that this makes things weird.'

'But you're still together?'

I pause. 'Yes.' My heart rate is escalating again.

'You don't sound too confident?'

I don't know what to say. 'I am just not sure I can keep doing this,' I whisper.

'Doing what?' Her voice is quite forceful.

'Being put on show like I am.'

'Oh yeah, I remember that.'

'I never knew it was like this for you.'

Mikaela's breathing is heavy. 'It was only in our last couple of months together. We used to have great fun together before that.'

I swallow hard. 'I wish he could always be the sweet, caring guy I see in him sometimes.'

'I regret not telling you more about what was going on with me at the time,' Mikaela says. 'I always suspected you liked Cooper. I didn't know how you'd take it if I told you what he could really be like.'

I sigh. 'Yeah, well, you're right. I probably wouldn't have believed you. I need to go inside.'

'Grace, wait.' There's an awkward pause again. 'I should have told you more about what was going on with me and Cooper. I'm sorry that I didn't, especially now…' Her voice is shaky. 'Look, I know I'm not in a place to be able to give you advice.'

Mikaela, sorry? Wow. 'No, it's okay… I could really do with some advice.'

Mikaela's voice is serious. 'Well, it's Cooper's birthday, so you don't have much choice but to play the part tonight. Cooper doesn't like it when things don't go his way and he'll do whatever it takes to make sure it happens. Regardless of how you feel, play the girlfriend tonight, Grace. Let him show you off. Remember the things you love about him and celebrate that.'

Hot liquid runs through my veins. 'Okay. Thanks, Mikaela. Thanks for ringing.'

When I walk into Cooper's house, he is dancing with a blonde from

Year 11. He's not touching her, but is moving with her suggestively. I'm not sure if it's his looks or the air of confidence about him that makes him appear so amazing. His dark curls flowing softly around his face in time to the music, his black jeans and a tight black shirt showing off his body. He's singing the song, or miming it, perhaps; his lips moving ever so slightly with the words. When he sees me, he immediately stops dancing, leaving the blonde girl dancing on her own. As he approaches, I notice the thin red tie hanging around his neck.

'Grace, you're here!' Cooper says way too loudly, but his eyes are lit up with excitement. He grabs me around the waist and pulls me into an embrace. He kisses me, hard, and I taste alcohol. He pulls back to look me over. 'You look fabulous.' His breath tickles my ear. 'Do you like it?'

'Yes, thank you. It's beautiful.'

His words slur as he whispers something that sounds like he loves me. He looks me up and down. 'Nice shoes.'

'I can barely walk in them,' I say. 'They're Nikki's.'

Coopers nods. 'Can't believe I didn't think of shoes to go with the dress. We'll have to make that a priority for our next shopping adventure.'

He's been drinking, but at least I know somewhat what to expect. I flash a flirty smile and break out of his embrace. 'Well, in the meantime, I'd love a drink.'

Cooper follows me into the kitchen, where a couple are busy getting to know each other up against the fridge. I ask them to move, but they ignore me. Cooper opens a special esky marked 'Grace' and holds up a bottle of raspberry lemonade. 'I made sure I catered for my girl, with her own special drink supply.'

I chuckle. 'Thanks.'

He pulls a fresh glass out of the cupboard. 'Come on, I'll introduce you to all of my friends.'

We walk around the house together, inside, outside, through

a variety of rooms I'd never seen before. He's saying hello and fist-pumping the guys, while I hang off his arm like an accessory to his winning persona. But he is also so sweet, holding my hand and drawing me into his conversations as much as he can. And every now and then, he pauses and smiles at me—that sweet, Cooper Dally smile.

'Cooper,' I say into his ear, 'I know you know a lot of people, but there's so many here and hardly any I recognise.'

'It's called networking—so important in the business world. I'm already working toward the day I own my surf shop. It's who you know in the business that will make or break you.' Cooper pauses and smiles at me, his dimples deep in his cheeks.

'Patty and your step-dad were okay with having so many people here?'

He laughs. 'They don't know. They're away for the weekend. Serves them right for leaving me alone on my birthday weekend. Do you need a break?'

I nod. 'My feet are killing me.'

Cooper caresses my hand as he leads me up to the landing that joins his and Sam's bedrooms. I'm disappointed to see no one else is up here, but relieved as well; I've had enough of the crowd. Cooper invites me to sit on the couch.

'I don't mind us escaping from the party for a bit,' Cooper says. 'Gives me a chance to show you just how much I appreciate the way you look tonight.'

'I'm grateful for some quiet,' I take Nikki's heels off and rub my aching feet. 'Mikaela was like that too, remember? She would have wanted to escape after a while.'

'She would have, but she's not here. You are—and you are sensational in that dress.'

Heat rises to my cheeks. 'Thanks.'

'And what's with the rainbow of ribbons in your hair? It's cute, but not the sort of thing you'd usually do.'

'They're the ribbons from all the presents you've given me.'

'Is that right?' He takes my hand and kisses it. 'That was a very sweet thing to do.'

I relax back into the soft couch.

Cooper puts his arm around me. 'Remember when we first sat here together?'

I snuggle into his chest. 'It was only a few months ago. You compared my eyes to Christmas trees.'

'I didn't, did I?' I hear him chuckle. He runs his hand softly up and down my arm. This is the Cooper I love. I could easily forget there are over a hundred people in the rooms below us. 'A lot has happened since then.' Cooper picks up his beer and raises it toward me. 'Here's to us?'

I pick up my glass and tap it against his. 'Cheers.' I take a few sips.

The noise of the party under our feet trickles up the stairs. 'Are you playing Keith Urban?' I ask.

'See, I remember a lot from that afternoon.'

'You know, I prefer Imagine Dragons.'

'Well, we can play them when we celebrate your birthday, okay?' Cooper takes my almost empty glass and puts it on the coffee table. He leans in and kisses me.

He pulls back and cups my face in his hands. 'You know I love you, Grace. I'll do anything for you. Anything.'

I giggle.

'What can I do to show you how much I love you?'

I run my hand down his face. 'I don't know. Tell me I don't have to go back to the party, that I can just stay here for the rest of the night?'

He smiles. 'You got it. You've done your part, wowing everyone at the party. You look spectacular tonight.'

He lies me back onto the couch and walks his fingers up my thigh and under the red dress, sending flashes of electricity up through my body. His other hand is behind my head, running through my hair. His kisses become more forceful as his body moves directly on top of mine.

'Come on, babe,' he coos. 'I love you so much.'

I push him upwards a little. 'I love you, too, Cooper.' And in that moment, I believe it.

He looks at me and smiles. 'You do?'

I nod.

He runs a hand up my stomach, across my body until his hand is tracing the neckline of my dress. 'You know it's my birthday, right?'

I place my hand on his chest, his muscles are firm under my touch. 'Of course.'

'Well, you know what I want.' His hand leaves the neckline of my dress again.

'Cooper, you know I'm not ready.' I move his hand to my stomach.

'If you love me, Grace, if you really loved me, you would give it to me anyway.'

I laugh. 'You're joking, right?'

'No. If you loved me like Mikaela loved me, you would, like she did.'

I try to pull back. 'Cooper, that's not fair.'

He kisses me harder. 'Come on. It feels so good. You wouldn't believe how good it feels. You'll wonder why you ever wanted to wait.'

He lifts me up and carries me into a room off the side of the landing. There's a huge bed, queen-sized at least, in the middle of the room. He lowers me down onto it.

'Cooper. What are you doing?' I go to sit up, but he moves himself so he's over me again.

'Let's just lie here for a bit,' he says. 'That couch is so uncomfortable.'

He starts kissing me again. I kiss him back but keep my hands up around his neck.

'Come on, Grace, you said you love me. Show me.'

I shake my head. 'I can't, Cooper. Not yet. Please, don't keep asking me.'

He keeps kissing me, running his hands over my body more forcefully. I pull my knees up to stop him, to try to protect myself.

'Stop it,' I say. 'You're being rough. I don't like this.'

'Just go with it. You'll enjoy it, I promise.'

'No,' I say.

'Come on, Grace. It's my birthday and you love me. I love you. What's there to wait for? I want this. I need you. This is what will make my birthday perfect. Please, Grace.'

I relax for a moment, a thousand thoughts running through my head. 'Cooper, I'm not ready. I want to know you better.'

His body relaxes over mine. 'That's what I'm talking about. Thank you, Grace.' He runs his hands up to my stomach and I can feel him doing something weird. I realise he's undoing his trouser button. I shake my head. He moves his hand up under my dress. He's so forceful it's ripping as he tries to pull it up.

'No,' I say. 'No, this isn't what I want.'

'Yeah it is, we're nearly there.'

I push hard with my hands. 'Get off me.'

He moves slightly but pulls himself back over me.

'Stop it!' I yell. I pull my knees up and get them between me and his body. I push hard with my hands again. 'Get off me.'

He falls over to the other side of the bed. 'What are you doing?' I can hear anger in his voice.

'I told you, no. I meant it.' I slide over the edge of the bed and sit on it, trying to get my breath back.

He thumps the pillow behind him. 'You could kill a guy doing this to him.'

My mouth falls open. 'Doing what?'

'Being so on and off. One minute, you're all over me and I think you do love me, and the next minute you go all cold.'

I shake my head. 'I have told you all along I'm not ready. I said no.'

He just looks at me. He gets off the bed and walks out of the room, adjusting his pants as he does. He comes back a few seconds later with our drinks.

'Here,' he says, holding out my red lemonade.

I shake my head. 'Just leave me alone.'

He puts the drink on the table beside me. 'You want me to leave? Why?'

'What do you mean, why? You just tried to force me to have sex with you, Cooper, just like you forced Mikaela.'

He grits his teeth. 'I told you, Mikaela wanted to. She was all over me the first night we slept together. If anything, it was me encouraging her to slow down, to make sure she was ready.'

I nod my head. 'Right. And what lies will you make up about me tonight, Cooper?'

Heat races across his eyes. 'I'll tell them you were begging for it; that you moaned the whole time.'

'You're ridiculous. I'll tell you what I'll say about tonight, Cooper. I'll tell everyone that you were the biggest mistake of my life.'

'And everyone will think you are a lunatic for saying it.'

The anger inside me comes out as a laugh. 'You know, Mikaela got to the point where she would rather kill herself than be trapped for another moment in a relationship with you. The difference is, I am not afraid of you, Cooper. You can say all you want, but none of it will matter because I will always know that you are the lowest kind of human being, and what you say about me means nothing. You are everything on the outside, but nothing on the inside. And what is on the inside matters most.'

'You underestimate me, Grace.'

'I always have, Cooper. I never would have believed you're as big a jerk as you are.'

I pick up my drink and leave the room but once I'm on the landing I hear him coming up behind me. I spin around and face him, his eyes red. 'You owe me, Grace.'

'For what?'

'Well, we could start with that dress.' His eyes look me up and down. 'I gave you so much and you have given me nothing in return.'

'You're such a jerk. I owe you nothing. You want your things back? Here—' I rip the ribbons from my hair and throw them on the floor. 'You can keep them as your trophy. Everything else I'll give to charity with a note to say it's from you.'

He grabs at my dress, but I throw the rest of the lemonade in his face. He starts going crazy, yelling something about the carpet. I make my way to the stairs.

My head is starting to feel fuzzy, confused, as I head down towards Cooper's guests. I can hear Cooper swearing somewhere above me. I get to the bottom stair and don't look back.

But just before I reach the front door, Hayley steps into my path. Brad is watching from a distance.

'Wow, Grace, I hope you're not bailing on your boyfriend's party. Man, you look plastered.' She laughs. 'And your hair's all over the place. You haven't been giving Cooper his birthday present now, have you?'

A wave of nausea sweeps over me. I go to speak but when I open my mouth, I throw up on Hayley's feet.

Hayley screams. The eyes of every person in the room are on me. They're all laughing with wild eyes and enormous mouths. None of them are standing still, which makes my head spin and hurt.

Brad's eyes are sad as he takes a step forward, then stops. I push past Hayley and take the final steps to the front door. I hear my name being called. It could be Nikki, but I don't wait to see.

I run down the street, my legs struggling to keep going, with a vague thought about not having anything on my feet.

Chapter 32

My head is swirling as I open my phone and look at my contacts. Most of the people I'd call for help are at Cooper's party. I can't ring Mum, she'll still be at work, and I don't want Lisa Marie to see me like this. The number of people in my contacts who can drive is seriously low.

Jack Oskar is one of the last names in my list. I run my thumb over his name.

I push the call button, but then hang up. I don't remember if Jack even has a phone. It might be his mum's number. I lean heavily on a tree. Perhaps I can just sleep here for the night and call someone in the morning. But then my phone vibrates.

'Grace?' It's Jack's voice.

'Is that you, Jack?'

'Yes. You rang my phone.'

'I did. But then, I've never seen you with a phone and I wondered if maybe it was your mum's. So, I hung up.'

'It's my phone. I just don't bring it to school.'

'You should. Then you could call someone if you get into trouble. Like I am now.'

Silence. Then, 'Are you in trouble?'

'Ummm,' I say. 'Yes.'

'Why?'

A surge of anger bursts from my mouth. 'Because Cooper Dally is a jerk and actually a complete arsehole and I shouldn't have gone to his stupid party.'

'Why does that mean you're in trouble?'

'Because I've run away from the party and now I have no way of getting home.'

Silence again.

'Are you still there, Jack?'

'Yes.'

'Why aren't you talking?'

'I don't know what to say. You sound angry.'

'I'm not angry at you, Jack. I'm angry at Cooper. And, I guess, myself.'

'Oh. Well, I should go now.'

'Hang on, Jack! Don't hang up.' I hold my hand over my mouth as it fills with saliva. I spit it out. 'Please, I need help.'

'Do you mean from me?'

'Yes, Jack. I hoped you could pick me up, since I'm in trouble and have no way of getting home.'

'What do you mean by pick you up? Can you not walk?'

'In your car, Jack. Could you come and get me?'

'I haven't driven since the accident.'

'It's your left foot that's broken, Jack. You don't need it to drive an automatic.'

'But I've never driven on my own, even when I had two feet working properly. And my mum's gone out.'

'Did your mum take the car?'

'No.'

'So, there is a car in your driveway?'

'Yes.'

'So, you could come and pick me up in it.'

'Well, not really.'

'Jack. Did your mum tell you that you should always take care of other people?'

'Yes.'

'I need you to take care of me now, Jack. Please.'

For some reason, Jack does what I ask. He turns up in his mum's car, hitting the kerb slightly as he pulls up opposite my tree. He leaves the car and hobbles around to help me get the passenger-side door open. He doesn't even say hi, he just says, 'Are you alright?' He's not asking, like, am I well, but, mentally stable.

'Not really,' I say. 'But I'm better now you're here.'

He slams the car door shut, narrowly missing my foot. He gets in the driver's side. 'I'm not even supposed to be driving, let alone on my own. I've borrowed Mum's car without her permission. I've left my house without letting anyone know.' He looks at me, deadpan. 'Have you been drinking?'

'No, I don't drink. Other than water and red lemonade, though I'm not sure I'll ever be able to drink red lemonade after tonight.'

'Why is that?'

I shake my head. 'Because of Cooper and what he did.'

'What did he do?'

'Can we just go, Jack, please? I don't want anyone to come out from the party and find me.'

Jack nods and pulls out from the kerb.

I can see him looking at me out of the corner of his eye. 'You don't look very good, Grace.'

I look down at myself; the dress is split up the side. I pull the material down so less of my leg is showing.

'What happened to you?'

I look out the window, at the houses with their tidy gardens and neatly mown lawns. I barely comprehend the words leaving my mouth. 'Cooper tried to force me to do something tonight.'

The car slows and I realise Jack's pulling the car over. 'He attacked you?'

I place my hands up to my cheeks, and hold my face as though it might fall apart with the admission. 'Yeah, in a way, he did.'

Jack keeps his hands firmly on the steering wheel. 'I should take you to the police.'

'No,' I say. 'No, no, no. That would be a bad idea, Jack. Please just take me home. No, don't take me home. I don't want to be left alone. Mum won't be home from work for ages.'

'Well, where am I going to take you then?'

'Can we go to your place?'

He's mumbling under his breath but pulling the car away from the kerb again.

'You're the best guy there is around, you know, Jack? You are kind and sweet. A true gentleman.'

The car does some weird swirling things, like there's a disco in it. My head feels all heavy and I'm having trouble holding it up. Then things go black.

When I wake, Jack's opening the car door and I'm kind of falling out, but he's catching me, except I'm trying to get my head past him so I can vomit somewhere he's not. His driveway becomes the recipient of the last morsels of my dinner. A lot of it is red lemonade. He's pulling tissues out of the glove box and telling me to stay in the car until he's cleaned me up. I tell him again what a lovely human he is.

'Where are your shoes?' Jack asks as I climb out of the car.

'I don't have any.'

Jack holds me up, a crutch on one side for himself, and me on the other, even though I insist I can walk properly.

'I don't know why I am so sick. I wonder if Cooper spiked my drink. Do you think he would do something like that?'

'I don't think anyone should do anything like that,' he says as I battle to keep my dress decent on the journey to the front door. 'But you are displaying some signs of having experienced trauma. What happened to your dress?'

'I don't know. It was a nice dress. It looked pretty when I first put it on.'

'You look pretty no matter what you're wearing. You seem to be having trouble remembering what happened to you tonight. Another sign you are experiencing some sort of trauma.'

Jack's house is very neat and it smells nice, like lavender or jasmine or something.

'Jade is in the spare room,' he whispers.

'Who's Jade?'

'Mum's friend. She's kinda, well, looking after me while Mum's out.'

I burst out laughing. 'You mean she's, like, baby-sitting you?'

Jack frowns. 'Shhh, you'll wake her.'

He stops in front of another room. 'I can't put you in Mum's room because she'll be home in a couple of hours. I'll take you to mine. But don't vomit in there, okay? I hate strong smells. I won't be able to sleep for a year if you vomit in my room.'

Jack's room has a single bed with a dark duvet on it. There doesn't look to be a thing out of place. 'Did you know I was coming, Jack Oskar, and clean your room for me?'

'My room is always like this.'

There is a shelf on the wall full of books in the shape of a wave. The books are colour-coordinated in the order of a rainbow. 'You need a few purple books,' I say, pointing to his bookshelf. 'It's not quite a rainbow.'

Jack's lips hold together tightly, curved at each end. He smiles more with his eyes than with his mouth. He pulls the cover back on his bed.

'I can't sleep yet,' I say. 'I need a shower. Is that okay?' Cooper and his hands are still all over me, resting on my skin, suffocating me.

He nods. 'Of course.'

He half carries me down the hallway into the tiny bathroom. Jack hands me a towel and closes the door behind him. 'Shall I make you a cup of tea, Graceland, for when you get out?'

'Thanks, Jack. I'd really like that.'

I turn on the hot water and pull off what remains of Cooper's red dress. Steam begins to fill the room. The bathroom has a long mirror on the back of the door, and I catch a glimpse of myself, still in my underwear, streams of mascara smudged across my face. I've never thought of myself as particularly pretty. But tonight, Cooper has made me feel like nothing. I run my hand down the outline of my body. What is it about a woman's body that makes her attractive to a man anyway?

I undo what is left of Nikki's hairdo and use the hair tie to put my hair up into a messy bun. I smile; I'm starting to look more like myself already.

I step into the shower and the water runs over me, stripping my face of makeup and washing away everything that had not really been me. I'm not Mikaela. I'm not Hayley. I'm not Lisa Marie, or my mother. I am Grace. Memphis Grace. Graceland MacKay.

I run my hands over my body along with the water to try to get rid of the feeling of Cooper Dally's hands on me. I push harder and harder onto my skin, trying to stop the feeling, trying to stop the memory. The reality of what nearly happened tonight washes over me in a wave of emotion. Tears begin to mix in with the water and I let myself cry, the big ugly kind of cry that helps you remember that you can feel something other than the pain, and that hopefully, you can cry the pain away.

I slump down onto the shower floor, the water pouring over me. I had thought that, with Cooper, I'd found a way out of the legacy my family was leaving me and that what he had been offering me was real. I thought I'd wanted to be Grace; Cooper's Grace.

That's not what I wanted. It's not who I want to be. But I'm also not the strong, independent Graceland I had hoped I was. Determined and sure. Taking control of my life. Finishing school. Going to University.

I'm somewhere in the middle. Something like, Memphis Grace. And I think that maybe, at least for now, that's okay.

When I step out of the shower, the house is quiet and the lights are off. I find my way back to Jack's room and redress in my underwear before crawling in between the lemon-scented sheets of his bed.

There's a mug on the bedside shelf. I pull myself onto my elbow and touch its warmth. I take a sip of the tea, clasping the mug in my hands as I look around Jack's room. I chuckle as I remember him that afternoon in my mother's kitchen, the mess, and how he couldn't let it stay that way. It's no wonder. His room is so perfect.

I lie back down, pulling the duvet up under my chin and snuggling down into the softness of his bed, close my eyes, and drift off to sleep.

Chapter 33

I wake up not sure where I am at first, but a thumping headache and Jack's rainbow-coordinated bookshelf soon bring some of last night's events back to me. I can hear people moving around on the other side of Jack's closed door. I'm not sure if I should introduce myself to everyone, sneak out the window or wait. Then I remember I'm only in my underwear, and I decide to wait, though I'm not sure how long I can—I'm also getting more and more desperate for the toilet.

Jack's bedside table holds a grey lamp, a small box of tissues and a mobile phone. My mug of tea is also there. I run my finger over the surface of the table, but there's nothing, not a speck of dust. Since he never takes his mobile anywhere he may not have a lock on it. How intrusive would it be to open it?

I'm still pondering the idea when there is a soft rumble of knuckles on the door and it creaks open. Jack pokes his head into the room. 'Oh good, you're awake.'

'Yes, only just,' I whisper. 'Does your family know I'm here?'

'I just told them a friend needed somewhere to stay. I didn't mention you are a girl.'

'So, I should stay hidden then? Sneak out the window?'

'No need. My family go to church, so they will be gone in about five minutes. Then you can leave via the front door like everyone else.'

I chuckle. 'Right-o then. Let me know when everyone's gone.'

Jack disappears again. I can hear voices and bumping around, a car starting, and then things go quiet. I get out of bed and pull the bed linen up over the pillow so it looks neat. There's a dressing gown on the back of the bedroom door that I pull over myself. Jack walks into the room, his Moon Boot knocking against things as he hobbles around.

'All clear. They're gone.' He looks at me strangely. 'You're wearing my bathrobe.'

'Just for a sec. Is that okay?'

He nods.

'Did I have my handbag with me when I got in your car last night?'

'Yes. It's hidden in the lounge room. I think you must have put it on the kitchen table when we got in last night. Fortunately, I found it before anyone else got up this morning.'

'Might have been a bit difficult to explain why your "friend" carries a handbag?'

'They would ask way too many questions. Many more than they already did when they found me asleep on the couch this morning.'

'What did you tell them?'

'That you're someone I know from school who'd got into some trouble last night and needed a safe place to go. I said I hadn't expected you to be here all night, but that you never woke up.'

'So, you told them the truth.'

'Of course.'

'But not the whole truth.'

'Do you think that is the same as lying?'

I chuckle. 'You're asking the wrong person there, Jack.'

I motion to leave the room, but Jack doesn't seem to get the hint. He just looks awkward, standing there not saying anything.

'Perhaps you could remind me where the bathroom is?' I say. 'I'm desperate for the loo.'

'Oh. Of course. This way. And, ah, do you want some breakfast?'

I rub my head. 'I think so. I'm hungry but my head is killing me.'

When I make my way down the hallway to the kitchen, smells of cinnamon and honey waft around. Jack is cooking.

'Smells good,' I say as I walk into the kitchen.

He stares at me. 'Now you're wearing my t-shirt.'

I look down at myself and give him a guilty smile. 'And a pair of your trackies.'

He nearly drops the glass he has in his hand.

'Sorry, but I could hardly put that dress back on. I'll wash them and give them back at school tomorrow.'

There is a four-seater round kitchen table next to a breakfast bench lined with three stools. I opt for the high-backed safety of the kitchen chair.

'You got them out of my wardrobe.'

'I did. But I didn't look. I just reached in and grabbed the first thing I felt.'

He frowns. 'That t-shirt is third from the bottom of the pile.'

I smile my guilty smile again. 'Okay, I peeked a bit. But I could hardly go home in just my underwear, could I?'

Jack blushes. He arrives at the table with a tall glass of water for me. 'Your headache is most likely dehydration. Water is the best thing you can drink.' He heads back into the kitchen, opens the fridge and pulls out a plate which he sets down before me. 'Do you like watermelon? It has a very high water-ratio, plus a small amount of natural sugars. It will also be very good for your headache.'

'Thanks, Jack. That's very sweet.'

'I'm cooking some porridge with fruit pieces in it. That's what I have for breakfast every day. I'm cooking extra for you, if you would like some as well.'

'Thanks, but just this watermelon will be great.'

Jack joins me at the kitchen table. 'I usually eat my breakfast at the breakfast bar, but today I'm sitting here so I can sit with you. It would be rude to sit somewhere else, especially since it is only you and me in the room. I'm telling you this because it makes me uncomfortable doing things a bit different, and sometimes I can do weird things when I'm uncomfortable. Mum says I should tell people these things, so they don't get weirded out by me.'

I laugh. 'Well, thanks for letting me know, Jack. We can sit at the breakfast bar if it would help.'

Jack looks up at the ceiling for a moment. 'No. Mum says I need to do things differently every now and then, so I can understand the feeling and get used to it. I have that feeling right now because you looked in my wardrobe and are wearing my clothes and sat at the table. And because we are alone in the house and I'm not supposed to be in the house alone with a girl until I'm married to her. This sort of thing is good preparation for me for when I might want to leave home to go to university or something.'

'You want to go to uni?'

'Yes. I'd like to be a scientist, but I'm not sure if I'll be able to. I have to be good at other things, not just Science, to go to university. But if I do get to go to university one day, someone else might do something like put on my lab coat by accident. That would make me feel like this. So now I'll know how I might feel and I can prepare for that. Am I acting normal, do you think?'

I burst out laughing. 'I'm not sure, Jack. Normal for you, I guess.'

He takes a mouthful of his porridge and closes his eyes to chew it.

'You mean things like English, don't you?'

He opens his eyes. 'What?'

'To go to university, you need to be good at English.'

Jack rocks and eats his food while looking at something on the wall behind me.

'I think,' I say, around a mouthful of watermelon, 'they should make an exception for people who are really good at Science, but not so good at other things, and give them a different way of getting to do the study they want to do.'

Jack keeps staring past me.

'Are you listening to me, Jack?'

'Yes.'

'You were ignoring me.' I take another bite of the watermelon.

'No. I was thinking.' He's looking out the window. There's an insect chirping outside.

'Were you thinking about Science?'

He starts looking around the room. 'Mum says I just have to do well in all my science classes over the next two years and that we'll worry about the rest later. She knows a professor who is a scientist at a university in New South Wales who might see me if I don't get into a university but have done well in Science.'

'That's why you need to do well in this term's genetics unit, too?'

'I have to prove that I can do well in Science, so they will let me do Biology, Chemistry and Physics. They think because my writing is not very good that I won't be able to do the subjects.'

I suddenly remember no one knows where I am, including Mum. 'Jack, sorry, can I have my phone, please? I need to check my messages.'

Jack gets my handbag. There is only a little bit of charge left on my phone. I open Messenger, but there is no message, which means Mum hasn't noticed that I didn't come home.

I open Snapchat. There is a Snap from Nikki. She's out the front of Cooper's house, and it asks where I'm going. There's another one to follow; she's back in the party with a sad look on her face, and it asks again where I am. Then another, sent only a few minutes later; she looks mad and it says something about me leaving her alone at the party. The next one she's in a car, saying she has no idea where I am but that she's going home, and that Hayley disappeared at the party too. The next Snap is just her with an angry expression on her face. She's in her pjs and I think her bed is in the background. There's another one of her waking up and asking where I am and saying she's worried that she hasn't heard from me yet.

The final Snap was sent only a few minutes ago, and it says to call her immediately.

'Jack, sorry, but I need to make a phone call. Can I go out the front or something?'

Jack leads me to the front door and indicates to a seat with a small table beside it on the verandah. 'Can I bring you a coffee?'

'Maybe some tea?' I say. 'That would be great, if that's okay?'

Jack disappears back into the house. I call Nikki's mobile.

'Grace! Oh my goodness, Grace, thank God you called me. Where are you? What happened to you last night?'

'It's a long story. I don't feel like talking about it now. But I'm okay.'

'Where did you go? How did you get home?'

'I didn't go home. I called Jack and he came and got me.'

'You slept at *Jack's* last night?'

'In separate rooms. He came and picked me up but I didn't want to go home.'

'Oh, man, what a mess,' Nikki says.

'What's a mess?'

'You and Cooper. You and Jack. Cooper and Hayley. It's all just a great big mess.'

'*Cooper and Hayley?* What have they got to do with anything?'

'Are you sitting down?'

'Yes.' Though my muscles are screaming for me to stand.

'Grace, after you left the party, Cooper and Hayley hooked up. Hayley never went home either.'

'You mean Hayley slept over at Cooper's last night?'

'More than that, Grace. Hayley slept *with* Cooper last night.'

And with that, my phone goes flat.

Chapter 34

Jack appears at the front door with my cup of tea just as my phone dies. He cringes. 'I'm no expert on facial expressions, Graceland, but that one does not look good.'

I bury my face in my shaking hands. I can sense Jack standing there, my cup of tea still in his hand, his giant Moon Boot sticking out in front of him. But all I can see is Cooper and Hayley, together, up on the landing, her sympathetic smiles, her gracious, understanding coos as he pours his heart out to her about his useless girlfriend who wouldn't give him what he wanted.

I look up at Jack and smile around tear-stained cheeks. 'Thanks,' I say, and reach up to take the tea. He frowns at me, and instead, places the tea on the table. He sits in the chair beside me.

Hayley would have been all sweetness, no doubt, as she explained to him the error in his choice of girlfriend—extolling her own virtues at the same time. I shake my head to rid it from my thoughts.

'You don't drink tea?' I ask Jack, taking a sip; it has too much milk, but I tell Jack it's great.

'No. I don't like hot drinks. But Mum says I should remember to offer them to people. She says it is unusual to not drink at least coffee, but I can't stand the smell.' His eyes are focused on my cup of tea the whole time he's talking. 'I am glad you prefer tea. I don't really know how to make a cup of coffee.'

I nod, but in the silence Cooper and Hayley rush back into my thoughts. Her stroking his cheek, moving in for a kiss. I put my hands over my eyes and press hard, begging them to stop seeing the images playing in my head.

'Did you get some bad news on the phone just now?' Jack asks, his hands sitting clasped together in his lap. 'Mum says when someone is sad, I shouldn't pry into other people's business, but that it is good to ask questions in case the other person wants to talk about it.'

'I guess it was bad news,' I say. 'I don't quite know what to do with it—it is too difficult to think about.'

'Are you talking about Cooper?'

Insightful, Jack. 'Yes. Cooper and Hayley. Last night.'

'Did they kiss?'

'Yeah, something like that.' It hurts to hear it said out loud. 'So much for them being my friends.'

So much for Cooper being my boyfriend.

'I don't think Hayley is a very good friend to you, Graceland. She has been sending nude pictures of herself to Cooper for weeks.'

My jaw drops open. 'Pardon?'

'The boys were talking about how Hayley has been sending nudes to Cooper, even though he's your boyfriend. They were talking about whether Cooper should stop her, whether it was being unfaithful to you by encouraging her to still send them.'

I stand up and pace the verandah. 'You heard them talking about this?'

Jack looks worried. 'I shouldn't have told you that. I've made you more upset.'

'No, Jack, it's important that you told me. Thank you. But it has helped me realise what an idiot I've been for trusting Hayley. And Cooper.'

'Cooper was not a good boyfriend to you, either.'

I blurt out a laugh. 'There's the understatement of the year.'

'He was acting different with you, but still being mean to people when you weren't around. People should be the same whoever they are with.'

'You're right, Jack. People who care about you don't do the sorts of things Hayley and Cooper have done to me. Especially Cooper. He hurt me, Jack. Really hurt me.'

'How?'

'He tried to get me to sleep with him last night. In a bad way. He tried to force me to do something I didn't want to do.'

Jack rubs his thumbs into his hands. 'Did he want you to have sex with him?'

'Yes, he did. And he tried really hard to make me.'

'You should report him to the police,' Jack says. 'You should file a complaint against him so that doesn't happen to anyone else.'

I nod slowly. 'You're probably right, Jack. But I don't think the police will take much notice. I stopped him.'

'You should still report him. People should know you aren't allowed to do that to other people.'

I put my head down in my hands and breathe deeply. Would anyone care about what Cooper tried to do to me last night? Probably not. If only Mikaela had said something when it happened to her, then the police would take more notice.

'Mum says that sometimes when people get bad news they cry. Are you going to cry? I'll go and get some tissues if you're going to start crying.'

I laugh. 'It's okay, Jack. I'm angry. And I'm hurt. I'm just glad I found out what Cooper Dally is really like.'

'This shows why you should not have sex before you get married. You can't know how committed someone is to you until you are married to them. It saves you getting hurt if you wait.'

'Is that what your mum tells you?' I ask dryly.

'Yes. Mum does say that. Though we don't talk about it very much.'

'Yeah, well, it's not as easy as you say it is, Jack. Not everyone can live up to your high standards.' I'm getting angry, but I don't know why. 'And just because you get married doesn't mean you don't get hurt. My mum didn't know my dad was going to yell at her until after they got married. And believe me, she got hurt. She got hurt here, in her heart, every time he left her. And he left her plenty of times. It was only after Jesse died that she had the strength to make him leave for good. Marriage doesn't guarantee anything. Love doesn't even guarantee anything. Nothing is a certain in life except yourself. You are the only one who you can trust.'

'That's not true, Graceland. There are people you can trust in this world. If you live a good life and do the best by others around you, you can be—'

'—Hurt. Abused. Taken advantage of,' I yell. I don't mean to, but I can't keep the anger back. 'You know your problem, Jack? You live in this idyllic world, where girls don't sleep with their boyfriends and no one tells lies and men don't hit the women they're supposed to love, and people fall in love and stay together and live happily ever after. But that's not the real world. Once you step out of your safety bubble you will find that people hurt you and lie to you. People will break your heart. Especially the people who love you.'

Jack stands up, his arms crossed. His face is twitching around his lips, as though he wants to say something but can't get his mouth to work. And then it all comes together and he says, without the slightest bit of hurt or anger in his voice, 'I know about hurt, Graceland. I know about people leaving, about them not wanting to stay. People hurt me physically. They hurt me emotionally. But I have hope. Because I know I can do better than that, and be better than that, and that by being better and doing better, I know I can change my world. And I thought, Graceland, that you thought that too. I thought you wanted more than just what the people around you were offering. I thought you wanted to make your world a better place.'

'I do, Jack. But people are still going to hurt me, they always will.'

'Perhaps. But the only thing you can change is you. That's where our DNA is all the same—we all have the biological ability to choose to stay, to choose to love, and to choose to change our world by not passing our hurt on to others.'

I pick up my cup of tea and take a few sips, while Jack comes and sits back down beside me. The occasional car drives past on the street below.

'You *are* Graceland, Graceland.'

I laugh. 'Yes, Jack, I am.'

He looks up at the sky. 'I mean, you are Graceland, the mansion.'

'I don't get it.'

'You are hope. You've had lots of terrible things happen to you, but you are going to change your stars and make things different for you and for your family. Just like Elvis did. You just have to make sure you are chasing after the things in life that will make a difference, and not settle for anything else. Being with someone like Cooper is not going to make you happy, no matter how much money he has.'

An old man walks by with his dog and I think of Jesse, and how he loved to watch the world go by from his blue chair in our front yard. The memory warms my heart. It may be too late to change things for Jesse, but Jack's right. In changing my world, my stars, I'll be changing my family's future as well.

'Thanks, Jack,' I say.

He looks somewhere close to my eyes and smiles.

'You have brown eyes,' I say.

'Hazel, actually.'

'You have a sweet smile. It's a kind smile, like Ellen's is.'

He looks uncomfortable.

I put my hand on his arm. 'Thanks for being my hero.'

He looks at my hand but doesn't move away. 'I'm not a hero.'

'Yes, you are. Thanks for rescuing me last night. For giving me a safe place to come home to. For kind of lying for me, and for giving up your Sunday plans to hang out with me for a while.'

'Any time, Graceland,' Jack says, and I think he really means it.

Chapter 35

Mum's at home when Jack drops me off later that morning. I don't realise until it's too late and she's heard me come through the door.

'Mum,' I say, 'you're home.'

'Graceland. You're just getting home now? You didn't sleep over at that boy Cooper's house, did you?' She looks me up and down. 'Whose clothes are you wearing?'

I pull at Jack's ill-fitting clothes.

'And why aren't you wearing any shoes?'

I make Mum a cup of tea and we sit at the kitchen table opposite each other. Her eyes are worried and carrying big bags under them.

'Sorry for not coming home,' I say. 'I hadn't meant to do that. I fell asleep at a friend's place.'

'Not your boyfriend's place?'

'No. Promise.'

She nods. 'I don't know if I feel worse that you didn't care to let me know, or that I didn't even know you weren't home until you walked in the door.'

Tears well in my eyes. 'It was not a good night, Mum.'

She takes a sip of her tea. 'You look like it wasn't a good night. Is that Cooper boy still your boyfriend?'

I shake my head. 'I'm done with him.'

'Do you want to talk about it?'

I shrug. 'Why aren't you going to work?'

She points to the calendar on the wall. 'It's Jesse's birthday. He would have turned twelve today.'

'Oh, it is too.' I can't believe how distracted I've been; I didn't even notice the date creeping up on me. 'Twelve, huh.'

A heavily weighted blanket of sadness rests across my shoulders. How could I have forgotten it was Jesse's birthday this weekend? How could I not have noticed Cooper's birthday was so close to Jesse's? I pinch myself on my thigh and it turns red. I won't let Cooper, or anyone else, make me forget what is really important ever again.

I look at Mum. 'Wanna watch *Follow That Dream* with me?' I ask.

Mum smiles. 'Always.'

By the end of the movie I'm crying; I don't know why. There was an inspo quote going around Instagram a couple of months ago that said crying is a way of letting your eyes speak when your mouth isn't able to say how broken your heart is. And I get it. No words. Only tears can express this level of hurt.

The credits roll across the screen with Elvis singing in the background.

'I miss Jesse so much, Mum.'

She puts her arm around me, wiping her nose with her sleeve. 'Me too.'

'There's this boy at school who knew Jesse from the special school. He said this was Jesse's favourite movie.'

Mum's cheeks glisten. 'It sure was. He knew all the songs, could quote half of Elvis' lines.'

'Why do you think Jesse loved the movie so much?'

'Oh, well, he loved how the family, when they ran out of petrol, just pulled over on the side of the road and set up a home there.' She laughs. 'He thought it was hilarious. A home right on the sand, by the water. I think that was his dream—that our family would all be together forever, looking after each other, carefree, like that.'

'And that people would just randomly break out in song from time to time.'

She laughs again. 'Exactly. He begged me to let him learn guitar when he started school, but do you remember hearing that kid sing?' She's laughing hard now. 'He was hopeless! He couldn't hold a tune to save himself.' Mum's face is alive with a mixture of sadness and the happiest of memories. 'Watching the movie helps me feel like he's still here with me. I know I need to let him go, but I just can't.'

'I know, Mum. I can't let go either. I'm scared that if I let him go, I'll make the same mistake again.'

'What mistake, Graceland?'

'That I'll forget how, when I love someone, I have to do better to look out for them.' I shake my head. 'If I'd been more careful and looked after Jesse on that day, I might have been able to save him. I might have noticed something sooner. I should have been with him, stopped him from putting the battery in his mouth.'

A deep groan comes from within Mum. 'Oh, Graceland. Jesse was not your responsibility. He was mine! And your father's. We're the ones who let him down. We were so wrapped up in our problems that we forgot to stop on the side of the road and sort things out together—by being a family. We were too busy trying to get back to where everyone thought we should be.'

'I still feel like it was my fault.'

'You were twelve years old, Graceland. Hardly able to look after yourself, let alone a little brother with Down syndrome.'

I breathe in deeply and exhale the pain. 'Maybe we don't have to let Jesse go, Mum. We can still remember him, talk about him.' Tears continue to roll down my cheeks. 'I've been trying to get away from the memories because they hurt, but maybe they're only hurting because I'm trying to stop them from getting out.'

'Maybe,' she says. 'Maybe we should talk about him more.'

'What if we ask Lisa Marie and Tom to come over on Tuesday night for dinner and they can talk about him too?'

'That's a lovely idea. You could also invite your friend who went to school with him.'

'Oh yeah, Jack has some funny stories about Jesse.'

'Jack is the boy who knew Jesse? Not Jack Oskar?'

My eyes nearly explode out of my face. 'You know him?'

'Well, I used to. He was Jesse's best friend, so I saw him a fair bit at school drop-off and pick-up times. Jesse talked about Jack all the time. Jack has autism, if I remember right.'

'That's right. You'll like him.'

Mum tucks my hair behind my ear. 'You've always been a bit different to the rest of us, Graceland. You've always been a planner and had dreams. I want you to be different from me. To live a different life to the one I have. To go out and find the love you need by following your dreams.'

'I'm trying to, Mum.'

'I'm sure you are.' She wipes my cheeks with her thumbs. 'I don't know what's going on with you at the moment, and what happened with you and Cooper, but don't let anything stand in the way of your dreams. Nothing and no one.' She looks at me with intensity, like her life depends on it. 'I need you to follow your dreams.'

I go to my bedroom and write up a new inspo quote to hang on my wall: *We all have the biological ability to choose to stay, to choose to love, and to choose to change our world by not passing our hurt on to others – Jack Oskar.*

I open Spotify and push play on my Chill Times playlist. Then I take a photo of Jesse out of my scrapbook and Blu Tack it to my wall. I give it a kiss and whisper, 'Happy birthday, little bro.'

Chapter 36

I make sure I'm up early to catch the school bus on Monday morning, so I can be there to see Cooper. I pack a little dignity into my backpack, and as we travel the streets of Maroochydore toward school, I use a pen to write up my arm, *Believe in yourself and follow your dreams.*

Ellen meets me at the front of the school.

'Hi, lovely,' I say.

'I heard about Saturday night. Are you okay?'

I do a slow nod. 'I think so. It's taken some processing, but I'm working through it.'

'Good. And what's the plan?' Ellen asks.

I scrunch up my nose. 'School. Form. Classes.'

'I mean, with Cooper. You know, from here.'

I shrug. 'Ignore him. Pass Science exponentially well.'

She puts her hands on her hips. 'Come on, that can't be it.'

'Jack thinks I should report him to the police. Do you think I should too?'

'Who, Cooper?'

'Yeah.'

'What, for sleeping with Hayley?'

'No, for what he did to me.'

Ellen cocks her head. 'What did he do to you?'

And I realise, Ellen doesn't know. No one knows. Hayley doesn't know, Nikki doesn't know—no one will know, unless I tell them.

'He tried to force me, Ellen. To sleep with him. He did

everything to try and convince me I had to, like as if it was what was owed to him. Just like he'd done with Mikaela.'

Ellen takes two steps backwards and sits on a bench, her hand covering her opened mouth. 'And how does Jack know about this?'

'He rescued me from Cooper's party.'

Ellen shakes her head. 'I shouldn't be so surprised, after what happened to Mikaela, that Cooper would try a similar thing on you.'

'Mikaela telling me what happened to her did help me be more cautious of him. Maybe it helped stop it from happening to me too.'

Ellen stands up, her fists clenched on either side. 'You have to report him. You can't let him get away with what he did to you. We have to find a way to stop it from happening again.'

'I don't know, Ellen. I mean, nothing happened in the end.'

'He tried to coerce you into doing something you didn't want to do, Grace. That's attempted rape. You have to call it for what it was.'

I shake my head. 'It will be his word against mine. Everyone saw me go up to the bedrooms. Everyone saw me hanging off his arm, flirting with him.'

'It doesn't matter. I'll get Dad to drop us off at the police station after school today. Okay? And then we'll work out what else we'll do to expose Cooper Dally for what he really is. Not just for you, Grace; for Mikaela as well.'

I take a deep breath and hold it. 'Okay, I guess so.'

Ellen wraps her arms around me and squeezes me tight. 'Did you tell your mum?'

'No. I was going to—I just couldn't. It was Jesse's birthday yesterday.'

'Oh, it was too. Sorry I forgot.'

'That's okay, for the first time ever I'd forgotten too. I hadn't noticed the date.'

'Guess there's been a lot going on, hey.'

I nod. 'Mum didn't go to work; she just watched Elvis movies all day.'

'That might have been a good opportunity to tell her.'

'You didn't see her face. I don't think she would have coped if I'd told her. She gave me this talk about how she wanted me to live a different life. Change my stars. If she knew what happened to me, or the situation I'd gotten myself into, she'd have been so disappointed. It's important to her that I'm different.'

'You *are* different, Grace. This doesn't change that.'

I shrug. 'Maybe.'

'What about Miss Krensky? You could talk to her about it. She's cool.'

'What's she going to do? Besides, if I do go to the police, if they think it is serious enough, won't they pass the information on to the school?'

'I guess so. But telling the school yourself might at least see Cooper get suspended or something.'

'What would that achieve?'

'A few days without the milkshake duck around.'

'What the?' I laugh. 'What the heck is a milkshake duck?'

'It's a very apt description, if you ask me,' Ellen says, hugging her text book and laptop to her chest. 'It's someone you think is okay, but later find out they have some serious faults. Though, if you remember, I did warn you getting with Cooper was a bad idea.'

'I'm nervous enough about being around Cooper as it is. Let's just get through the day, okay?'

We head up to Form, watching everyone standing around talking while we wait for Miss Krensky to arrive. Cooper completely ignores me, which is a relief. I wouldn't know how to act around him anyway. He's showing off an attempt to grow some facial hair; the dark across his jaw line gives him an air of intelligence. My chest burns as I watch him; all I want to do is take his gorgeous face and smash it against the concrete post.

I notice Brad doesn't come over to say hello to Ellen.

'What's with Brad?' I ask.

'He texted this morning; said we need to cool it for a few days while the storm blows over.'

'What storm?'

'You and Cooper.'

'Cooper and I are a storm?'

Ellen chuckles. 'You're a cyclone.'

Nikki comes bounding up. 'Grace, you're here. I thought you might not come.'

'Why wouldn't I?'

'Because of the thing.'

'I'm not going to let Cooper Dally stop me from following my dreams for one second more. I'm done with him.' I look at Ellen. 'This afternoon I'm going to report him to the police for what he did to me. And I'll mention what happened to Mikaela, too, and see what they say.'

Nikki pulls out her phone. 'Whatever you mean, it's not what I'm talking about, Grace. You haven't been on any social media this weekend?'

I shake my head. 'I didn't recharge my phone after our phone call yesterday morning.'

'Well, maybe just as well. You might want to sit down for this.'

Miss Krensky bustles by. 'Come on, everyone.' She unlocks the door. 'Inside, inside. I think it's about to downpour.'

The class streams inside. Everyone is looking at their phones, except Jack, who has put his headphones on and is sitting with his head down. I slip into my usual seat up the back. Hayley's seat is empty. I can sense Cooper's gaze from the other side of the room but I refuse to acknowledge it.

'What were you going to show me?' I ask Nikki.

Ellen shakes her head. 'I don't know what's going on, but I don't think this is the place to find out.' She looks sideways at Brad.

'What? What is it?' It's like every eye in the classroom is on me. Miss Krensky is up the front prattling on about something. I wish I could be like Jack, with his headphones on, blocking the world out.

'It's a video on YouTube,' Nikki says. She looks at Ellen. 'But Ellen might be right. Let's wait until recess, okay?'

'We've got HPE and then Science to get through this morning,' Ellen says. 'You don't want to be distracted.'

A knot tightens just below my ribcage. 'Don't leave me alone today, will you, girls? I don't want to talk to Cooper. And this time, when I say don't leave me, I mean it. For fear of your lives, and for mine.'

Chapter 37

It's not Nikki or Ellen's fault that I've been left alone when Cooper finds me and pulls me into an empty, unlocked classroom. Realistically, they couldn't be with me all the time, especially since Ellen doesn't even do HPE most days.

Cooper had been lying in wait; there's no other explanation for the way he is able to grab me and pull me into the classroom when I go back to my bag to get my drink bottle. I jerk my arm away, but it's too late, and he's able to get between me and the door so I am trapped.

'What do you want, Cooper?' I ask, forcing some apathy into my voice, as though he is merely inconveniencing me. But my heart is about to burst from my chest and do what the rest of me can't— get out of here.

'You're avoiding me, Grace. It seems we have something to talk through.'

I shake my head, the adrenaline that's running through my body helping to build the anger I should be feeling. 'No, we don't, Cooper. You're not even worth the breath it takes to get the words out.'

He seems shocked. 'Excuse me?' His eyes narrow as he speaks. 'What's that supposed to mean?'

'It means, I don't ever want to look at you again, let alone say anything to you.'

His face is turning red. 'Don't you speak to me like that, Grace. Don't say things you will regret.'

'When it comes to you, there's nothing I'll regret more than what has happened between us over the past few months.'

Cooper steps closer to me. He grabs my arms. 'Come on, Grace. That's not how a girl treats her boyfriend.'

'Boyfriend?' I say. 'I don't have a boyfriend. I stopped having a boyfriend the moment you tried to force me to have sex with you, and then slept with someone who I thought was my friend.'

Cooper's eyes go dark. 'Who told you that?'

'Well, you may remember that I was there for the coercion part.'

'I was just trying to get you in the mood. You wanted it, you know you did. You're just frigid. I was getting you over that.'

'Frigid?' I say through gritted teeth. I can't believe he can't see what he did to me, to Mikaela, for what it is. Mikaela's words pop into my head: *My counsellor tells me it will empower me to tell the story, to use the word rape.* I take a deep breath. 'You tried to *rape* me, Cooper. You are the lowest of life forms. Lower, even. Just looking at your face makes me want to vomit.'

Cooper's face explodes into a darker shade of red. 'Oh come on, Grace. *Rape?* Really? I was just doing what you know deep down you wanted to do.'

'I made it clear that I wouldn't sleep with you until I was ready, until I was sure. You wouldn't wait.'

'I could have slept with fifty girls in the time I was with you.'

'Well, that's what you should have been doing, if that was what you wanted from this relationship.'

'This—' he points in my face, '—how this relationship has worked out, is your fault. It's your fault I slept with someone else. What would the boys say if they knew my own girlfriend wouldn't sleep with me on my frigging birthday?'

'My fault?!'

'I was trying my best to be this "better person" for you. A good guy. But you couldn't give me what I wanted most.'

'What are you talking about?'

'The decision, remember? To be more kind. I wanted to show

Mikaela Harper I was the kind of guy that any girl would long to be with. That I could be all the things she told me I wasn't. And I could be happy again. But you couldn't give that to me.'

'You need to choose to be happy yourself, Cooper. You can't leave your own happiness to other people.'

He paces back and forth in front of the door. 'Well, w-what about the Hayley thing?'

'I didn't mention Hayley. I just said you slept with one of my friends.'

'Yeah, well, Ellen wasn't there and I hardly would have slept with Nikki, would I?'

I shake my head in disbelief. 'You really are a jerk. There's no better word to describe you. At least none that Ellen would approve of.'

I push past him and grab the door, but he grips the handle and holds it shut.

'I'll ruin you.' His face is so close his breath mingles with my own. 'If you walk away from me, you will pay for it. I will crush you. I'll make sure that you never get anywhere on the Sunshine Coast; you'll never amount to anything. You'll end up exactly like your mother. Just like Lisa Marie and the rest of your miserable, hopeless little excuse for a family.'

'Is that what you said to Mikaela, too? Did she try to break up with you and you threatened to ruin her as well?'

Cooper snarls. 'Mikaela Harper was a selfish bitch who deserved everything she had coming to her.'

Tears sting my eyes. 'Well, at least I now know that the Cooper who is drunk and high on drugs, the one I despise, that's the real Cooper Dally. Everything else is just you trying to pretend to be something you're not. And there is nothing—nothing—you can do to me now.'

He drops his hand from the door handle and smirks. 'You haven't seen it yet, have you?'

'What are you talking about?'

His lips curl on one side. 'You'll find out soon enough.'

I open the door and step back out into freedom.

Chapter 38

At recess, Nikki leads Ellen and me to a corner up near the science classrooms, where students aren't allowed to hang around in breaks.

'It's a video.' Nikki's phone is shaking in her hand. 'It was uploaded to YouTube by SevenPackages.'

'I've never heard of it. Whose do you reckon it is?' I ask.

Nikki shrugs. 'I suspect it's a fake account.' Nikki clicks the Play button and Ellen and I crowd in closely to watch.

It's titled *Conversation with Voles*.

My throat tightens as two voles appear on the screen, and Jack's voice comes through the speakers. *Voles are a type of rodent.*

Jack's voice is followed by mine. *And what do voles have to do with anything?* The two voles dance across the screen as each one speaks.

Some scientists believe there is a repetition in a string of their microsatellite DNA that influences them so they are monogamous.

'Is that Jack Oskar's voice?' Ellen asks.

'Just watch.' Nikki says.

I search my memory—Jack and I—when did we have this conversation?

My voice in the video: *They're what?*

They are faithful to their partner. They find a partner and stick with them for life, Jack's voice continues. Then I remember, *the library.* The recording. Jack's evidence of learning video. *Some humans do choose to stay together for life. I'm going to be like that. I will meet someone, marry them, and never leave them.*

The voles stop and look at each other. A different voice, female, high-pitch, begins. *Really, Jack? Will you really never leave them? How can you be sure?*

Jack's voice: *I will not even kiss a girl until I think I will most probably ask her to marry me.*

The female voice says, *Jack, I would do anything to be yours.*

A male voice, also slightly high-pitch, says, *Oh, Graceland, you are the only girl I've ever thought I could be with.* I try to suck in breath, but it hurts. Everything hurts.

The female voice says, *Then kiss me now, Jack.*

The vole leans in, as though it's going to kiss the other vole. But then Jack's real voice says, *I want my girlfriend to wait, too. I don't want her to have had sex with anyone else before she has sex with me.*

The female voice giggles and says, *You are safe with me, Jack. My virginity is all yours.*

I lock Nikki's phone and pace the hallway with fists clenched, my heart beating so fast the blood feels like it could blast its way through the veins in my neck.

'I'll murder him,' I say.

Ellen tries to pull me into a hug. I shrug her off.

'I'll get his puny little excuse for a brain and smash it against the pavement.'

Nikki laughs. 'Come on, Grace. Don't take it so personally. Laugh it off.'

I glare at her. 'Laugh it off? This is a betrayal on so many levels. That recording, that's part of Jack's evidence of learning video. Where would he have even got it from? And who is the girl?' I'm lightheaded. 'How many people have viewed it?'

Nikki checks her phone again. 'Not many.'

I grab the phone. 'Two hundred and forty-seven? When was it uploaded?'

'Sometime late yesterday,' Nikki says.

I pace again.

'Grace, it will be okay,' Ellen says.

'Did you know about it?' I ask. 'Did Brad say anything?'

She shakes her head. 'No, but I guess that might be what he meant about the storm.'

'He better not have had anything to do with it,' I say, glaring at Ellen. 'Did you tell him about me recording Jack?'

'Why would Brad have had anything to do with it?'

'Brad—Cooper's lead guitar—master hacker?'

'What, Grace?' Ellen looks genuinely perplexed.

'Brad told me he's a hacker. Or at least he was at his previous school. He could have got into the school email system. If he knew it was there, that I'd emailed it to Mr Van, he could have hacked it.'

Ellen's staring at me with wide eyes.

'Grace,' Nikki says. 'Come on, that's a long shot. Why would Brad do that?'

'Cooper,' I say. 'He said he'd ruin me. What better way than through my friends? Hayley. Brad. You. Ellen. And Jack will never speak to me again if he finds out about this.'

'Jumping to conclusions isn't going to help anything,' Nikki says. She looks at Ellen. 'Cooper found out about the video, but we don't know how. That's not what this is about.'

'Nikki's right.' Hot tears roll down my face. I turn to Nikki. 'You saw the video this morning?'

'I saw it on an Instagram post and was going to report it as inappropriate. I didn't so I could show it to you first.'

'This is Cooper humiliating me,' I say. I look at Ellen. 'And hurting my friends. We can't let that happen.'

'Yeah but you can't let him get away with this, Grace,' Nikki says. 'What I want to know is, what are we going to do as pay-back?'

'I agree,' Ellen says. 'This is just another reason why Cooper needs to be exposed; he can't do this to you or to Jack. Or to any of us.' She leans over and gives me a hug.

'For a start, we need to report it,' I say. 'Get it off social media before Jack sees it.'

'I'll do that now,' Nikki says. 'It shouldn't take long.' I look doubtfully at Nikki. The knot is still tight in my stomach. Jack's not on most social media, but if everyone is talking about it at school, he could hear about it that way. I rub my fingers into my palms and wish all over again that Cooper Dally had never taken any notice of me.

I sit on the edge of my bed and put my head between my knees, trying to slow my breathing. It's been a rough couple of days at school, with snickers behind my back and 'in jokes' that everyone except Jack and the teachers seem to get. Jack seeming to stay unaware of what is happening around him has been the only thing keeping me sane. I read over my inspo wall, reminding myself this experience will just make me stronger … eventually.

I shove some earphones in and lie back on my bed, staring up at the ceiling. It's patchy and discoloured. The window in front of me is dirty. A door on the old wardrobe, the only brown thing in the room, has come off its hinges—all imperfect things I hadn't really cared about before in my room.

My bedroom door opens. Lisa Marie sticks her head in.

I remove an earphone. 'What are you doing here?'

'Nice to see you too.' She sits on the bed beside me. 'It's Tuesday. Mum said you wanted a family dinner or something. To talk about Jesse?'

'Oh, yeah. Is Tom here too?'

'No,' she says. 'Tom and I had a fight. Nothing too serious, but I needed a break. Might be nice with just the three of us anyway, don't you think?'

'Sure.' She stays on my bed. I look at her with raised eyebrows. 'What?'

'Is there anything you want to talk about?'

'Not really. Why?'

'Well, have you been on any social media lately?'

I groan. 'I've been staying off it for mental health reasons.'

'So, you've seen the videos?'

There's a weight in my stomach, so heavy it is hurting; I manage a nod.

'Who did it, do you reckon?'

I shake my head. 'It had to be Cooper.'

'Makes sense. Whoever it was obviously has plenty of support behind them, for how quickly this one took off.'

'Don't tell me. I don't want to know.' I frown. 'Hang on, you said videos. Plural. There's only been one.'

'No—another one went up a couple of hours ago. That's what I'm talking about.'

I swallow, dread filling my stomach like wet cement. 'I've only seen the one from Sunday.' I open my phone. 'Ugh, no data.' *And no Cooper to top me up.*

Lisa Marie pulls out her phone and hands it to me.

'Is it bad?' I ask.

Lisa Marie does a half-smile. 'No?' She raises her eyebrows, a hopeful expression on her face.

I notice the video is on a different account, but using the title *Conversation with Voles* again. I don't recognise the new account. I push the Play button and two voles come onto the screen.

Jack Oskar, did you just smile? My voice sounds light-hearted.

I smile. His voice sounds tight.

When? I rarely see you smile.

I smile when I'm at home. Oh, crap. I remember this conversation.

Really? And what makes you smile at home?

One of the voles is moving erratically around on the screen. *You.*

Me? I hear myself laugh in the video. *But I've never been to your house.*

When I think about you when I'm at home, Jack's voice says.

Why don't I make you smile when I'm around you then?

The high-pitch male voice starts. *I told you you're the only one for me, Graceland. I want to be with you forever.*

Okay, comes the female voice. *But first, I'll have to break up with my really hot and gorgeous boyfriend.* There's laughter off screen.

Is that Hayley's laugh?

Oh dear, the voice continues. *I just got a text. My boyfriend is having a big birthday party. I have to go to it. Jack, will you come with me?*

Oh, I don't think so. I'm too much of a cowardly chicken.

My own voice returns to the voiceover. *There'll be lots of people there. You could come along. No one would notice an extra person.*

They'd notice me, Jack's real voice says.

You could come anyway.

That would be one way to end my life, I guess. But, I'm not ready to die yet, at least not death by— and the video ends.

I place my hands over my head and rock, just like Jack would do.

'See, not so bad,' Lisa Marie says.

I place my head back between my knees. 'This is bad. Really, really bad. I'll kill them both.'

'Both?'

I pop my head up. 'You didn't hear it?'

She shakes her head.

'Hayley's laugh in the background when she says "I need to break up with my hot boyfriend". If she's not the girl in the voiceover, she was at least there. Her and Cooper—they're both behind the videos. And I bet she's the one who uploaded it. Cooper was at school today, but Hayley wasn't. She's Cooper's new Barbie doll.'

Chapter 39

I text Ellen and Nikki to meet me near the science rooms before school.

'You both saw the new video?' I ask.

They both nod. It's been taken down now but not before it reached 800 views.

'And did you hear what I heard?'

'What do you mean?' Nikki asks.

'Hayley. She laughs in the clip. It's her, I'm sure of it.'

Ellen shakes her head. 'No, Hayley wouldn't.'

I look at Ellen and then at Nikki.

'Actually, I kinda think she would,' Nikki says.

I pull out a pad and pen. 'I've been thinking about what you guys said, and I agree. I've reported Cooper to the police, but without Mikaela's testimony, they said they needed more evidence before they could do anything. And since Mikaela is still saying she won't file a report, it's up to us to make sure this doesn't happen again. It's not enough to just sit back and take whatever Cooper feels like dishing out. Get those creative juices flowing, because it's time we exposed the jerk for what he is.'

Nikki puts her hand out into the centre of our circle. 'For you, Grace, and Mikaela, and for all the girls who are yet to be broken by boys like Cooper Dally.'

I put my hand on hers.

Ellen puts her hand in and smiles. 'Let's do it.'

Nikki looks at her phone. 'Hayley's just arrived at school.

Should we go and meet up with her?'

'Great idea,' I say.

'You're back,' I say, as Hayley walks across the school parking lot. 'No new videos to upload this morning then?'

She gives a wry grin. 'Not today.' She flicks her hair about and puts her hand on her hip. 'Do you have a problem with me, *Graceland*?'

'Well, you did sleep with my boyfriend.'

'At least someone did. And man, was he *gooooood*.'

I clench my fist so hard my nails dig into my hand; pain surges up into my wrist. 'It was you, wasn't it? You're the female voice.'

She opens her mouth and places her hand on her chest. 'Me, Grace? How could you think such a thing?'

'You're laughing in the background of one of the clips. I know it was you.'

She shrugs. 'You're a bit precious about it.' She tries to walk off.

'Where did you get the video from, Hayley? I deleted it off the camera and emailed it to Mr Van straight away. No one else has a copy.'

Hayley raises her eyebrows and runs her fingers along her lips. 'Loyalty can be a fickle thing.'

'That won't work, Hayley. However you guys found out about the video, however you got it, that doesn't matter. What matters is, that video was to help Jack pass Science,' I say, trying to keep the anger from my voice. 'And you dragging him into this is not okay.'

'Really? Gee, sorry Grace. It was just a bit of fun.'

I hold my fist tight against my leg. 'You know full well it wasn't for fun. I don't understand why you're doing it. I thought you were my friend.'

Hayley's eyes flash hurt, then sadness, but only for a moment. 'Why do you think, Grace? You had Cooper; he was all yours. But you couldn't appreciate what you had. He was giving himself to you, and you kept throwing it back in his face.'

My dropping jaw forces my mouth to open. 'You're in love with Cooper?'

She brushes hair out of her face. 'Shut up. What would you know about love?'

'I know Cooper Dally isn't capable of feeling it. Unless he's loving himself; he's real good at that.'

Hayley shakes her head. 'You've got no idea.'

'Well you didn't have to involve Jack in it. You could have done whatever you wanted to me; drawing Jack into it is low.'

'*Jack?* If it wasn't for Jack Oskar, none of this would have happened. I could see that it was Jack who was beginning to ruin everything for us.'

I stare at Hayley. 'Ruining *it*? Ruining *what*?'

'The social life Cooper brings with him is worth far more than some useless boy who can barely string three words together.'

'Jack Oskar has a lot more to offer the world than people like you.'

'That's where you're wrong, Grace. You know, you were right in History that day when you said people with disabilities have nothing to offer the world and shouldn't be alive.'

My mouth falls open again. 'It was you? You tampered with Jack's brakes!'

Hayley laughs heartily. 'Yeah, that's right. Mystery solved, well done, Grace. Took you long enough.'

I shake my head in disbelief. 'You could have killed him.'

Hayley shrugs.

'You're worse than just a horrible person. You're evil.'

Hayley laughs. 'No, Grace. Just determined to get what I want.'

'Some would say Adolf Hitler was the same.'

She rolls her eyes. 'I wasn't about to spend the rest of my high school life in loserville because of you. I've been there and I wasn't going back again for anything. Or, anyone.'

People are gathering around us and whispering, but I don't care. 'There is more to life than going to parties and being popular.'

'You're wrong, Grace,' Hayley says. 'You might be satisfied hanging out with the likes of Jack Oskar, but I want more from life. I want to be loved and admired and to have people saying, "Gee, I wish I was more like Hayley Thompson". I deserve more than what I have. I deserve more than the shit life I've been given.'

'Yeah well, you might end up with people saying that about you, Hayley. But you won't be remembered for the right reasons.' I take a deep breath. 'You make your life the way it is by the choices you make. You take the bad stuff and make sure it doesn't happen to other people. You don't make it worse for everyone else—that's not changing the world.'

'Don't quote one of your stupid Instagram-mantras at me, *Graceland*. You live with your head in the clouds, chasing dreams. We're born the way we are and who we are and there is nothing we can do to change that.'

'Not true, Hayley. People can change. People can choose to be kind or mean, grateful or spoiled, smart or stupid, no matter where they have come from. That's what Jack has taught me—that in choosing to make better life-choices, I am changing not only my future, but the lives of others around me ... for the better.'

Hayley bursts out laughing. 'We're done, Graceland McKay. Go and play with your little friends and pretend your life will be something it will never, ever be.' She starts to walk away but then adds, 'Oh, and check your phone.'

I realise Ellen and Nikki are standing behind me. They wrap their arms around me. Ellen whispers, 'Well done, Grace. That was amazing.'

My heart still pounding from the confrontation, I unlock my phone and it connects to the school Wi-Fi. No new messages. No secret Snapchats or private Instagram messages. Just a couple of emails—Mrs Higgins with a reminder that we have an assignment due today. My heart sinks; I had meant to finish it last night. There's just too much happening at the moment to keep track of. I don't know what Hayley meant …

I go to close the app when I notice another email further down with voles in the subject line. I don't recognise the sender. I open it. It has two attachments, and simply says *Thought you'd like a keepsake*. They're the two voles videos. And then I notice it. It hasn't been sent to me, but to the whole Year 10 cohort.

My breath catches. That will include Jack.

Chapter 40

'You watched the videos, I'm guessing?' I ask Jack that afternoon. He hadn't been at school, which just about killed me as I stewed all day about talking to him. There was no escaping it; I had some serious apologising to do to him. I'm lying on my bed with my phone on speaker. He is silent on the other end. 'Please talk to me, Jack.'

'I did.'

I bite my lip. 'I'm so sorry, Jack.'

'I didn't even know you were recording me.'

'I know.' Tears roll down my cheeks and land on my bedspread in damp, salty puddles. 'I have no idea how they got hold of it. The recordings were supposed to be for your Science portfolio, to show Mr Van Hayden how much you know.'

Jack remains silent.

'I forwarded the videos to Mr Reyl and Miss Krensky, and told them Hayley virtually confessed to being involved in your accident. I also told them I've filed a report against Cooper at the police station for attempted rape, just like you said I should. Mikaela is thinking about letting the school in on what happened to her, too. I hope it is enough to have them both expelled.'

Silence.

Then, finally: 'You know, Graceland, how Elvis started off really poor, in that little house?'

'Yes, I remember.'

'His parents had to get help from neighbours just so they could eat sometimes.'

'That's intense.'

'And then he became really rich. He became obese, unhealthy.'

'Yes, you told me that.'

'Yeah, well, do you think Elvis died happy?'

'I don't know, Jack.'

'I think he probably wasn't happy, even though he got everything he thought he wanted. They reckon he had an affair and was using drugs. He got divorced. Graceland, I think that even when you get money and everything you think you want, that doesn't mean you become happy. Maybe it would have been better for Elvis if he had never been so rich.'

I choke back tears. 'Why are you telling me this, Jack?'

'Because it's one thing to want to change your stars, and another thing to be happy. They're not always the same thing.'

'I've made some stupid mistakes lately, haven't I, Jack?'

'I guess so.'

'Ones where I haven't thought about you. But you have to believe me that I only recorded that video for Mr Van Hayden. I never thought, not even for a moment, that anyone else would see them. I just wanted him to see that you were so smart, even if you couldn't write it all down on paper.'

'I believe you.'

I chew the skin beside my thumbnail. 'And forgive me?'

He is silent.

I nod my head over and over, stifling the sobs. 'I need to tell you something else.'

He is silent.

'Are you still there?'

'Yes.'

'In Science last week, when we were talking about what we should say on the video voiceover …'

Silence.

' … I was recording you so it could go on the video. And in class

239

today, when you were away, Seb and I put your voice into the video.'

Silence.

'Jack?'

'Is that all?'

'Please, Jack. Is that okay?'

'Why are you asking my permission now? You did it anyway.'

I sob. 'I'm sorry. I'm so, so sorry. Please, Jack.'

'I guess when we want something bad enough and we get it, sometimes we realise it was never really what we wanted at all.'

'What, Jack; what are you talking about? You don't mean that about me, about being my friend, do you?'

'I need to go now.'

'Jack,' I say. 'Wait. I'll see you at school—?'

But Jack's not on the line anymore.

Chapter 41

I organise for the girls to meet me at Nikki's on Saturday afternoon. When I arrive, Ellen is already there.

'I came half an hour earlier,' Ellen says. 'Mum's still mad at you because of the night you left me at the party. I thought it best to avoid her seeing you, just in case.'

'Encouraging. Thanks, Ellen,' I say. 'As if I don't have enough to feel bad about at the moment.'

Ellen shrugs. 'It is what it is.' But she wraps me in a bear hug. 'You're a different person now, Grace.'

'Thanks, Ellen. I think I am too.'

My phone vibrates in my pocket. I pull it out and look at Nikki and Ellen. 'It's Mikaela,' I say. Nikki's eyes widen, but Ellen nods.

'Hello?' I say.

'Hey.' Mikaela's voice sounds sweet, calm. 'Thanks for picking up.'

'Why wouldn't I?'

Mikaela chuckles. 'I dunno. I wasn't sure if you would after our last conversation.'

'You didn't say anything I didn't need to know,' I say. 'In fact, it was probably stuff we all needed to know months ago.'

She doesn't say anything for a moment. 'Sorry, I was nodding.'

I laugh. 'Good one.'

'I hear you're plotting revenge?'

'Well, not so much revenge, more of an awareness campaign,' I say.

'The truth revealed?'

'Exposing him for who he really is.' I take a deep breath. 'Ellen said she's been trying to convince you to go to the police.'

'She has. Every time she calls she brings it up.'

'You know I filed a report with the police. They said my testimony alone isn't enough to press charges.'

Mikaela pauses. 'I just don't think I can, Grace.'

'What happened to me with Cooper would be so much stronger if you told your story, too. The police would have to do something.'

Mikaela is quiet for a moment. Then she says, 'Okay, I'll think about it, Grace. But, can I be involved in your plan to expose him?'

'Sure. This isn't about getting Cooper back for what he did, though,' I say. 'This is about preventing it from happening again.'

'Yeah, I know,' she says. 'Ellen told me all about it, and I've got an idea. I've already organised a couple of friends here to help me,' she says.

'Okay, well, the plan is to have the clips up by tomorrow night, so if you could do the same?'

'Yep, will do. And Grace?'

'Yes?' I say.

'It's nice to talk to you. Let's do it again soon, yeah?'

'For sure.' I hang up the phone. 'Mikaela's keen to be involved,' I say. 'She's going to put up a clip of her own.'

'Maybe it will inspire others to do the same,' Ellen says.

I shrug. 'All I know is, knowledge is power. If girls know what Cooper is like, they'll be wary. And maybe there are others out there, staying quiet about what's happened to them in relationships, who'll be inspired to do something similar.'

'And maybe force some decency into the guy at the same time,' Nikki adds.

Nikki takes her phone out of her back pocket and holds it out for us to see. 'It's time.'

'Look, I want to take the fall for this on my own. Cooper is already targeting me, I don't need him targeting you guys too. Especially you, Ellen.'

'Yeah, agreed,' Nikki says. 'We don't need any extra pressure being added to that tender heart of yours.'

Ellen laughs. 'Do you mean physically or metaphorically?'

'Both,' Nikki and I say at the same time.

'Okay,' I say. 'We'll do all the filming on my phone. And both of you, complete silence while we record, okay? Everyone will assume at least one of you is involved, so don't give them any clues as to which one of you it is.' I pause and look at the girls. 'Are you sure we should be doing this? I don't want to see you guys get hurt.'

Ellen squeezes my hand. 'This *is* a good plan, Grace. We need to do this. I don't care about the consequences; the world needs to know what type of person Cooper Dally is, so no one else gets treated like you and Mikaela have been.'

'I've got nothing to lose anyway,' Nikki says. 'You girls are my rock. It's all or nothing; I'm with you a hundred per cent.'

I close my eyes. 'Okay. Let's do this.'

We head out into the warm Queensland day. As we begin the walk, I regret wearing jeans—I don't want to be all sweaty on the video. Ellen is also looking uncomfortable in her skinny jeans.

'It's a bit of a walk,' I say. 'Mostly uphill from here on. Maybe I should call Lisa Marie and see if she can drive us? It's warmer than I thought it was going to be.'

'We'll be right,' Nikki says. 'We are women! Hear us roar!'

Ellen and I burst out laughing. 'True,' I say. 'But Ellen has to be careful about walking too far, especially uphill.'

'I'll be right,' Ellen says with a chuckle. 'My doctor says my heart is heaps better lately. Besides, it's more of a danger if I'm given a sudden fright; I just can't walk very far because I get super tired. It's not going to land me in hospital or anything.'

The hike to Cooper's house in the hills is pretty intense, and we have to make frequent stops for Ellen to rest. It makes for great views, but we're pretty spent by the time we get there.

'Okay,' Nikki says, bending over to catch her breath. 'We're here now. Let's do it.'

'Are you okay, Ellen?' I ask. 'You're really pale.'

Ellen nods. 'Just dizzy. Go on, do the filming.'

'I'm all red in the face, aren't I?' I say. There's moisture under my arms, despite the antiperspirant I'd put on this morning. 'I want to wait until I don't look so ridiculous.'

'You don't look that bad, Grace,' Nikki says. 'Not as bad as Ellen, anyway.'

Ellen laughs.

'Yeah, but Ellen has an excuse. I'm just hugely unfit.'

Ellen sits down in the gutter. Nikki elbows me and whispers, 'I think we should just do it. Probably best to get Ellen home.'

I position myself out the front of Cooper's house. Nikki takes my phone and holds a thumb up to show she's hit record. I hold up a sign that says, *A lesson in trust*. I hold up another sign. This one says, *He'd asked me to be his girlfriend*. As Nikki films, I drop the first sign to reveal another. *Even said he loved me*. I rip the page up. The next one says, *He hit me*. Then, *He tried to rape me*. And the final card, *No means No. Coercion is Rape*. Nikki stops the recording.

'Then, after the photos, I'll hold up the red dress,' I say. 'It's got a big rip down the side from that night, so it will be pretty dramatic.'

'Awesome,' Nikki says. 'I love how you ripped up the *he loved me* page. That was great.'

Ellen's wheezing as she speaks. 'Which photos did you decide you'd put in it?'

'A few of Cooper and I together from his party,' I say. 'Someone must have taken them as we were walking around meeting everyone. I got them off his Facebook page, but they're nice photos. And of course, I'm wearing the red dress in them, so it will tie it together.'

'And how are you going to end the video?' Nikki asks.

'I'm not sure yet. When we get back to mine, I thought I'd record a little spiel about how having sex with someone who doesn't want it is rape, and encourage everyone to go to the police with their story.'

Nikki nods. 'That's awesome, Grace.'

'And then you'll start the hashtag?' Nikki says.

'Yeah, I'll add it to the end of the clip. Lisa Marie has organised some girls from Year 12 to comment with the hashtags to get it going. I was thinking simply #Voles to link it in with Cooper's. And also use that celebrity one, #MeToo, and get views that way.'

Nikki rolls up the signs and puts them in her backpack. 'And whose account will you upload it to?'

I feel a smirk sneaking across my lips. 'I've created a new YouTube account just for this project. I've called the account Memphis Grace.'

'Huh?' Nikki asks, her head tilted.

'It's a nickname Tom gave me. I didn't get it at first. But, you know how Graceland is the name of Elvis' mansion? It's in Memphis, Tennessee. Tom calls me Memphis Grace because I don't like people outside my family calling me Graceland, so he thinks it's a kind of in-between name.'

'That's cute,' Nikki says.

'I don't get it. In between what?' Ellen asks.

'Not quite Graceland, but not Grace, either. And that's who I think I am at the moment. I've been so busy trying to not be Graceland, that I've become someone else. Someone I don't like as much. As Memphis Grace, I am moving back—I'm somewhere in the middle.'

'By exposing Cooper?' Ellen says.

'By reminding people that we can become whatever— whoever—we chose to be, even if bad stuff happens along the way. Just like Elvis' mansion Graceland reminds the people that they can become whatever they want, despite what they were born into.'

'And how Cooper doing bad stuff isn't going to stop you from doing everything you want to do,' Ellen says.

'Exactly,' I say.

'It would be awesome,' Nikki says, 'if we could get Cooper to come out of the house, like super-mad, to show the world what he's really like.'

I shrug. 'I could phone him, let him know I'm out the front.' I laugh. 'I'm sure that would set him off.'

Ellen shakes her head. 'Bad idea.'

'Ellen, are you sure you're okay?' I ask.

She nods. 'That last hill was full-on. I haven't pushed myself that hard for a long time and I'm having trouble catching my breath. I might just call Brad and ask him to come get me. Justin is home this weekend with his car.'

'Sure, good idea,' I say. Ellen stands up and walks over to a nearby tree, while Nikki and I take her place in the gutter out the front of Cooper's house. The sun is colouring in the sky with pinks and purples. 'This sure is a nice part of the world to live.'

Ellen joins us. 'Brad can't get me. His parents aren't home and Justin is at uni today.' She still sounds out of breath. 'I think I stressed him out by calling him.'

'I could call Lisa Marie?'

Ellen nods. 'I might need you to, if that's okay.'

'Sure.'

I call Lisa Marie, but she's just starting a shift. 'Tom's dropping me off, though,' she says. 'He says he's happy to come get you all.'

I bite my lip and look at Ellen. 'Sure. Thanks, that would be great.'

The three of us sit in silence. 'Do you think,' Nikki asks, 'that Mikaela really meant it when she took those tablets?'

I shrug.

'She was pretty messed up,' Ellen says. 'Cooper was playing all sorts of mind games on her, as well as what he did to her physically.'

'How do you know?' I ask.

Ellen shrugs. 'I never said anything, because I didn't want you guys to be mad at me. And it wasn't my story to tell.' I can still hear the wheezing. 'Mikaela rang me after she got out of hospital. She'd been in the psych ward for about a week. She said the doctor was helping her to work through all the lies Cooper had been telling her about herself.' Ellen takes a few shallow breaths. 'It was sad.'

I jump to my feet. 'Oh, he just makes me so mad!' I pace back and forth. 'I can't believe we got to this stage. Promise me, girls; promise we'll tell each other about what's going on in our lives. That we'll be honest with each other. Promise?'

'Sure,' Nikki says.

'In that case,' Ellen says. 'There's something I probably need to tell you both.'

Suddenly a door slams and Cooper bursts onto his front porch. He's swearing his head off in some sort of rage. He makes eye contact with me and rushes straight in our direction, a baseball bat rising skyward in his hand.

I grab Ellen up out of the gutter and pull at Nikki. 'Run!' I scream.

We take off down the street, my feet struggling to keep up with the sharp descent of the hill and the gravity pulling me down it. Ellen's face has gone deathly pale. Cooper is not far behind us, still swearing and waving the bat. We're halfway down the hill when Tom's car comes around the corner.

He pulls into the kerb and jumps out of the car. 'Grace,' he says, his eyes wide as he looks at Ellen. 'Are you okay? What's going on?'

Ellen falls towards the car.

I look back, but Cooper isn't there anymore. 'Cooper,' I say, bent over, catching my breath. 'He was chasing us. With a bat.'

Tom helps Ellen into the back of his car. 'What, Cooper Dally?'

I nod. 'He's a jerk.'

Tom tilts his head. 'Yeah, I kinda knew that already.'

Nikki is tapping Ellen on the face. 'Something is wrong with Ellen. She won't open her eyes.'

'No shit,' says Tom. 'What's wrong with her?'

'She has a heart condition. It looks like she's passed out.'

I climb into the car. How did Cooper know we were there? Would Brad have called Cooper to tell him? But nothing else matters now.

'We need to get Ellen to the hospital,' I say. 'Fast.'

Chapter 42

The next few hours fade in and out; some things are real, others surely couldn't be. Like the look on Ellen's mum's face as she rushes into the hospital emergency room, past us, and through the doors we were told to stay out of.

People rush about, eerily similar to the last time we were here, to hear what had happened with Mikaela. Except this time, we know why Ellen is here. And we know it must be serious.

Brad arrives at some point. I don't know how long we'd been there for. Not long after, Tom leaves, promising to get some takeaway and bring it back for us.

As people come and go through the Emergency room doors, Mr Maple appears, dressed in a suit, his eyes wide; Ellen's younger sister, Aimee, is trailing behind him like a lost kitten. She joins us on the seat as her dad disappears behind the same doors.

'Hey,' I say, rubbing my thumbs into the palms of my hands.

'Hi, Grace.' She smiles at Nikki. 'I don't suppose you guys know what's going on?' Tears are forming in her eyes.

I put my arm around her. 'Not really. Ellen kinda passed out on us this afternoon.'

'Mum said this might happen,' Aimee says.

'Oh?'

'I heard Mum and Dad having a fight one night when they thought we were asleep. They were fighting about Ellen. About whether she should be allowed to go out now.'

'Oh,' I say.

'They were fighting a bit about you too,' she says, looking at Brad.

'Yeah,' Brad says. 'Ellen told me about it.'

It's sometime later that Mr Maple, Ellen's dad, comes back through the doors and stands in front of us. His face is solemn and tired. Aimee flings her arms around him. 'Thanks for staying, everyone,' he says.

'What's going on, Mr Maple?' Brad asks.

He sits down beside us, pulling Aimee onto his knee. She's fourteen years old, but somehow it looks completely normal for her dad to be wrapping his arms around her. 'Her heart is doing some pretty crazy stuff,' he says.

'She's going to be okay, though, isn't she?' Brad seems to be begging more than asking.

Mr Maple's whole face droops. 'I'm sure she will be, Brad. The doctors are going to do some pretty major surgery in the next couple of days to try to make it right. But she's tough, our Ellen. She'll pull through.' His eyes are red and puffy around the edges.

'Can we see her?' I ask.

'Just quickly and one at a time, once they've got her settled into Intensive Care.' Mr Maple looks at Aimee. 'You can come in, of course, sweetheart.'

Mr Maple takes us to a different part of the hospital and into a different waiting room. It's not long before he comes back to tell me I can see Ellen.

My breath catches as I walk into the room. She looks tiny on the hospital's long white bed, tubes all over her, monitors beeping. The glaring light illuminates Mrs Maple, sobbing, as her head rests by Ellen's side. I cough, and Mrs Maple looks at me, beckoning me to come in.

I walk over to Ellen and place my hand on her arm. She opens her eyes and moves her mouth slightly. Her face has no colour, like the sheets around her.

'Hey, drama queen,' I say.

She chuckles but it makes her cough.

'Hey,' she says. It's like a whisper of trees.

I bend down to kiss her. 'You get better real quick, okay? You know I can't survive in this world without you.'

She nods.

'We're only allowed in for a second,' I say, 'but you knew we'd all be here, didn't you?'

She nods again.

I go to stand up straight but her fingers are holding my shirt, just lightly, but enough to pull me back in.

'Make the video,' she whispers. I look at her. 'Be Memphis Grace.' I promise her I will and she lets go of my top.

Tom comes back with a variety of noodles; we sit and eat them in silence in the ICU waiting room. He eventually stands and says he's going to head home. Nikki and I pop in to say a quick goodbye to Ellen, and follow Tom out to his car. But we leave Brad behind; he refuses to leave the hospital without Ellen.

We drop Nikki home, then head to my place. My phone, with the afternoon's footage, burns in the pocket of the jeans Cooper paid for. As Tom pulls up out the front, I thank him for all he did.

'No problem, Memphis Grace.' He beams. 'We are going to be officially family soon, after all.'

'Oh, yes, of course, congratulations on the baby,' I say.

He nods. 'I can't wait. I always wanted kids and I knew Lisa Marie was the girl I wanted that life with. She's the best.'

I nod and smile. 'You're a good guy, Tom. I'm sorry for giving you a hard time in the past.'

'All good, sis,' he says, a cheeky smile on his face. 'And hey, I really hope your friend is going to be okay. I don't reckon I've seen anyone look that sick before.'

'Thanks. I really hope so too.'

I walk up the front path of my house and pause. I look at Jesse's blue chair and wander over to sit in it.

The air has cooled a little and the stars are joining with the moon to diffuse a gentle light over the front yard. I think of Mikaela; how she ran away without telling anyone the truth about Cooper— and how one person can tell a story, but its power grows when other voices join it. Ellen's words repeat in my mind: *Be Memphis Grace.* She's right. I have to tell my story and remind the world that coercion is rape, and it should be reported.

I head straight to my bedroom, open my laptop and log in to my Memphis Grace account. #Voles, here we come.

Chapter 43

'We're over five hundred views and thirty #MeToos already,' Nikki says, as school carries on around us. 'Mikaela's clip is awesome and has heaps of views too. Did you see it?'

'I did,' I say. 'She did a great job. Very powerful. She's been texting just about every day too, to find out how Ellen is. I think the whole thing has really shocked her.'

'Yeah. It has for all of us.'

We walk around the school athletics track. I can see the substitute teacher yelling at us from the other side of the track, but I pretend I don't. Walking the track with Nikki seems a much better option than the ball skills everyone else has moved on to.

'I have something to add to the hashtag stuff too,' Nikki says. 'Another video. But I thought I'd better talk to you about it first.'

'What is it?'

She pulls out her phone and hands it to me. A video starts playing. It is jumpy footage, but I can see it's Cooper, running at us with a bat in his hand.

'How did you—?'

'I started videoing when he came out of the house. I kept it going as we were running.'

I can hear our footsteps amongst heavy breathing, and me, asking Ellen if she is okay.

None of us are in the footage. Every now and then Cooper's face flashes across the screen.

'Do you think it is, you know, morally okay for us to add this to the hashtags?' Nikki asks. 'You can't see Ellen.'

'I had no idea you had this, Nikki. Can you send me a copy?'

'Sure.'

We receive the expected lecture from the substitute teacher, then part to go to our different Science classes. But my heart is not in it. No amount of evidence against Cooper will help Ellen get through her operation.

The science lab feels empty with neither Ellen or Jack sitting beside me. Jack has hardly been at school since the *Conversations with Voles* clips were emailed out. Ellen's group looks lost, scrambling on computers to pull together their presentation.

I move my shoulders around in an attempt to loosen the tension. Mr Van Hayden looks as lost as the rest of us.

'Class,' he says. A few people stop, but most people ignore his attempt to gain their attention. He tries again, 'Class!' Everyone stops and looks this time. He runs his hands through his hair. 'I understand the events of the weekend, with Ellen being in hospital, have impacted on some of you substantially.' He looks at me. 'For those of you directly affected, I'd like to give you the opportunity to delay today's presentations.' He looks over at Ellen's group. 'Michael, I take it your group is not fully prepared?'

Michael holds his hands up. 'Ellen has our finished video on her laptop. We have bits and pieces, but Ellen was in charge of pulling it all together.'

'All good,' Mr Van Hayden says. 'We'll talk after class. Okay?'

The group looks relieved as they take their seats behind the bench.

'I see Brad Armstrong is away,' Mr Van says, looking to the group up the back.

Joe says, 'He's been at the hospital since it happened, sir. Says he's not leaving without Ellen.'

I swallow the lump in my throat and beg my eyes to not release the forming tears.

Mr Van Hayden continues looking from group to group. 'Hayley Johnson's group; who's in that?'

A few people, including Joe, raise their hands.

'You'll need to sort out your project without her.' There hasn't been anything officially said, but everyone knows she's been asked not to come back until the police investigations have been completed. Thanks to my email to Mr Reyl, the police have been investigating her involvement in Jack's car accident, as well as the original Voles videos. Well, according to Miss Krensky, who wasn't supposed to tell us anything.

We haven't heard anything about Cooper, but he hasn't been back at school since, either.

A knock at the lab door takes Mr Van Hayden away for a moment. He returns with Jack hobbling in behind him. Jack's head is down. He doesn't look up the whole time, even though he sits just two chairs down from me.

Mr Van Hayden looks at Jack and then at me. 'Would you like more time too?'

I look at Latisha and Seb, and then I look at Jack. His blond hair is falling down over his face, his thumbs rubbing his palms with great force. He looks emotionally exhausted, just like me.

'I think we should still go ahead, especially since Jack is here. It must have taken a lot for him to come in today.'

Jack's thumbs stop rubbing.

'Thank you, Grace.' Mr Van Hayden gestures to the front of the classroom. 'Would your group like to go first then?'

I pick up my laptop. 'We might as well. As long as Jack and the others don't mind.'

The four of us stand up the front. On the whiteboard beside us, Latisha's first drawing appears on the screen and my voice introduces our presentation. Jack is looking at the floor as my voice reads my lines.

Then Latisha's drawing of a brain flashes across the screen.

It has been discovered that children with autism have larger-than-normal brains. Jack's voice says on the video. *One theory is that this is because when the brain is growing, it doesn't cut-out the unneeded connections that other people's brains do. Because of this, people with autism have brains that often go into overdrive, taking in too much of the information around them.*

My voice comes on as a large blue and pink DNA strand, like a ladder, appears across the screen. *Although autism is considered a neuro-developmental disorder, there is evidence to suggest it is genetic, often passed down from one parent to one or more of their children. Researchers today are finding links between changes in the DNA of people with autism, substantiating the theory it can be hereditary. Some even say it is the next stage in human evolution.*

The class erupts in whispers. Jack's face glows but continues to focus on the floor.

His voice comes on again. *Rather than it being seen as another form of disability, people with autism are increasingly recognised for their heightened ability to focus, problem solve and over-empathise with others in their social network and workplaces.*

The video continues but I stop hearing our voices. The class is captivated, their attention moving between the video and Jack, who is now looking up at the ceiling. I hear my voice mention Jesse, and Down syndrome, but I can't watch it. I stand back behind the rest of my group and lower my eyes, so I don't have to see anyone looking at me.

At the end of the video, the class erupts in enthusiastic clapping. Seb's song plays and in the final moments, the credits roll, causing another burst of applause. A few of the groups even come up the front to shake everyone's hands and congratulate them on the presentation. Three girls are talking to Jack; he looks like he wants to sink into the linoleum. Perhaps the *Conversations with Voles* videos have done more for him than against him.

'I'm very impressed,' Mr Van Hayden says. 'With all of you.'

He asks us to return to our seats. 'I'll look forward to seeing all your learning portfolios now.'

Jack casts a sideways glance at me.

'I know, I know,' I say. 'We'll sort something out, okay?'

Jack just looks away.

As Science ends, Jack heads out to meet his mother, who is waiting outside the lab. I rush to catch up with them as they walk off.

'Jack, wait,' I call. He slows but doesn't stop. His mother turns and frowns at me.

'Mrs Oskar, hi,' I say.

She gives me a half smile.

'Please, can't Jack stay just a little longer?' I say. 'We still have to hand in our portfolios of learning to Mr Van Hayden.'

'I don't have anything to hand in,' Jack says, his eyes to the ground.

'That's not true,' I say. 'We've been working hard to get through it and haven't got much left to do. I thought we could work on it together at lunch. Maybe Miss Krensky would even let us work on it in the library during English.'

'I'm not sure I'm keen for Jack to be doing any more study sessions today, Grace,' Mrs Oskar says. 'It was enough for him to come in for the presentation.'

'I know, and I'm so proud of him for doing that. But please, the portfolio is also important for him to be able to get a good grade this term.'

'Okay,' Jack says.

'Jack,' his mum says. 'Are you sure? I mean when you think of all you've been through …'

'I'll stay,' he says. He looks at my cheek. 'But no recording. At all. Of any kind.'

'Agreed, Jack. Totally. Not even a little bit. Okay?'

Jack nods.

'I won't let anything happen to him, Mrs Oskar,' I say. 'I promise.'

'I'll come back after lunch then, shall I?' Mrs Oskar says.

Jack mumbles, 'Thanks.'

'Meet me in the library,' I say. 'I'm just going to tell Mr Van what we're doing, so he knows he'll have your portfolio by the end of the day, okay?'

When I get to the library, Jack is sitting at the far end, down near where the Year 7s hang out.

I smirk. 'Not taking any chances, hey?' I say.

He looks around. 'There's no way you could have a video set up here that I can't see.'

'I really am very sorry, Jack,' I say. 'And I promise you, there are no videos, no recorders, nothing. We're just going to get as much information out of your brain onto my laptop as we can in this time, okay?'

Jack seems to relax a little.

'Okay, let's start with, *What is replication?*'

Jack takes a deep breath. 'Replication is when a double-stranded DNA molecule produces two DNA molecules which are exactly the same as the originals. That means they have to contain the same genetic information as the original, or parent, cells contain.'

We work through the worksheets: me asking the questions, Jack talking as I type. Mostly I can't keep up with the speed of his words, but I don't care, so long as Mr Van Hayden was true to his word and is standing behind the wall in the entrance way to the library listening, as he promised he would be.

When the bell rings to announce the end of the break, I pause. Jack stops talking. 'You have an amazing brain, Jack. You know that?'

He looks up at the ceiling.

'Jack, why couldn't you tell Mr Van Hayden all this?'

Jack shrugs. 'I can't talk to him properly. He makes my brain turn foggy and I forget things.'

'You're usually pretty good in class, though.'

'Maybe,' he says. 'We should finish. Mum will be here soon.'

'I think maybe we have enough.' I raise my voice. 'What do you think, Mr Van Hayden? Is that enough?'

Mr Van Hayden comes out from around the corner with a clipboard in his hand. He looks at Jack and then at me. 'Yes, thank you, Grace. That is plenty.' He looks again at Jack. 'You really know your stuff, Mr Oskar. I've caught glimpses of it before, but nothing like you just showed me while talking to Grace here. Definitely enough for me to give you a very good grade, and highly recommend you continue studying Science next year.'

Jack's mouth is open wide, his eyes smiling with the rest of his face.

'And me?' I ask.

'You've proved me right, Grace. I knew there was more to you than you were letting the world see. I haven't looked at your portfolio yet, but the way you've pulled this group together has been remarkable.'

'The miracle you were looking for?'

Mr Van Hayden snaps shut his clipboard. 'Yes, Grace, very much the miracle I was hoping for.'

Chapter 44

Jack is sitting on the library chair rocking slightly while we wait for his mum. He's not comfortable around me anymore. I've broken things between us. Mr Van Hayden leaves us sitting alone in our silence, despite our success, our victory.

Ellen should have been out of surgery by now. I pull out my phone and flick open Facebook, but there is no update on her page from her mum. I bite my thumbnail so short it hurts.

Jack has his head down.

'I hope that was okay,' I say, 'you know, to do that with Mr Van Hayden. No videos, no recordings.'

He places folded hands on the table. 'I guess I should say thanks.'

'It's great you'll get to do those science subjects you want to do next year.'

He nods. 'I don't think I'll be coming back to this school, though. Mum's talking about home-schooling me.'

'Really? Jack, why? After all your mum did to get you to come to a regular school, moving up from Victoria and everything?'

He looks at me but doesn't say anything. I know why.

'We don't know what is going to happen with Cooper,' I say. 'Hayley's gone. Cooper might leave too.'

'Why would he do that?'

I tilt my head. 'I've started something; maybe it will stop him from wanting to come to school.'

Jack puts his head down. 'I don't think revenge is okay.'

'I'm not getting revenge, Jack. I don't want anyone else to go through what I've been through these past few months.' I open my backpack and pull out a parcel. 'I got something for you, by the way,' I say.

He frowns at me. 'Why?'

'Friends do that,' I say. 'They see things that remind them of the person, and they buy it for them. Especially if it might be funny.'

Jack looks at the parcel sitting on the table.

'I found it at an op shop. It didn't cost me much. Are you going to open it?'

He shrugs but picks it up. He pulls the book out of the wrapping. '*The Art of Conversation*, by Judy Apps,' he says. He opens it to the chapter content.

'I know you're still trying to work out the whole *how people talk* thing,' I say. 'I thought it might help.'

'Thanks,' he says, though he doesn't look very happy. 'And why might this be funny?'

I turn the book on its side and point to the binder. 'It has a purple spine. For the bookshelf in your bedroom.'

I think I almost see him crack a smile.

My phone vibrates. I look at the screen. 'It's Ellen,' I say, my heart in my throat. I swipe it open. 'Hello?'

'Grace?'

My heart sinks. 'Oh. Hi, Mrs Maple. I thought you were going to be Ellen.'

'Ellen wanted me to call you,' she says. 'She's come out of surgery.'

'Oh, good,' I say. 'She was in there for longer than I expected.'

'Yes, she was,' her mother says. 'The surgery didn't go well. I'm ringing you because Ellen asked for you after she woke up.'

'Can I visit her?'

Jack's eyes are on my phone.

'Yes, she is very keen to see you.'

'Okay. I'll come straight after school.'

'It would be better if you could come straight away,' she says. 'If you can get here. If your mother wouldn't mind you missing some school.'

'Why's that?'

'I think she'd like to see you as soon as possible, that's all,' she says. I look at my watch. Mum should be getting ready for work. 'I'll do my best. Thanks for ringing.'

I hang up. Jack keeps his eyes on the phone. 'Is Ellen okay?'

'I'm not sure,' I say. 'I don't think so.' I run my hand through my hair. 'Mrs Maple says I should go up to the hospital as soon as I can.'

Jack looks worried. 'I'm sure she'll be okay,' he says and places his hand on my arm.

Mrs Oskar walks into the library and looks around frantically. She heads over to Jack and I, and frowns when she sees Jack's hand on my arm.

'I know I'm early, but we need to go now, Jack,' she says. 'We have to go to the hospital.'

I look at Jack. 'Ellen?' I turn to Mrs Oskar. 'You know Ellen?'

'We go to the same church,' she says.

I stand up with Jack. 'Mrs Maple just rang me,' I say, 'asking me to come to the hospital too.' My eyes plead with Mrs Oskar. 'But I have no way to get there. Could you take me with you, please?'

Mrs Oskar shakes her head. 'No, I don't think so. We'd need to get permission from your mother.'

'Please,' I say. 'Ellen is one of my best friends. She asked her mother to ring me specifically.'

Mrs Oskar looks at her watch. 'Fine. But if we can't get hold of your mother, I'm not hanging around to wait, understand?'

I grab my stuff and rush out of the library, straight to the office.

Chapter 45

Ellen looks the same after the surgery as she had before.

Mr Maple looks forlorn as he sits on the side of Ellen's bed, but he smiles when Jack and I walk in. 'Hey, guys,' he says. 'Sorry, but they've given her some pain relief, so she's just gone to sleep.'

'How is she?' Jack asks. Her eyes are closed and she's lying motionless.

Mr Maple tilts his head from side to side. 'She's not real great, Jack. She'll be glad to see you both, though, if you don't mind waiting?'

'Of course.'

'You just missed Brad,' he says. 'He's gone home to shower. I don't think he got any sleep last night.'

'It's really great of you to let Brad be here,' I say. 'It must be a bit weird for you guys.'

He looks confused. 'Why's that, Grace?'

'Well, because they're not supposed to be dating. Not that they are, not officially. Not until Ellen is seventeen.'

'Why not until she's seventeen?'

It's my turn to be confused. 'Because she's not allowed to date until she's seventeen?'

He shakes his head. 'But we've never said that.'

My jaw drops open. 'No dating, no parties. That's what Ellen said.'

'As difficult as it was sometimes, we trusted Ellen to make the right decisions for herself, Grace. If she had those rules, they were rules she put on herself. Not us.'

'So, all those parties she said no to, that was her choice?'

'I guess so,' Mr Maple says. 'We just thought she wasn't invited out much.'

I shake my head and smile. 'That's our Ellen.'

A nurse comes in, pushes some buttons on Ellen's monitor, then leaves again.

'She looks so pale,' I say.

'The operation didn't go as well as the doctors hoped,' Mr Maple says. 'Her heart still isn't doing what it's supposed to.'

I sit in a chair opposite Mr Maple and touch Ellen's hand. It's warm.

'They had planned to do this surgery after she turned eighteen,' Mr Maple says. 'But turns out we couldn't wait that long. She's been deteriorating the past few months.' Mr Maple has tears running down his face. 'We had to decide whether we let her be a teenager and enjoy life, or wrap her up at home and make her miserable in the hope she'd do better with the operation when she was older. We decided to let her live life.'

'I'm so sorry, Mr Maple,' I say. 'We had no idea. I mean, we knew she had to be careful, but she had told us she'd be okay. I never would have let her come out with us if I knew it would hurt her.'

Mr Maple leans over to rub my hand as I hold on to Ellen's. 'We didn't always approve of the choices she was making, even if she was saying no to parties every now and then. But we needed to let her make some mistakes. You guys let her live a relatively normal life, and we're grateful for that.'

He wipes his face and the tears stop flowing.

'What is going to happen now?' Jack asks from behind me.

'Oh well—' Mr Maple runs his hand down Ellen's face, '—she's been on the organ transplant list for over a year, but now she's been bumped closer to the top. It's a matter of waiting until the right heart comes along.'

Jack's eyes are glued to the ceiling.

'A heart transplant?' I say. 'Aren't they kinda rare?'

'They are. She may have to hang on for a long time yet, Grace. At the moment, this machine is helping to keep her heart beating regularly. But she is weak, as is her heart.'

'Will her heart not just get better, like, on its own?' I ask.

'Well, ideally, yes,' he says. 'It would be great if her heart recovers enough for them to try the same operation again later on, to avoid needing the transplant. But it would take a miracle.'

Jack says, 'We'll give you a break, Mr Maple, and come back in a bit. I'll let Mum know she can pop in, though, if that's okay?'

He nods. 'Ellen usually only sleeps for an hour at a time. I'll let you know when she wakes.'

As Jack and I wait out in the hospital waiting room, my phone buzzes. It's Mikaela.

'Hey,' I say.

'Hey,' Mikaela says. 'How's Ellen going?'

'She's not doing great,' I say. 'She's so pale and is sleeping heaps.'

'Are you at the hospital now?'

'I am.'

'Cool. I'm on my way there.'

'You're on the Sunny Coast?'

'I'm on my way back to see Ellen,' Mikaela says. 'And, to go to the police.'

'Really?' I sit up straight. 'With your story?'

'I'm not promising anything, Grace,' she says. 'But I've talked it over with Mum and Dad and they agree it's the right thing to do. Especially after making those videos, it would be hypocritical to not tell my story after encouraging others to.'

'I'm proud of you.'

'Will you come with me?'

'Of course, I will.' I hang up the phone and do a little fist pump into the air.

Jack gives me a funny look. 'I take it that was Mikaela?'

I nod.

'And she's going to the police?'

'She is.'

Chapter 46

Hospitals are not quiet places, especially the waiting room, but they're horribly lonely. People come and go all the time; doctors, nurses, patients with walkers and family members bustling around them. It's a long wait. Mrs Maple is in an adjoining room, sitting at a table writing something down. She smiled when we came in but hasn't spoken to us. She's been crying the whole time, so I figure it's better to leave her to whatever she's doing.

After a while, she heads back into Ellen's room, and Jack and I are left on our own. I'm grateful for his company and for the fact that he is happy to sit with his own thoughts, as am I.

A good half hour passes before Mrs Maple returns to the waiting room.

'Grace,' she says. 'And Jack. We're hoping you might be able to sit with Ellen for a while in case she wakes up.'

'Of course.' I jump up, followed by Jack. 'Anything to help.'

'Mr Maple and I need to meet with her team of doctors and it's better if we're not all in her room when we do so. But I don't want her left alone.'

'We'd love to,' I say. 'Where's Aimee?'

'She went with Brad. They'll be back in an hour or so. The cuisine in the hospital cafeteria is okay in small doses but I think they were both keen for some proper food and showers.'

While Jack and I sit by Ellen's bedside, she stirs and opens her eyes.

'Ellen,' I say. 'Hey, lovely.' She frowns and blinks a number of times. I rub her hand. 'It's Grace. And Jack.'

She looks from one face to the other. 'Hey.' Her voice is barely a whisper.

'How you feeling?'

She smiles a little. 'A bit so-so.'

Tears flood my eyes. 'I'm so sorry, Ellen. We never should have had you walking around or put you in danger like that.'

Ellen moves her hand onto mine. 'It was my choice, Grace. I could have said no.' She closes her eyes for a moment. 'I feel bad for putting you through that. And Brad.'

'Looks like he's sticking by you.'

She coughs a little, wincing as she does. 'He's a keeper. But he feels as though this is all his fault. He told Cooper we were there that day.'

'What!' I couldn't believe it. First the emails, if it was Brad who'd hacked the system, and now this? Ellen brushes my hand with hers, but I can't hide the anger I know is on my face. 'If Cooper hadn't come rushing out of the house like that …'

'No, Grace. No *if*. This isn't Brad's fault.' Her voice is forceful. 'He didn't know why we were at Cooper's house, he just knew I wasn't well and needed help. He was really worried about me.'

I hang my head. I'd been running through every single *what if* since Saturday afternoon. Ellen closes her eyes again. I can barely see her chest rising and falling, and she is so pale and still. I wonder if she's gone back to sleep when she says, 'Did you get the video done yet?'

'Yes,' I nod. 'It's uploaded and is already taking off.'

'Good. We need to make sure the girls around here are aware of the type of guy Cooper is—to stop him.'

'Oh, don't worry,' I say. 'I'm telling them. The hashtags are working well, but not as well as word of mouth. I've had heaps of girls, people I don't even know, message me with support or to say they're going to the police with their own story. Including Mikaela.'

Ellen raises her eyebrows. 'Really?'

'She's on her way back to town to see you, and we'll go to the police station together for her to file her own report.'

Ellen sighs and coughs a little. 'I'm proud of you, Grace. You've got guts.'

'Either that or I'm crazy.'

'Or,' Jack says, 'a little bit of both.'

Chapter 47

Ellen's recovery is slow and painful. She is out of hospital within a couple of weeks, but it is months before she is able to leave the house. She hasn't come back to school, leaving Nikki and I on our own.

There's been other changes at school as well. After Mikaela went to the police with her story, Cooper was charged with rape and attempted rape. Between that and the Voles videos, the school suggested he didn't come back until the court case was over. Even though Mikaela did an amazing job testifying against him in court, he was only given a suspended sentence. My testimony supported Mikaela's story, but Cooper's lawyers convinced everyone Cooper didn't really know that what he was doing was wrong. The school thought differently, and expelled him.

Brad ended up leaving around the same time. His parents were convinced he'd managed to get himself in with the wrong crowd again, and moved him to the Catholic College down the road. Although, I'm still not sure about Brad and his role in all that happened, moving him was hardly necessary with Cooper out of the picture. Brad seemed like such a genuine guy. I'm not sure if he rang Cooper on purpose to tell him we were at his place, or if it was out of concern like Ellen believes, but for Ellen's sake I'm letting it go.

All our videos got taken down off social media but they did the job. Girls and guys are sharing their stories of being coerced into sleeping with their partner before they were ready. Mikaela had led the charge of calling coercion by its real name …

Rape.

School is winding up for the Christmas holiday break now, and things are easing for me. People are still talking about the videos, but I've been able to let it go. It isn't our campaign anymore. It isn't about Cooper. It isn't about me. It's about trying to be a young adult in today's world and protecting those who need to be protected. It's about everyone.

And I'm glad to have it all behind us. Getting Ellen better, getting on with life and *following that dream* of mine; passing Years 11 and 12, going to uni and helping others are what's important. Having the big house and money and clothes, that isn't happiness. Elvis found that out. I'm starting to work it out too.

Mr Van Hayden catches me as I leave the final Form class for the year. 'Grace, are you going away over the break?'

'No, too much happening at home,' I say. 'My family don't really do holidays.'

'Do you have a summer job lined up, then?'

'Not yet. But Lisa Marie has set me up with an interview at her café next week. Hopefully they'll give me a go.'

'How is Lisa Marie?'

'Really well, actually. Only a couple of months to go until the baby is due. She's really happy.'

'Good. And I see you have your report there.'

I pull the white envelope out from under my arm and nod.

'Have you looked at it?'

'No. Thought I'd read it on the bus home.'

'Well, I hope you'll be pleased with your Science grades. Certainly, they're enough to get you into Biology next year.'

'Thanks, sir.' I play with a piece of bark with my foot. 'I, err, I wanted to say thank you. For putting me in a group with Jack.'

'You weren't too happy with the idea at the start.'

'I wasn't, but he grew on me.' I curl my lips. 'And it's been really great talking about Jesse again. Jack has amazing memories of him. He remembers things so much more clearly than I do.'

'I'm really glad to hear that, Grace. You have a good summer break, won't you?'

'Thanks, sir. You too.'

Chapter 48

I finish my shift at the café and ask if Lisa Marie can drive me to Maroochydore Surf Club.

'Are you sure?' she says. 'Isn't that, like, where you used to hang out with the boy band?'

'Yeah. It's just another step, another healing thing I've been meaning to do since the court case.'

Lisa Marie barely fits behind the steering wheel of Tom's car these days. 'I've got so much to do before the baby comes, so I'll be around the shops for a while. I can pick you up when you're done if you need. Just call.'

'Nah, all good. Mum's going to come and get me.' I flash a couple of yellow squares from inside my handbag.

'You got your learners?'

'Finally. Mum's going to take me for my first driving lesson this afternoon.'

'Nice.' Lisa Marie pulls up along the esplanade and rubs her large belly. 'I can't wait to finish up work. Though, I gotta admit I'm going to miss hanging out with you.'

I lean over and give her an awkward hug. 'Same. You promised I could be there when the baby comes—so the slightest twinge, and you call me, okay?'

I open the car door.

She puts her hand on my arm. 'Are you sure you don't want me to come with you?'

'I'll be fine.'

'Okay, but I won't be far away, so yell if you need me.'

As I round the path leading onto the beach, the sand whips around my ankles. Images of that day, back when Copper Dally came bustling into my life, fill my mind. I lower my glasses over my eyes and place a large floppy hat on my head. There are people everywhere. Families, young people, surf lifesavers. Girls in bikinis and boys in board shorts. I take a moment to look over at the surf club, before turning to head down the beach.

I don't get far before I see some familiar faces. Brad Armstrong and Cooper Dally are standing in amongst a group of bikini-clad girls. My chest tightens. The girls speak in strong accents and laugh as they head back down to the water.

Brad says hello. Cooper looks the other way.

'Hi,' I say. 'How's your holidays?'

Brad runs a hand through his thick hair. 'Okay, I guess.'

'Have you seen much of Ellen?'

Brad shrugs. 'It's a bit weird around her parents. They're cool and all, but I can't help but feel like they blame me for her getting so sick.'

'Yeah, well, I was going over there every few days, but it's been tricky over the holidays, now I'm working. She's getting stronger, though. She misses you.'

Brad nods.

'She's meeting a few of us this morning at cafe De Ju Vu, if you wanted to join us.'

'When's that?'

I look at my watch. 'In a few minutes, actually.'

Brad looks at his feet as he makes patterns in the sand.

I gesture toward Cooper standing nearby. 'I didn't realise you were still hanging out with Cooper.'

He looks surprised. 'No, actually, today's the first time, since …' He looks out over the water. 'We came across each other at the beach this morning. It's been a bit weird seeing him again after everything that's happened.'

'Why's that?'

Brad gives a melancholy smile. 'There's a lot of regrets, Grace. Losing Cooper as a friend isn't one of them.'

I look again at Cooper, knowing I don't have to acknowledge him; knowing I could ignore him, or give him a hateful stare. But instead I adjust my disposition, lower my shoulders and widen my lips, so sweetness leaks from between my teeth. 'How have you been, Cooper? I hear you're leaving town. Another new school to get used to?'

He looks at me. 'It's just school. No doubt as useless at one as it is at the other.'

'Fair enough,' I laugh. 'Nothing new there … for you anyway.'

He looks around uncomfortably.

'You know, you're lucky you only had to leave town,' I say.

He sighs deeply, the puff of air dispersing his lips. 'I don't have to leave town, we're choosing to. There's much more money to be made in the city than here. And remember, *Graceland*, despite all your accusations, no one found me guilty of anything other than having a temper.'

'Oh, I don't know. I think the court proved pretty clearly that you're an ignorant, and somewhat stupid, jerk.'

Beside me, Brad stifles a chuckle. Cooper glares at him and walks away.

I breathe in the warm air, filling my lungs and holding it, then releasing it.

I take a step backwards. 'Well, good to see you, Brad. Enjoy the rest of the summer break.'

'Grace, wait.'

I stop.

'Maybe,' he says, avoiding eye contact with me but looking me in the face at the same time. 'Maybe I'll come along some other time for coffee with you and Ellen. If she wants me there.'

'She'll be very glad to see you, Brad. Whenever you're ready.'

As I walk away, my phone vibrates. I glance at my watch, smile, and swipe the phone to answer it. 'Jack, what's up?'

'Well, I'm bored,' he says.

'Sorry, I am coming,' I say. 'I saw some people and stopped to chat. Are you in the coffee shop already?'

'I am.'

'Is Nikki there yet?'

'She's always late. You know that.'

'And Ellen?'

'Her dad is looking for a park. That's why I rang you.'

I chuckle. 'I'm sorry, I'll be there in a few minutes. It will take that long for Ellen to get herself from the car to the café.'

'Okay.'

'You remember that Mikaela is joining us today as well?'

'I know. You won't be long?'

'I'm almost there. I'll see you in a minute.'

I slip my phone into my bag and head up the warm, soft sand toward the path that leads out to the shops.

Chapter 49

Jack has chosen a table out the front of De Ju Vu.

'We're sitting outside today, Jack?' I say.

He's relieved. 'You're here. Yes, I thought it would be easier for Ellen if we are outside.'

'How are you? Having a good holiday?'

'The same as it was last week, Graceland. Did you come from work?'

I chuckle. 'I did. It was just a three-hour shift and I was on at the same time as Lisa Marie, so that was cool.'

'I like your hat,' he says, pointing to my head.

'Oh,' I take it off and my sunglasses. 'Thanks.' I run my hands through my hair.

'You look pretty,' Jack says.

'Thanks.' I continue to fiddle with my hair.

'Your hair looks fine.'

'Oh, okay,' I muse. Nikki approaches the table and gives me a kiss. She smiles at Jack and he waves stiffly.

She takes up a seat on the other side of me. 'You made it.'

'I did. Is Ellen not here yet?'

I look at Jack, who says, 'Her dad couldn't get a park. I saw them drive by a few times.' He points down the street. 'But that's the car there. I haven't seen them get out yet.'

'I'll go help her,' Nikki says, bounding off.

Nikki returns, pushing Ellen in her wheelchair.

'Hello, beautiful,' I say, kissing her on the cheek.

'Hey, everyone,' Ellen says, waving, her smile taking up half her face.

'The wheels are a nice addition,' I say. 'I've never seen you move so quick.'

Ellen laughs. 'They're awesome. Mostly.' Jack moves a chair and she pulls up to the table. 'Moving through cafés is pretty tricky.'

'Hey, I have some news, everyone,' I say. 'Someone else is joining us today.'

Expectant faces look back at me.

'Mikaela is back in town.'

Nikki looks surprised. 'She is?'

'Yeah, her family got home from picking her up a couple of days ago. And—I think she might be back for good.'

'Are you serious?'

'She said her parents have been impressed with how well she's doing and think they might move her back here.

'That's awesome.'

'I'm going to order a coffee,' Jack says. 'And probably a burger because of that bacon I can smell. I'm starving. Is anyone else ordering?'

Nikki stands up. I hand her some money. 'Can you get me an Earl Grey please? Ellen and I will save the table.' Ellen hands some money over too.

Nikki and Jack disappear into the café. I sit back and let the salty breeze kiss my face. The sky is speckled with clouds which drift lazily across the sky. Nearby, palm trees try to wave but don't manage much movement.

'You doing okay, Graceland?' Ellen asks.

I nod. 'So much better now, seeing you out of the house.'

'You are looking very thoughtful.'

She knows me well. 'I saw a couple of people on the way here.'

'Oh?'

'Brad. And Cooper.'

'Oh,' Ellen says. 'That must have been awkward, seeing Cooper?'

'A little.'

'Is it the first time you've seen him since court?'

'Yeah. It was the first time I'd seen Brad too, since we were all in court together.'

A little spark leaves Ellen's eyes.

'Brad's still not contacting you?'

She shakes her head. 'After all he did while I was first in hospital, I really thought I meant something to him.'

'You do, Ellen. I think he's struggling with his own regrets and feeling guilty about what happened to you.'

'I thought he was a bit torn, between having a fresh start at his new school, and trying to sort himself out.'

'Yes, I got that impression, too.'

'You spoke to him for a while then?'

'I could see the hurt in his eyes when I talked about you.'

Ellen puts her head down.

'Don't give up on him just yet, Ellen.'

I look out across the water and remember us all on the beach that day all those months ago. That day when Brad set his heart on Ellen, and Cooper swept like a hurricane into my life. That day was the start of a horrible train-wreck for me. But it was the start of something beautiful for Ellen.

'He'll come back to you if it was meant to be, Ellen. You're worth too much to not come back for.'

She smiles and wipes a tear from her cheek. 'Maybe.'

Mikaela arrives at the same time that Nikki and Jack return to our table with our drinks. She brightens the mood immediately, as she always did, with stories of her life at boarding school. I'm on my last mouthful of tea when I notice a figure walking towards us. It takes me a moment to realise it's Brad.

I stand up. 'You came.'

'Yeah,' he says, looking at Ellen. 'I figured I could do with some coffee. And some friends. Real friends.' He moves around to her side of the table. 'Do you mind me being here?'

She indicates the seat beside her, and the spark returns to her eyes.

Chapter 50

There's a knock on the door. I leap from my bed and run down the hallway, calling out, 'I'll get it, Mum!'

I open the front door and Jack is standing there. He has a bunch of wildflowers in his hand.

'You brought me flowers, Jack?'

He shifts from one foot to the next. I open the wire door and he goes to hand me the flowers, but then pulls back.

'What?' I ask.

'Um. The flowers … I brought them for your mum.'

I burst out laughing. 'Come in, you idiot.'

He frowns. 'That's not very nice, Graceland.'

'Jack, don't you know calling someone an idiot can be a term of affection?'

He frowns and looks down.

'Come on, Jack. You know I think you're one of the smartest people on the planet. I wouldn't call you an idiot and mean an idiot.' I take his hand and squeeze it.

His eyes start flittering from the ceiling to the floor and back to the ceiling again.

'It's okay, Jack. I know you're nervous, but Mum will be so excited you're here. You don't need to be worried, okay?'

He nods and walks into the kitchen, where Mum greets him with a handshake.

'Jack brought you some flowers, Mum,' I say.

Her cheeks flush. 'Oh, Jack, they're beautiful. Thank you.'

He thrusts them into her hands. 'You're welcome, Mrs McKay.'

Mum smiles and grabs a dirty glass from the sink. She fills it with water and puts the flowers in it, watching Jack the whole time.

'You've grown up,' she muses.

Jack looks down at his feet. 'Yes.'

'I hear you want to be a scientist?'

Jack looks at me and then says, 'Yes, I do.'

'Jesse would have liked that. He liked science stuff.'

'Not as much as he liked Elvis, though.'

Mum chuckles. 'No, not as much as he liked Elvis.'

'Graceland is going to be a nurse,' Jack adds.

Mum looks at me. 'You still want to be a nurse?'

My heart aches as I remember my unread Set Plan papers lying on the kitchen table for a week, before I forced her to sign them, unread.

'You've wanted to be a nurse since the day Jesse was born,' Mum says. 'You were so fascinated by the nurses running around looking after him, poking and prodding your new baby brother.'

'They looked after him really well.'

'They did.'

'Graceland will make a great nurse,' Jack says.

'Jack,' I say.

'It's true.' He looks at Mum. 'You know she helped me pass Science this term.'

'Grace did?' Mum says.

'Even though no one else thought I could do it.'

Mum slowly nods, looks at me and smiles. 'She's pretty determined when she wants to be.' She presses the button down on the kettle. 'I'm about to have a cuppa. Do you have something planned for the afternoon, before Lisa Marie and Tom join us for dinner?'

'Well,' I say, looking at Mum, 'Jack's come over to watch an old classic with me: *Follow That Dream*, Gordon Douglas, 1962. Do you know it?'

Mum's face lights up. 'Are you really?'

I laugh. 'Would you like to join us, Mum?'

'I'll make some popcorn,' she says, and starts rustling around in a corner cupboard.

'Then,' I add, 'I thought we could cook dinner together. What do you think, Jack?'

Jack's eyes roam around the kitchen. He leans in and whispers, 'Can I clean up first?'

I smile. 'I'll do that.'

The author wishes to thank:

Writing a novel doesn't happen on its own, though plenty of alone time is required to write it. My family have continued to be a blessing of patience, understanding and encouragement throughout this writing project. Larry, Emily, Anna and Molly, you guys are all I could have asked for in this life, and so much more. Thank you for loving me.

Likewise, my parents, Jim and Elaine; thank you for your continued love and support, for encouraging me in everything despite how crazy it might sound at the time.

To my writing family that is Rhiza Edge – Emily and Rochelle, and everyone one else who spent time reading, refining and making this book the best it could be. Thank you.

To my wonderful friends on #TeamCate – Michelle, for therapy coffees that kept me sane, and Jax for cheering me on from afar. Love you girls; couldn't do life without you.

A big thank you to the writers (and in particular that crazy strain, Christian writers) I share a passion for words with, especially those in my Omega Writing Group. Thanks, too, to all those who have read parts or wholes of this novel throughout its various forms and given the feedback I've needed to make it through the numerous *throwing it all away* stages. There are many of you, and I'm grateful for you all.

To my heavenly Father—where would I be without you? You called me to write novels of hope for teenagers and then walked with me to provide the people wisdom and guidance I've needed along the way. Despite my unfaithfulness, thank you for your faithfulness.

And a special thanks to those children, students and families touched by ASD. You have taught me so much about passion, education, inclusion and God's plan for humanity to love as He loves, without limitations.

More by Catriona McKeown

The Boy in the Hoodie

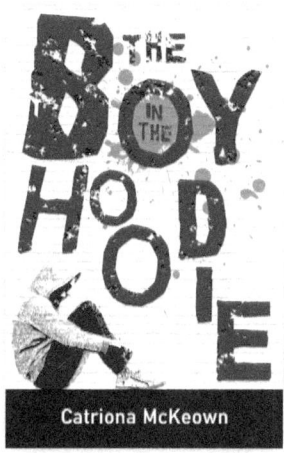

Good-girl Kat knew drinking alcohol at school would have serious consequences. But to protect her friend from being expelled, Kat lands herself a term's worth of detentions.

Inside the detention room, she meets a strange boy who obsessively draws dark pictures and covers his head with a grey hoodie. Little does she know, the hoodie hides a dark past ...

An unlikely friendship forms between Kat and the boy in the hoodie. When she discovers a sinister truth he's been hiding, she somehow feels compelled to help him—but at what cost? And how much is she willing to risk in order to keep him safe?

The Boy in the Hoodie is a real, unforgettable story about past scars and how the ones we love can sometimes heal them.

www.rhizaedge.com.au

www.ingramcontent.com/pod-product-compliance
Lightning Source LLC
Chambersburg PA
CBHW020948260626
47169CB00006B/1881